BLINKINGREDLIGHT

BLINKINGREDLIGHT

A NOVEL

MISTER MANN FRISBY

RIVERHEAD FREESTYLE
NEW YORK

RIVERHEAD FREESTYLE

Published by The Berkley Publishing Group
A division of Penguin Group (USA) Inc.
375 Hudson Street
New York, New York 10014

PRINTING HISTORY
Previously published by Skye Larieux Publishing, Inc. 2002
Riverhead Freestyle trade paperback edition: May 2004

Library of Congress Cataloging in Publication Data

Frisby, Mister Mann.
  Blinking red light / Mister Mann Frisby.
    p. cm.
  ISBN 1-59448-019-2
    1. African American men—Fiction. 2. Male friendship—Fiction. 3. Philadelphia (Pa.)—Fiction. 4. North Carolina—Fiction. 5. Sex crimes—Fiction. 6. Extortion—Fiction. I. Title.

PS3606.R575B55 2004
813'.6—dc22

                                                                    2004041793

Printed in the United States of America

10 9 8 7 6 5 4 3 2 1

For my godmother
Mae Frances Ligon (1942–1994)
(aka The Juicy Fruit Queen)
Thank you for making me the center of your world
until the day you left this earth.

HERE WE GO . . . Writing this book was the easy part. This is where it gets tricky. Sure, everyone who knows me will read it from the prologue to the very end with great interest, but I know the real deal. I know that everyone who knows me will really be reading this page closer than anything else. Everybody wants a shout out. Just listen to the radio for five minutes and you'll see what I mean. And when folks feel like they ain't been shouted out, that's when the drama starts. With that being said, I'll try my best. . . .

I figure that I'll start right off the bat with the most important people. I want to thank Lindsay Wagner for her many wonderful years of portraying Jaime Sommers, The Bionic Woman. I had a ball watching that show. And of course what would I be without the guidance and mentorship of the most influential sports entertainment figure of all time, Hulk Hogan. I am still saying my prayers and eating my vitamins to this day because of the Hulkster. Much love goes out to the brown-skinned lady at the post office with the head full of silver-gray hair who told me I was going to be very successful just because she liked my see-through blue folder from Kinkos.

But really though . . .

So much has happened since I left my newspaper job to be-

come a novelist. I have seen the birth of my first child, Skye Larieux Madison Frisby. I lost a track coach who was very influential
and supportive of me during my high school years. Monique
Legette went above and beyond for me and I am eternally grateful that God put her in my path. And of course, right in the middle of me completing this novel the terrorist attacks of September
11, 2001 occurred.

The year 2001 was so important to me because I figured out
that I can do whatever I set my mind to. I know it sounds cliché
and after-school-specialish but I truly learned a lot about myself.
Sure, my car was repossessed. Sure, there are very irked credit
card companies, utilities, credit unions, and banks. But I don't regret a thing. Those people will get paid when I get paid, so I stress
over it as little as possible. I try to keep my heart open to what
God wants me to do and if it means going broke for a minute and
writing my heart out, then so be it. Yes, there are curse words, yes
there is sex in this book, but hopefully all of you will be able to
make sense of all of it and be inspired.

So many people have come through for me that it has been
overwhelming. I love music so I was particularly thrilled about the
industry cats who supported my efforts. Mad shouts to Cheryl
"Salt" James, the spiciest, bestest, most flyest female rapper ever.
Big ups to the staff at the Axis Music Group for believing in me
and supporting my vision wholeheartedly. Thanks a million
Chauncey, James, Angela, Taayib, Vikter, and crew! Thanks to
Hammer and Play for all of the words of encouragement. Both
of your stories inspire me greatly. Dyana Williams of IAAAM,
thanks for setting me straight that day we were rapping on the
phone. I will never bitch about a rainy, dreary day again!

I can't forget Hank Wilson of Allstate Insurance who supported a brotha like me when he ain't even know me all like that.
I hope I can do the same for someone else one day.

ACKNOWLEDGMENTS ix

Much, much love to my Overbrook Panthers all over the world, especially the track & field alumni. Thanks to my "Grain," Philip "Scooter" Kiszie, and the rest of my MID crew. Big ups to all of my crew from Penn State, especially DINO. It seems like an eternity since we all snacked and layed to the best of our ability, but I still feel y'all. (A-bababa)

I am grateful for the support of the track & field community, namely Beverly Kearney, who is a talented black woman on a mission. You're my role model, Bev, and sure 'nuff one of the best track coaches in the world. I couldn't have functioned without the Internet, and my favorite Barbados native, Obadele Thompson, hooked me up on that end. Although you were only good enough for bronze in Australia, you have a heart of gold, Oba. Thanks to Nanceen Perry for enduring that hickory-smoked macaroni and cheese and for critiquing my stuff. Thanks Shakeema Walker, the skinniest hop, skip, and jump South Philly girl in the world. To the Clown Prince of Track & Field, Jon Drummond, thanks for taking the time to pick my brain and pull out some great ideas. And mad, mad thanks to one of my best friends, Toya Brown-Milburn, the "Quarter-Horse" extraordinaire. Them track chicks don't want it with you when you're at your best.

And of course, all of the athletes that I coach at the Oak Lane Youth Association. Kaloma Cardwell shamelessly begged me to put his name in this section. Also, much thanks for the years of support and encouragement from my assistant coach, Michele Brooks. Khalil Snell represented for me and put together a bangin' website and I really appreciate that too. I cannot say enough about the confidence that Rico Joseph showed in my dream. Thanks for believing in me, Rico. Now let's do this . . .

Big ups to all of the black-owned businesses that have shown love and support for this book: Baltimore Crab and Seafood (Nita and Tank), Kinki Kreations (Jena Renee Williams), and

Jagged Ends barber shop (Steve White). Where would I be without the media? Thanks to *Upscale Magazine*, the *Philadelphia Tribune,* and Ivory Clinton II of *People* magazine for looking out.

My inspiration for writing this novel came fast and furious, and if you're one of those people who I talk to every day on the phone then you know I appreciate you! Big thanks to Steven, Roxxanne, Dior, Corey, Chynell, Kesha, and JD for making me hustle to get this book done. Y'all had me heating up the keyboard, every night, all night. . . .

I can't even begin to stress how monumental my writing group has been in this process. I was harassed, corrected, encouraged, supported, corrected, edited, yelled at, corrected, and basically pulled right along by some very fine writers. Karen E. Quinones Miller ("Satin Doll," "I'm Telling"), Jenice Armstrong, Hillary Beard, Kamal Rav, and Sheila Simmons kept it cracking every Wednesday night at seven (. . . and we still are). I finished two and a half books in a year because of them cats.

A very good friend of mine, Natalie "Sound Girl" Clarke has reminded me throughout my unemployment and throughout the writing process that there has to be someone praying for me. All of your prayers and support in every form, be it monetary or simple words of encouragement, has not gone unnoticed. I'm still in awe of how God gave me the courage to quit a very decent, high-profile job to pursue a career as a novelist. A lot of people looked at me out of the side of their eyes like I was an idiot for following my dream, but I don't hold any grudges. I just figured that I would do my thing and let the result speak for itself.

I have been blessed with some very good friends. Mad love goes out to Steven "Manski" Willoughby, Alexis "Hooter" Drake, Dionne "South Philly" Craig, Alahyo "Yeti" Young, Malika "India" Canty, Shondell "Tardy" Ayala, Patrick "2-Cool"

Weston, Brian "the Dr." McNeil, Bryan "the Dancer" Oliver, Delano "Butterfly" Shane, Sheka and Nichole "Doublemint" Bartley, and Blakeley "Game-Cock" Cooper. Oh yeah, and the little puppy boaw who's always with Blake. I think his name is Jibri. I know I forgot somebody and it'll hit me after this has already gone to print.

I have a very big family and so much extended family that it would be sickeningly impossible to remember everybody. I will say this, if your name ends in Poindexter, Willoughby, Drake, Lark, Branch, Craig, Davidson, Snell, Edwards, Milburn, Brinkley, Scott, then you know you are very much loved and thanked!

Specifically, I have to thank my sister Larneice for coming through for me big time. You're far from rich but you acted like it when Skye was born, and I really appreciate all that you've done. And Joycelyn, don't think I forgot about you. Even though you're way out in the country woods of Texas, I feel you every single day. I can't wait until the day when you step foot back on South Philly soil. Now go ahead and put it in the puppy pan! My little brother Malcolm has gone through way more than I could've handled but he still managed to get through school without ever getting left back, and got into Lincoln University. You are a dream in the making.

I have to thank my mother, Joyce "Starr" Poindexter, for keeping a library in the back closet of our project apartment in South Philly. It seemed corny to me at the time but who would've known. . . . To those of you who are parents, please take note: video games are cool and fun and all that (Lord knows I put Ms. Pac Man's kids through college with all them quarters), but there is nothing wrong with giving your kid a book every now and then. Thank you, Mom for all of your undying support, especially over the last year when I really needed it. I couldn't have pulled this off without you.

"FOR THE LOST"
by D.I.R.T.

What goes around comes, but some choose to ignore this rule.

What goes around comes, but some choose to ignore the fool that they are and gain the whole world and lose their soul. In the midst of these last days, they place their bid for their space in hell kuz on earth they wanted to live their life so cold.

When I needed you the most, I couldn't find you, so I dove in your soul and fell straight to your feet. You were empty inside. I fell straight to your feet, shivering from the cold bliss showering from your heart. It froze my body and split my mind into three parts.

They were each led a separate way which showed me tomorrow hence, why I can't be with you today. The first part was taken away by man. He called Himself the Father. He showed me the beginning and the end, yesterday and tomorrow, last month's laughs, and next month's sorrow.

He said that He knew all that I was thinking, and left me puzzled when he told me it would be blinking. While I was still in a state of confusion, the second part was led away by another man.

This man, well he called himself the Son. He showed me all my mistakes and wrongdoing but said he would forgive me. He showed me how prosperous I would become if only I would let him in. This Man told me he'd shed his blood for me. He then asked me what the color of blood was. I replied red . . . he disappeared.

As if this revelation was not weird enough, I began to hear a whisper. However, no one appeared. The voice proceeded to speak to me and told me that it was a Spirit, and that I need not see a face. All I needed to do was just respect the words that it spoke. It revealed to me all of the snakes in my life, and spoke of how all of my dark days would soon become bright. The spirit told me that all I had to do was remain humble and beware of the light. . . .

PROLOGUE. It felt like I was raping the second one.

She was with it at first, or at least she was acting like she was with it. But when I started to pull her panties off and grab her titties she was acting all tense like it was the worst thing in the world to be getting some dick. And from a fine-ass brotha like me at that.

I was thinking, what woman in her right mind would front on a chance to get with me? Especially since her husband is a shrivel-dicked little white man from Jersey who probably only can get it up twice a week at the most. He was the one who got her into that shit in the first place, so I figured it was him she should've been mad at. I was just doing my job.

Anyway, my cousin Dex was tripping me out because he was just sitting on the edge of the bed with a towel wrapped around him sweating like he just ran in a marathon. He was staring at us all hard like a kid watching cartoons on Saturday morning.

We had already nailed this Jewish chick from Willingboro, and he was just chilling. She was long gone but I still had to get it in with this bitch who was as stiff as an ironing board. She was acting like she wasn't with it, and to make shit worse Tony Salvatore was all up in her face with his camcorder. He was the coolest Italian cat that I ever met.

I remember there was a Lil' Kim song playing on the radio and that shit was getting me hype. It was the one where she be gruntin' and talking about giving head, so it had me mad horny. I guess Maria wasn't a hip-hop fan all like that, because it wasn't doing shit for her. She was just sitting there making me do all the work. I was doing my best to make it all right for her under the circumstances, but she was making me so pissed that I started getting mad.

I was like, "Look bitch, you better act like you know and get with the program," and she just rolled her eyes and looked the other way. That's when I grabbed her chin and made her look at me right in the eye. Now see, I wasn't going to make her suck my dick at first, because I think that's just something you should really wanna do, nah mean? Just because she was trippin' though, I had to do it.

Anyway, I told her I want head and she told me that she didn't do that and I told her, "What, you scared you gonna choke?" She just wrinkled up her face and folded her arms across her chest all tight like I was supposed to give a fuck. She was all right for a white girl. She had a small waist and a black-girl ass almost with some big-ass titties. I figure she was about a size six because she was a little bit bigger than my ex.

She had long blond hair and her perfume was off the hook. I didn't tell her though, because I wasn't in the habit of complimenting the jobs. Well, one thing led to another and before you know it I was standing in the middle of the bed getting my dick sucked by Maria. She was working my jawn like a champ when Dex got up and got in the action. I guess he couldn't take it no more.

So there we were, standing up on the king-size bed in a DoubleTree Hotel suite with our hands up getting a BJ from Maria White, the wife of Harry White, the New Jersey accountant who should've stopped gambling when his ass was ahead.

After we got our shit off, I laid her down and nailed her like I was getting paid to do. Tony was loving every minute of it. He was maneuvering that camera so close to us that I thought his fat Italian ass was going to get butt-naked and jump on the bed with us.

It's funny now that I look back on it, but he was hooting and hollering and talking shit, rooting me on like I was Jerry Rice or some shit. Dex was cool with the BJ she gave him so he went and got in the shower.

I was tearing it up for about five minutes when she finally started to moan and show some kind of reaction to the work I was putting in. She was one of the weakest lays I'd ever had. I knew she was faking it but I didn't care. I mean, I know she was probably upset and all, but damn. I look at it like she should at least make the best of the situation. She tried to stroke my ego by saying I was too big for her and that she couldn't take it, but I know game when I see it. I mean, I ain't the smallest brotha, but I'm sure she could handle it. She should have been counting her lucky stars that Tony didn't make her fuck Dex. I think cuz injected horse blood into his jawn when he was a teenager, but that's a whole different story.

Right when I was about to bust she tensed up real bad and it looked like she was holding her breath. I was gripping the back of her legs and could feel her tightening up every time I hit it. I was just smashing it like a superhero or some shit and thinking, damn, get this shit over with before she starts to cry or something. I busted again in the condom and stood up from the bed. I didn't have no more rubbers, and that was cool with me because Maria was the last job of the night before me and Dex were going to roll out to the club to crack on some honeys that we really wanted to get with.

She jumped up and grabbed her clothes and stormed into the

bathroom all dramatic and shit like she was on the soap operas. I think she was crying but she turned her face away before I could really see.

When she was leaving the suite, Tony said some ol' ignorant shit to her like, "Tell your husband that dark meat tastes better," and me and Dex were just cracking the fuck up. Tony paid us in cash, as usual, and said that a copy of the tapes would be sent to their husbands, as usual.

The crazy thing about that night is that I think the first jawn was really into it. That was the first time a job ever gave me her number. She slipped me her cellie number after she got dressed and blew me a kiss on the low. I blew one back but I knew damn well that I wasn't going to holla back. She was a job, and I don't mix work and pleasure.

1. Now I know that Tony thought I was just a simple ghetto dude when we first met, but he didn't really know the real deal. I mean, I ain't no rocket scientist or nothing like that but I graduated from South Philly High with B's and C's and I went to community college for a year and a half. I had a 2.8 GPA after the first year but I ain't never been one to have my head buried in no books. Life passes you by that way.

It's so much to be done and so little time as some scholarly nigga once said. I dabbled in a little bit of everything. I hustled weed for a minute but that street shit wasn't for me. I threw parties at Eden Rock with my man E to make some cheese before he got sent up to Graterford on some aggravated assault–type shit. He damn near killed his son's mother last winter and the judge, who was a woman, wasn't trying to hear that shit. Get that ass upstate, no pass go, no collect $200. That was my man and all but you can't be beating on no sista like that. That's one thing about me. I don't disrespect women.

Anyway, my most recent hustle before I started working with Tony was chipping up cable boxes and selling them for about $250 or less on the street if I knew you like that. Everybody had free cable, thanks to me. Shit was sweet until the companies got hip to it and started sending out bullets through everybody's boxes and scrambling their signals. That wasn't my problem, because everybody knew I had a no refund policy. That was a sweet hustle until my cousin Dex put me down with Tony and it was smooth sailing for a while. He was like, "Yo, I got this gig where we can make a lot of money and it's all legit."

First off, I have to say that Dex ain't my real cousin. He's just somebody that I grew up with in South Philly who always used to roll with me. He's twenty-seven and he thinks he knows every damn thing. I used to tell him all the time, just because you got me by a year or so, don't think you're the man. One thing I can say about Dex though is that he always came through in crunch time. And the hookup with Tony was right on time.

The way he explained it to me at first was that all we had to do was bang these chicks and that we would get $600 a pop. Of course I was like, count me in, and we went down Fifth and Catharine in South Philly to his apartment to hear what he had to say.

To this day I'm not sure how Tony and Dex ever met. They are total opposites. Tony was a fat-ass Italian dude in his early forties who wore truck jewelry on his fat fingers and sweated a lot. He reminded me of the boaw Captain Lou Albano who used to be on wrestling when I was a young buck. Dex is a thug-type cat who is damn near blacker than Wesley Snipes and the spitting image of the boaw from *Boyz 'N the Hood*. The jawns around the way can't keep their hands off of him. That's why his ass has three kids between two girls we grew up with. He might look like Morris Chestnut but he ain't got cheddar like that cat.

But back to Tony. This guy invited us up into his crib, which was phat as hell, and made us feel like kings. He ordered a seafood platter and cracked open a bottle of Cristal. Dex had me tripping because he was acting like he drinks Cris like that all the time knowing damn well both of us only heard about that shit on the radio.

This man's living room was like something out of a catalog. He had a zebra print thing going on, but it wasn't as ghetto as it might sound. Everything from the living room chairs to the coffee-table coasters had the same print. The walls were the whitest damn walls I'd ever seen in my life. If there was one dirt spot on the walls it would stand out. That's how white the walls were.

Tony gave us the scoop while we stuffed our faces with these mini crab cakes. He said that he wanted us to bang about two or three women a week and that we would be paid for each hit.

All of the women were the wives, girlfriends, sisters, or daughters of some unlucky stiffs who did Tony wrong. The women were down with what was going on and everything, because from what it seemed they really didn't have a choice. Yeah, there were a few that acted all tight like they didn't want to be there, but nobody put a gun to their heads. They could've skipped town or just told their men that they weren't with it. Shit, I know if I ever got into some heat and another cat said he wanted to nail my jawn I wouldn't have it. That shit is dead.

I didn't understand everything that was going on in the beginning and how deep that shit would get. All I knew is that I was going to get paid for getting my freak on. Damn! How sweet could it get?

He told us from the gate that he would be videotaping it but that nobody would see it. Dex was with that right away, but I wasn't feeling the part about him taping it at all. I guess I was noid about it because you always hear stories about shit like that coming back to haunt you when you're running for president, and I didn't want that to happen to me. Not that I'm president material, but you never know. I could be a contender one of these days. I like to get head, and I have a way with the ladies, so what other qualifications do I really need? Anyway, after Tony started talking about all the money that we could make and how easy it would be, I was sold.

Now I assumed that Tony was in the Mafia or some shit right away, but then I kept telling myself that I was getting into them stereotypes. Yeah he lived in South Philly, yeah he had a lot of jewelry and money, but that don't mean shit. I wear FUBU and Phat Farm every day and I rock a fake platinum chain but that don't mean I'm a black rapper. I'm sure that all the white folks on Tony's block think that I'm Puff Daddy or P. Diddy or Little Biggie or whatever the fuck he's calling himself these days.

I could tell by the way they looked at us when me and Dex strolled up to the door of his crib. Just to show us that he was serious, Tony broke me and Dex off with $300 a piece just for agreeing to do it. After we got our cash, we shook hands and relaxed for the rest of that Sunday afternoon. We watched the Sixers lose to Toronto in the first game of the play-offs on the flat-screen television that hung on Tony's wall. I was pissed that AI and crew lost, but I had $300 in my pocket, so it was all good.

2. I know that Dex hooked me up and all, and I know we call each other cousin, but he was nickel-and-diming me to death. Every time I looked up he was trying to borrow twenty-five dollars here or thirty dollars there. That shit was getting tired after a while.

I don't know why I was so surprised though because he always been like that. Ever since we was young boaws he was obsessed with getting cash. And when he got it, he always got stingy with his. If his mom gave him a dollar he would buy me ten penny cookies and get his self ten and then hide the rest of the loot. I should've took a hint then. Dex lived for the green.

And what made it so bad is that when we would do jobs for Tony I would be the one doing most of the work. Dex would start banging one of the jobs and then he would like run out of steam. Of course I was left to pick up the slack, which meant going all out for the camera.

Even if I didn't feel like it I had to put my back into it and look like I was loving the coochie. Tony said that when I grunted a lot and was rough when I hit it that it made the tapes look better and when the tapes looked better he even threw in some extra loochie. I could stand an extra forty or fifty dollars on top of the gravy we was pulling, so it was cool with me.

All of that shit was worth it except for the one time we nailed the jawn at the Hyatt near Penn's Landing. If I knew then what I know now I would have passed on that shit. Six-hundred and fifty dollars or not, it don't matter.

Her husband ran up in the spot with a burner in both hands, and he was itching to pull the trigger. He was a stocky white boaw who looked like he could have been mixed with black. He had on fatigues and black Timberland boots, the whole damn nine. Sweat was dripping off his large bald head like crazy. All I could think was, "Damn I'm about to be sprayed by Rambo up in that motherfucker and I was butt-naked."

To this day I don't even know how he found us. Tony would set up everything so smooth so that the chick didn't even know where we were going. He would always meet the job at a neutral location and then bring her to the secret hotel. Well that time, I think her man followed Tony on the down low.

He was crying and shit and said that he was going to blow all of us the fuck away. I found out later the cat owed Tony a lot of money and had offered up his wife, like most of the cats that owed him money did. It was like a little extra insurance that Tony had taken out to make sure these clowns came through with what they owed. He threatened to send the tapes to their family, friends, or jobs if it came down to that. Tony spared their lives or limbs with the threat that if they didn't come through with what they owed with the quickness, they would be embarrassed.

I guess the dude at the Hyatt snapped at the thought of his woman getting nailed to the wall by a brotha. Tony was sweating bullets up in that bitch, even more than he normally sweats. But I could still see that he was trying to keep his cool. Dude was tripping but Tony was not about to be played.

He said, "Listen here, buddy. Why don't you put the gun down and relax yourself. You can knock all of us off if you want but chances are you won't make it to the lobby of the hotel. I got so many guys on the perimeter of this hotel that you and your old lady would be finished before you got to the parking lot."

I could tell that dude wasn't gangsta all like that, because after a few minutes he put the burner down. He didn't have a ounce of common sense. If Tony had that much backup, then how did he just roll up in the hotel room all easy like that. A duh!

Dude told his girl to get dressed and he was out in a flash. I just knew that Tony would be hearing from him again, but man was I wrong. That shit blew my fucking mind when I was watching the news one day and saw that same dude flash across the television screen. That same nutcase who ran up on us at the Hyatt when we was smashing his wifey was found not too far away in the Delaware River. Now the cops didn't know that it was him right away because he was drenched in acid. I think they said hydrochloric acid or some shit, and stuffed in a sleeping bag.

As for the chick, ain't nobody seen or heard from her ass ever since.

3. Me and Dex were moving like zombies just grabbing and stuffing every damn thing that we could get our hands on.

Looking back, I wish I would have snapped out of the trance I was in and come to my damn senses. I should have stayed my ass in the house and watched the Sixers game like I planned in the first place.

I remember hearing horns honking outside Tony's window and motherfuckers in the street just buggin'! My mind was on what we were doing, but I couldn't help but get caught up in the action out on the South Philly streets. I knew right away that the Sixers must have beat the Lakers in the first round of the play-offs.

Any other time or place I would have been ecstatic, but being as me and Dex was walking back and forth over Tony's dead body like it was nothing just had me all fucked-up in the head. Iverson and crew would have to wait until later to get my attention. I was in some serious shit.

My mother always said that greed always gets the best of stupid-ass people and it usually leads them same damn people to their downfall. She wasn't talking shit either. Now you would think I would have turned my ass around and walked right out of the boss's crib when we saw his ass lying on his back—butt-naked with his arms tied behind his back and dead—on the living room floor. Big-ass patches of his skin was missing from his legs and arms and stomach. There was no skin on his legs or stomach, just blood, and the stench in that living room was worse than anything I had ever smelled.

And that's saying some shit, considering that I lived in the projects all my life. It smelled like a combination of old crabs that sat out in the sun too long and a backed-up toilet at one of them filthy-ass gas stations. I was trying my best not to throw up and Dex was just pacing back and forth like he was walking through a field of daisies. I ain't no autopsy examiner but it seemed like Tony had been up in there for a minute. His face looked melted away and there was craters all over his damn body. I wasn't ready for that shit but when I looked down and saw that some of his toes were missing, I almost lost it.

There Tony was. He was just laying in the middle of that ridiculously white and zebra-print living room, a hot, bloody mess. Damn! I was in South Philly with a corpse when I should have been screaming my head off at Iverson and McKie on the TV screen. Why didn't I just go over Terrell's house and watch the game like I started to in the first place? Damn! Oh well, I can't change the past. Especially since so much shit has gone down since then.

Anyway, I told Dex that we should just get up out of there and be on our way. I wanted to bounce and call the pigs from a phone booth and tell them to check out his house just so that they would know he was dead. But no. Dex insisted on staying up in that motherfucker. I was headed back to the door, when he grabbed my arm and spun me around like I was a rag doll. That boaw turned into Hulk Hogan whenever cash was involved. He looked me dead in the eye and started trippin'.

"That nigga dead already, ain't nothin' we can do about it, yo. Let's just look in his bedroom and see what we can get."

As soon as he had turned and hustled his way through the living room to the bathroom, I should've hurdled over that damn body like I was back on the high school track team and been out. But the dumb-ass side of my brain made me stay and root around that apartment like a crack fiend.

I hit the jackpot when I found a platinum Rolex covered in diamonds and a money clip with $300 in his sock drawer. Dex grabbed a few of his credit cards out of his Kenneth Cole wallet and scooped some rings and other jewelry that he found on top of his dressers. There was no cash in the wallet though.

Me and Dex figured out right away that whoever offed our boss was not out to stick his ass, that's for sure. All of his goods was easy to find. The hot shit was in all the obvious places. Ray Charles could have rolled up in there and found all the shit. It was easy. At first, I was glad that we stayed.

I looked over my shoulder one last time when me and Dex were leaving Tony's crib and chills ran up and down my body. Man! It's not like that nigga was my family or nothing but he did hook us up with mad loot just to nail jawns that we would never have to see again.

I felt some kind of way that he was dead, but there was no time to stop and mourn. Dex yanked at my arm and told me to come the fuck on, and we bounced. I can't help but laugh now, but I remember cuz telling me how important it was for us to leave Tony's spot and get back to North Philly unnoticed. Yeah right. That was a joke.

The Sixers were in the NBA finals for the first time since '83 and had just won the first game of the series against Shaq and bitch-ass Kobe Bryant. There were so many people in the streets it was sickening. The Italians around Tony's way were ripping and running up and down the streets. Niggas was on top of their whips—everything from Navigators and Benzes to busted-ass squatters—waving towels and screaming at the top of their lungs. Even the Chinese boaws on Seventh Street was out in the mix. And Dex was talking about some damn, "Try not to let nobody see us." If I had a dime for everybody who saw us walking down the street that night I would be on some ol' Bill Gates shit right now.

Just like Dex, I was banking on the fact that everybody was so caught up in celebrating for the Sixers that nobody saw our asses.

When we got back to my mother's house we called up a couple of bitches that we knew and told them to come over. Dex got with Loretta and I hit Trina. I don't think I'll ever have sex like that as long as I live. I came so hard that every single muscle in my body tightened and loosened ten times before I pulled my jawn out and collapsed on the bed. I needed that.

4. The next four days was nerve-racking as a motherfucker. Every time a door slammed or a cop car rolled through the hood, I was about to shit myself. I was so damn shook about what we took from Tony's crib that I just took $150 from the money clip and gave the Rolex to Dex, so that he could get us something for it. He said that he could pull in some major ends for that watch and jewelry he found and that we could split what he got up the middle.

I didn't even care after a while. I just wanted to be able to go to sleep at night again. As soon as my eyes would close, it seemed like they were popping back open again. I was a mess.

Looking back though, I guess I was doing all right compared to how my whole shit just got flipped around shortly after that. And I thought my life was falling the fuck apart already. It seemed like I was losing five pounds a day. I'm not one to be on my own dick, but I consider myself to be a thorough brotha. I'm a little over six feet and weigh 205 pounds. My skin is smooth and bitches always tell me how much they love my smile and my big muscle booty. I guess that came from all of those years of running. I got these jawns in Philly open.

Every time me and my boaws go to the club—or the "let out" I should say, because we never pay to go in—the honeys be on my dick. All I got to do is kick some game and let 'em rub on my six-pack and they're gone after that. They be tripping over my chocolate skin and smooth-ass goatee like I'm the last boaw on earth sometimes.

I've always been popular around the way. Ever since I was little, the jawns would say they loved my name because it was so exotic and unusual. They say I look like a dark version of the boaw from *Dead Presidents*. I think I look better than that chump, and I damn sure think that I would look better laying next to Nia Long. Much better than that clown did with her in *Love Jones*.

Anyway, so then I was starting to look like a smoker. I lost at least five pounds in no time. I ain't want nobody to think I was smoking that shit, so I got back on my game. I didn't want my mom to start worrying either. I ate every cheesesteak—smothered in ketchup, fried onions, and mayonnaise—that I could get my hands on. When I wasn't eating a steak, me and Dex would make a run to the church at Twelfth and Poplar and get a platter. You can't beat $6.50 for smothered pork chops, macaroni and cheese, string beans, and cornbread. We would take our plates back to my crib and watch the news like fiends.

When my mom would ask us why we were so interested in the news all of a sudden we would just say that we were watching because of the play-offs. Jaime Arthur wasn't suspicious at all. I had my eyes glued to the news to see if they mentioned anything about Tony in South Philly. Four days went by and there was no word from any of them cats on the news about Tony. They were so damn wrapped up in the play-off shit. Damn!

I wanted to know how he died and what the fuck happened to him. Maybe all bodies looked like that when they were sitting around for a while. Maybe. It's not like I ever seen a dead body before, so what the hell did I have to go on?

5. I only felt that way one other time in my life. It was the time Donovan, some dirty-ass boaw who lived up the street, sucker punched me and knocked me off my bike. I was like twelve or thirteen then, so that's saying some shit.

But that's what it felt like when I rolled over and rubbed the sleep out of my eyes one Friday and saw a picture of Tony on the television screen.

It was like somebody caught me with a mean-ass right hook. The news chick said that it was a home invasion. That he had been brutally murdered and robbed. She said that huge patches of his skin were removed from his body with a potato peeler or something like that while he was still alive. She said that he was tied up and that his killer poured hydrochloric acid all over his face and body while he was still alive.

I don't think I breathed at all the whole time she was talking. The screen went from a picture of Tony to a picture of all these detectives walking back and forth in front of the house. Just when I was about to exhale and get out of bed to call Dex, she dropped the real bomb.

She said that two African-American males in their mid-twenties are being sought for questioning. I was fucking numb. I couldn't believe that shit. My whole stomach knotted up like a ball of hard, cold clay and I started to sweat right away.

I love the way them bitches always add, "They are being sought for questioning and are not considered to be suspects." Give me a fucking break! They must think that niggas just came off the truck with the morning milk. Whenever I watch the news and hear "sought for questioning" I think that they must be the dudes who did it.

I lifted my legs up one at a time. They felt like lead, like I had a hard-ass track workout. I called Dex up on his cell phone but of course he was still asleep. I think he was laid up that day under some new chick that he hardly knew but that I'm sure he nailed. I whispered what I had just seen on the news, and that nigga woke right the fuck up. Even though he was like six blocks away I could see the crazy-ass look on his face over the phone.

"Are you fucking serious?"

Those were the only four words my cousin could put together. He repeated himself like five times before we hung up with each other. He was on my doorsteps in like twenty minutes.

He asked me again, and I told him the story again. Then I asked him whatever happened to the loot that he was supposed to get from the Rolex, and he said that he was still working it. He didn't want to go to a pawnshop just in case the shit was reported stolen. He said he wanted no more heat to be on us than there had to be. I could believe that. I just knew that we were going to need some extra money just in case we had to lay low for a minute.

The shit about Tony was on the news about every ten minutes. They would interrupt the soap operas and everything else for updates. Not that they were saying anything new though. It was the same shit at every newsbreak. Mob shit is big in Philly. It makes the news at the drop of a dime.

They kept saying that their police sources claim that Tony was killed over mob business but I wasn't feeling that explanation at all. I had a feeling it was something else. I mean, just because the nigga was Italian and he was ballin' don't mean it had to do with the Mafia.

Dex was acting weird as shit. I think he was trying his best to keep his cool but he wasn't doing a good job of it at all. I told that motherfucker to stop getting up at the crack of dawn to buy the *Daily News* and the *Inquirer*. That just looks suspicious. Especially coming from a cat that never fucking read any of that shit. The only thing I ever saw him read was the back of the cereal box while he ate his Cap'n Crunch.

I mean, I ain't no scholar but I sit down every now and then to read the paper or crack open a book. Dex just looked plain ol' guilty of something when he strolled into Mr. Dang's corner store and snatched up Philly's two biggest newspapers every day like clockwork.

Me, I was cool. I never acted pressed to know what was going on with the case, and I didn't talk about it with nobody. I backed off of watching the news while my mom was around. Dex was sweating bullets since he had bragged so damn much to the boaws around the way about our hookup with Tony. When we were doing the jobs I told him to keep his mouth shut, but he went on about how he knew who he could trust and whatnot. I just said, fuck it. I was getting paid and I was happy, so I didn't sweat it.

Then came the reward. Out of the motherfucking blue, it came up that Tony had a family. A wife, two teenage sons, and a grown daughter. They were all over the news crying and carrying on about how their father was great and how he was respected in their community. They said he coached little league football in Northeast Philly and that he used his own money to buy their uniforms and equipment. There was a large picture of his house in the *Daily News*. The two-story row house was dead smack in the middle of the Northeast.

I figured out kind of quick that the spot in South Philly must've been where he bought all of his side jawns. I guess even Italian cats like to step out on wifey every now and then. The bad thing was, I knew that as soon as the news started talking reward money that the phones down at the Roundhouse would start lighting up. Black people will turn in their own damn moms if the price is right. It was only a matter of time.

The look on Dex's face made me know right away that we was in some major shit. He was talking all fast and in circles while he was pacing back and forth across my mother's living room. I remember he was wearing a pair of dark denim jean shorts, a red Phillies baseball jersey, and a pair of sand-colored Timberland boots. Every few steps he would snatch the hat off his head and twist it up in his hands.

"Yo cuz, Boo and them told me that the cops was around on Ridge Avenue asking about me. They said they had to ask me a few questions about a case and if they saw me to tell me they were looking for me."

I sat there without saying a damn thing. I just stared at the TV and pounded my fist into my hand. Where the hell was I going to go? Who could I turn to? Would I get out of this shit without going to jail?

I had all this shit racing through my head. I figured that if the pigs were asking about Dex then they had to know he was rolling with somebody, which meant they was going to be looking for me too. I was numb. My first instinct was to run upstairs and pack a suitcase. I just took a deep breath and told Dex that the whole thing would blow over. I was lying through my teeth though. I was just trying to calm him down in order to calm myself down but it didn't work.

I knew that me and Dex didn't kill no damn body, but the cops didn't want to hear that shit when there was a dead Italian man in South Philly who the news made out to be the best little league football coach in the world. Maybe they had found our fingerprints in the house and knew that we stole all that shit. That would be all they needed to put us at the scene of the crime and throw our asses up in Graterford.

I was petrified of jail. I knew that if the honeys on the outside was loving me that them sex-starved niggas on the inside would want to fuck me crazy if I got locked down. I couldn't do it. I would kill myself before I went to jail and let another man nail me to the wall.

We both knew that right then and there we had to be out for a while. But to where? I knew a whole lot of people but I was starting to think like a cop all of a sudden. I couldn't go to Pittsburgh to stay with my aunt Rachel and her husband, because that would be the first place they would look. She is my mom's sister.

Delaware was out of the question. My ex-girlfriend Farrah moved down there, and the last time we talked she told me how she was living in a two-bedroom apartment and how it was off the hook. She opened a hair and nail salon and was doing good from what I heard. One, I thought that the pigs would go there too. And two, I didn't really like the idea of her and Dex being under the same roof. I always had a feeling that she kind of liked my cousin. Bitches are scandalous. I wouldn't be surprised if they had fucked already.

Dex had no suggestions of where we should go, because the farthest his ass had ever been out of Philly was to Atlantic City every other weekend in the summer. That, and he went to see the Pentagon on a class trip in D.C. in eighth grade.

Anyway, after a couple hours of racking my brain, I came to the conclusion that me and my black-ass cousin would have to live among the white folks for a little while.

6. Driving to State College was the longest three hours of my life. Dex let this chickenhead named Meka roll with us, and I wanted to choke her ass before we were even at the halfway mark.

She was a bona fide clucker. The long-ass nails, the long-ass weave, and the long drawn-out conversation were dead give-aways that she was a clucker. She yapped about what rapper she heard was fucking whoever and yapped about who was pushing the most weight up in Brooklyn. I don't give a fuck who them cats are nailing or how much drugs they're selling, as long as their shit is tight when it hits the record store.

That jawn talked about absolutely nothing for most of the trip, and Dex entertained her dumb ass by acting interested. Anything for some ass was his motto.

There was no telling how long we would have to be up in that lily white-ass town. Meka had her knockoff Fendi bag packed in like ten seconds flat when Dex asked her to roll with us.

I knew that she was going to be trouble from the moment I saw her. There was something shady about that jawn, but I couldn't really tell Dex that because I'd never met her before. I just knew that it was going to be some shit with her though. I don't know why he brought that jackal along for the trip anyway.

Meka reminded me of that rap chick Foxy Brown, and obviously a lot of other niggas told her that too, because it looked like she was going all out to look like Foxy. She had smooth dark skin but her eyes made her look Chinese. Her teeth were real white and she had fat-ass titties. The black weave that she had in her head hung down past her shoulders and looked like it grew right out of her own damn head. I knew it was fake though, because my ex-girl used to do hair in my basement and I would see the miracles she would work with some of them jawns from around the way.

I have to give it to Meka though. She looked good. It's just that when she opened up her mouth, I was turned off. She popped her gum real loud and quoted the gossip chick Wendy Williams like the gospel. I was around her for five minutes before I knew that she was definitely the gold-digging type. It had me fucked-up in the head why she was with Dex though, because he was not that boaw. She would be lucky to get a pack of Oodles of Noodles or a box of pumpkin seeds out of that nigga.

I couldn't be too mad at first, because she was nice enough to drive her own whip. Me or Dex didn't have a credit card to rent a car, plus we didn't want to blow all of our money on that shit.

We left a little after midnight so that the whole damn hood wasn't watching us bounce. I told my mother that I was going to watch my boaw's house in South Philly. I hated lying to her, but I wanted to keep her out of it as much as I could.

We made a pit stop in Harrisburg to take a leak and Meka told me I could drive the rest of the way. They were in the backseat kissing and feeling all over each other in the dark. I knew that he had hit it already, so I was surprised how hard he was sweating her. I ignored them and just listened to my Jadakiss CD. There was too much on my mind at that point.

There I was, on my way to see one of my boaws from community college, and I had major baggage with me. I barely had the time to tell Kameron that my cousin Dex was coming along for the visit and now I had to explain why we had a bitch with us too.

I never told Kam why I was coming up to Penn State. He was up there trying to get his master's degree and working full-time for the school. We always used to roll together when we were at community. After I dropped out he stuck with it and graduated. Then he went to Temple and got an English degree. I guess that wasn't enough school for that nigga, because he applied to Penn State for grad school and got in.

For Kam to be all book smart, he was mad cool. That nigga could read Hemingway or some shit and then turn around and spit like sixteen bars from a Mobb Deep song without blinking. He was a bookworm back in the day, but he always kept it gangsta for his boaws, and that's why we was always so tight. I feel bad for fucking up his life the way I did.

7. I wasn't ready for Dex to be knee-deep in Kam's girl's pussy that night. I should've known that nigga was going to fuck up.

Everything was straight up until then. It was as smooth as silk until captain dick went buck wild. It was Friday night and the Kappa fraternity was sponsoring a jam over on campus. For it to have so many white folks up there, we was able to find a lot of shit to do with the niggas up in Happy Valley.

It was summer school and I guess a lot of them cats decided to stay up there and take some classes. From what Kam was telling me, a lot of them up there were failing out big-time. All of that freedom, liquor, and ass was making them fall off quick. Summertime is when they all got their shit back together I guess.

Anyway, the pool party was off the hook. It started out as a cookout near the pool at one of them big-ass apartment complexes up there where all of the apartments look alike. A couple of the fraternities were stepping and chanting and battling on the side of the pool. It was so laid-back up there. I wasn't used to that kind of atmosphere, but it was tight.

There were about twenty bitches dancing by the pool with bikinis on and their titties jumping all over the place. The DJ was wack but it was cool because I couldn't take my eyes off them jawns. Damn! They made me want to send for the rest of my shit in Philly and just move. I was playing it cool, just chilling on the side and nodding my head to Mystikal.

I didn't bring swimming trunks because it wasn't no vacation. I just chilled on the side. There were a few white girls there too and a couple of Asian jawns. They was all giving me rhythm, but I wasn't feeling them all like that. I mean, a few of them had fat asses but I would rather have some dark meat up on my plate, nah mean! I pocketed six numbers at the pool.

I caught a couple of them jawns at the pool cutting their eyes at Meka a few times. I guess they were gritting on her because they didn't know who she was and she looked good as shit in that bright pink bikini. Dex was all splashing around in the water with her and trying not to look whipped, but I know it was hard as hell for him not to be pressed. Her shit was proper.

We did the pool party for a few hours before all of us jumped in the ride and headed back to Kam's apartment to take showers and change into clothes for the party inside at some dude's apartment.

It was me, Dex, Meka, Kam, and Kam's girl Stacy. She was legit. Brown skin, short—about five foot two inches—with thick thighs and pretty full lips. Her hair was brown and her tatas were mouthwatering. Stacy was definitely a dime piece. She always wore Angel perfume and that shit sent me up the wall. Kam was the man!

Everybody was in a good-ass mood. It was the first time that I had gone that many hours without thinking about Tony's bloody, skinned body and all the drama that had us out of Philly.

Kam's apartment was tight. He had a two-bedroom about fifteen minutes off campus. He had a king-size bed in his bedroom and his own personal bathroom. The living room was tight as hell. Everything was black and gray and his television was thirty-two inches and hooked up to a digital cable box. His main couch was black and leather and turned into a full-size bed. That's where Dex and Meka crashed. I slept on the small couch.

That shit was tripping me out, because they would fuck like rabbits every night. I would lay there and act like I was asleep and watch, or half the time I really was asleep and the noise woke me up. One night I rolled over and saw Meka riding the shit out of Dex. She was moaning all crazy and grabbing her hair. Her nipples were big and suckable. My dick got hard just looking at her. She was a pigeon and all but I knew that I would fuck her in a heartbeat. I never told them I watched but I think Dex knew.

For a minute there I was wishing I had finished at community and went off to a four-year college. Kam was living phat and he wasn't even finished yet. I was cool with staying at my mom's until I saw how he was living. Maybe I should give that school shit a try, I was thinking. Naw, I thought my brain would explode if I had to sit through another algebra class. And I heard that they made everybody take math no matter what you wanted to be.

I took my shower first and got dressed real quick. I was ready to get back to that apartment complex so I could get on some of them honeys that I saw earlier on at the pool. I knew that I couldn't bring any of them back to Kam's since it was a crowded house, so I had to make sure my game was tight and I would get invited to one of their spots.

It don't even matter if I got lucky, like the white boys say. I was just tired of being up under Dex and Meka all the time. In the ten days that we were up there I only really got to spend a few hours alone with Kam. We ate at the Chili's and walked up and down College Avenue near the campus. It was cool getting caught up with my nigga.

Dex and Meka were the next to get ready. Kam came strolling

out of his room by himself and said Stacy was not going to go since she had a headache. She said she would just go to her own apartment and chill. I was hoping that Meka would follow her lead so that it could be a guys' night out kind of thing, but of course that wasn't happening. She was on my cousin's nuts real hard.

The party that night was jumping. There were way more people there than were at the pool party earlier that day. Black people were coming out of the woodwork up in white man's land.

It was a little after midnight when Dex pulled me and Kam to the side and said that he was going to get a room at the Motel 6 on Atherton Street. He said he felt like getting buck wild with Meka and he needed a room so that he could really get his freak on. I just smiled and shook his hand, but in the back of my head I was thinking, they already been knocking it out like they had a hotel room, so what's the difference? Whatever, fuck it. That's Dex for you. I told him that me and Kam were probably going to holla at a couple cuties ourselves and just like that him and foxy Meka were out.

Me and Kam held it down big-time after they left. We was dancing with them freaks for like two hours straight. I guess they were feeling us not only because our shit was tight but we were obviously older than the other young boaws there who were still cummin' after three strokes.

The party winded down a little after three. Well, on the real it didn't wind down. The damn cops shut that shit down. The white folks called and complained about the music. Me, Kam, and these two jawns that he introduced me to went to Eat 'n Park to get dessert.

After we busted a grub, the honeys dropped us off back at Kam's apartment. I got the digits and got Nydira to rub on my shit, but that was about it. She said that I couldn't stay the night since we just met. That was cool with me. As long as she knew that I was going to smash it up when she let me.

Me and Kam were wired when we got back to his spot at about four thirty. For some reason we weren't that tired. He said that we should watch a DVD in his room. What happened next changed every damn thing.

Like I said, I wasn't ready for Dex to be knee-deep in that girl's pussy that night. I should've known that nigga was going to fuck up.

Stacy was spread-eagle on the floor of Kam's bedroom and Dex was drilling away like a machine. It took about three full seconds before both of their sweaty bodies jumped off the floor and turned around.

She covered her face and jumped on the bed and was breathing all hard and crying and grabbing for the sheets to cover her face. Dex just stood there with a stupid-ass expression on his face and a rock-hard dick. He kept looking down on the floor around him like he was looking for his boxers, but they were nowhere to be seen. The only thing on that light gray carpet was a gold Trojan wrapper and her bra and panties. Stacy scooped up his red-and-black boxers off the bed and threw them at him. Dex put them drawers on so damn fast it looked like he was about to start break dancing. Kam was quiet at first and then he just snapped.

"Pussy, you done lost your fucking mind! I'm getting my fucking burner!"

He turned and ran out of the bedroom before I could reach out and grab his arm. I was too much in shock. I couldn't believe that Dex would do some ol' slimy shit like that. I mean, my boaw gave us a place to stay and didn't ask no questions. I know Dex didn't know Kam all like that and wasn't expected to be loyal and shit but that was just slimy. At that point I just knew that

Kam wasn't thinking straight and that he might wind up in jail if I didn't stop him.

I ran out the doorway to his room and into the living room. Kam was storming out of his computer room with a gun in his hand and the meanest look I have ever seen on anybody's face. It was like one of them cartoons when I was little and I would see steam coming out of somebody's ears. That's what he looked like.

I jumped in front of him and begged that nigga to chill. He was so damn pissed that I think he was ready to shoot me, but something inside of him made him put the forty-five down on the kitchen counter a few minutes later. He just screamed toward the room at Stacy.

"Get the fuck out of my house, bitch! Get your shit and get the fuck out of my house before I bust a cap in both of y'all asses!"

"Sit down on the couch, Kam," I said.

"Fuck that shit! I ain't sitting no fucking where! Tell your boy to come on out here so I can bust his ass!"

Dex walked out of the room a few minutes later with both of his hands on front of him pleading for Kam to listen to him. Stacy was still in the bedroom. Before Dex could get three more words out of his mouth Kam leapt off of the couch and started to whip Dex's ass. I'd never seen Dex get his ass whipped, but on that day he got his shit toasted. Kam flipped him over on the middle of the carpet and was stomping the shit out of that nigga. He was throwing blows at his head and his ribs at like a hundred miles per hour.

Dex was mostly just blocking because he couldn't even get any hits the way Kam was wailing on him. By the time I pulled Kam off him—and I was moving slow on purpose—Dex had a busted lip, his nose was leaking, and his jaw was tapped the hell up.

I dragged Kam into his computer room and screamed for Dex to pack him and Meka's shit and to meet me out in the parking lot. I grabbed the burner off the counter just in case Dex got any crazy ideas. I shut the door and held Kam in that room for at least fifteen minutes until he calmed down.

My man was huffing and puffing and cursing and then he just broke down and started to cry. It wasn't the kind of crying on the soap operas. It was the kind of crying that you don't see niggas do. He was shaking, and I didn't know what to say. He was really into that chick.

"I was going to give that bitch a ring one day! I was going to make her wifey!"

Since it was just us in that empty room his words echoed off the walls.

That skeezer-ass bitch of his must have crept out while we were in the room, because she was gone by the time I came out and started to pack.

Once I got everything together I gave Kam his piece and apologized again. He didn't even look me in the eye. I think he wanted to kick my ass too, but he knew that I didn't have anything to do with it. I shook Kam's hand for the last time and thanked him for letting us stay there. He didn't say shit to me.

8.   I was so pissed on the way home. I wanted to bash Dex in the head with a motherfucking bag of hot nickels. What he did was some ol' nut shit.

I mean, if it was ten years ago and we were still back in high school, then that would have been something different. That was cool back then, to try to nail your boaw's main jawn. But you just don't do that to somebody who looked out for you like that.

I remember riding down 322 and wanting to pull over and dump him and Meka out of the car. If being stupid was worth something, that bitch would be sitting on bricks of gold. Dex told her the reason wc were leaving so quickly was because his mother was sick and he had to hurry back to Philly. When Meka asked Dex how he got a busted ass, nose, and lips, he said that he got rolled on by these two racist white boys. She believed everything he said. I thought it when we were going up there, but I knew it for a fact when we were driving back, that her head screwed on and off.

When we got back to North Philly the first thing me and Dex did was ask around to see if the cops were still looking for us. As far as our boaws knew, it wasn't as hot as it was before we bounced.

My mom was happy to see me. She had a million and one questions and I just lied my way through all of them. All I wanted to do was go to sleep in my own bed and that's what I did. I was knocked out for like twelve hours straight.

When I woke up it was like nine o'clock. I remember because the Hot Boyz was just starting the countdown on Power 99. I washed my face and brushed my teeth and was out before they could get to song number seven.

I borrowed my young boaw's bike and rode around the corner to see if I could see what the deal was on the street. I wanted to know if the cops were still hunting for us the way they were the first few days. I started to call Dex and get the scoop from him, but I had a hunch to put down the phone, go there, and ask around for myself.

The cats out there was surprised to see me.

"Yo, I heard you on the run. Wassup with that?"

"Naw, not me," I said. "You got me mixed up with somebody else. I'm just trying to eat every day, that's all."

I was trying to play it cool and act like I wasn't pressed like a motherfucker to see what the streets was saying about me and Dex. After a while, one of the young boaws, Marquan, who used to hang on my block, told me that the cops was in the Chinese store two days before asking cats about Dex and his partner. It ain't take a rocket scientist to figure out that that partner was me.

Quan also told me how the jakes was all trying to intimidate the corner boys into telling where we were, since it was a big-time murder case that they wanted to question us for. I thanked the youngun for the information and I was out.

There was a lot of shit running through my mind that night when I was riding the bike back around the corner to my mother's house. The little trip up to Penn State had me wanting to just run to the library and fill out some college applications. I wasn't the smartest motherfucker but I knew I could hang enough to get that paper and get me a bangin'-ass job. At the same time I wasn't ready to be sitting up all times of the night reading books on shit I didn't really want to know about. I wanted to see the world a little bit first. Just chill. Get my thoughts together before I figured out what I wanted to do.

Anyway, when I got back to the crib I called Dex and told him what I'd heard. He didn't seem pressed that 5-0 was breathing down our damn necks. He didn't care that we were probably the last people to see Tony alive. He was cool just being all up under Meka and beating up that dark chocolate coochie.

Every bone in my body told me to make a run on my own. I wanted to do it and looking back I should have done it without even blinking, but when it came to it I didn't follow my gut. Plus I knew that I couldn't just leave Dex hanging like that. We had to ride this shit out together. He was my cousin.

I sat in my room that night and just stared at the walls, thinking. The phone had to ring at least six times but I just let the answering machine get it. My mom was over at my aunt's house and my sister had moved out to her own apartment at that point, so I had the spot all to myself.

When I finally did pick up the phone it was Dex on the other end. He was breathing all hard and shit. It sounded like he had just ran up a flight of stairs.

"Nigga, where you been? I called there three times tonight."

"I was knocked the fuck out."

"Well wake your ass up, boaw, because I'm about to get both of us paid."

"What you got crackin'?"

"I don't want to get into it over this cell phone but make sure you pack your bags for about three or four days and be ready to roll out tomorrow morning at seven."

"Aight then, Dex, but this better not be no bullshit. I need some loot. I'm trying to get me a whip before the summer is out."

"Aight bet. See you in the morning."

I made up another lie to tell my mother while I was packing my shit for the mystery road trip. I was having mad second thoughts about that shit after what Dex pulled at Penn State, but I needed the money. Besides, it ain't like I knew anybody in North Carolina at that point, so he couldn't fuck up again and make me lose another friend. I planned on just playing the shit by ear and if I wasn't feeling his plan then I would just bail out. I wish it was that easy. Dex always had a way of making a nigga do what he wanted to do.

When he came to scoop me the next day I still wasn't totally convinced that I was down for the trip. I told my mom that me and Dex were rolling down to D.C. for a hip-hop convention. She knew that Dex was always trying to get a record deal, like every other nigga from around the way, so she didn't even blink when I kissed her on the cheek and bounced that morning.

Dex was pushing a black four-door Honda Accord. It was tight but it ain't have no rims or nothing. It was clean on the outside and looked like it was about a '98 or '99. Dex popped the trunk for my bag and when I tossed it in there I noticed that there was already two bags up in that piece.

The first thing I noticed, other than the three strong-ass vanilla air fresheners when I got in the whip was a nigga in the backseat that I never seen before. Dex introduced me to the boaw Herb and we shook hands. I had mad questions at that point. Where the fuck did you get this car? Who is this nigga? And why is he rolling with us?

Before I could ask anything Dex blasted an old Funkmaster

Flex tape that he copped off Fifty-second Street and peeled out of my mom's block like Knight Rider.

"So what's the deal, Dex?"

He kept on nodding his head to this Nas track and grinning. I didn't think that shit was funny. I looked in the rearview mirror and saw that Herb was smiling too. It was too many teeth flashing up in that car. I was getting vexed.

"Listen, cuz, I got the hookup. We about to go on a little trip to get us a little ass and a lotta cash."

"What the fuck are you talking about?"

"One of my hookups got me a gig with a few freaky couples down in North Carolina. They into all that swingin' shit and they got money. They want some dark meat to spice up their love lives and we got the job."

"How the hell did you hear about this shit, and who are these fucking people?"

"I can't get into all that shit, but just trust me, cuz, this is going to be some easy money. These fools get their rocks off by watching black thug cats smash their wives."

"What? You telling me that we about to get paid just for nailing somebody's wife?"

"Three wives."

"And all of this shit is legit?"

"Yup."

"I don't know, Dex. This shit sounds crazy."

"Trust me, we gon' be in and out of this country-ass town so quick, and we'll be four and half large richer for that shit."

"What? This job pays $4,500?"

"Yup. It's $1,500 for each hit. Three couples in three days. Think you got enough balls to handle this shit?"

"Nigga, is you crazy? That's, let's see, that's $2,250 a piece. Hell yeah, I'm with it!"

"How you figure your share is that much?"

"What? Can't you add? If you split that shit up the middle you get $2,250."

"Naw, Herb is rolling with us, cuz. He's in on this too."

I turned around and looked in the backseat to get another good look at the motherfucker who was cutting into my share of the loot. Who the fuck is this nut? I was thinking. I couldn't believe that Dex was bringing a new face around when we already had so much heat on us.

He just looked back at me with this sly-ass smirk on his face like he was "that boaw" or some shit. I couldn't wait for me and Dex to be alone so I could get the scoop on this cat. I was grilling the shit out of Dex when we stopped at the Maryland House off 95 south to get some gas and something to eat. I pulled Dex to the side while Herb was waiting in line at the Sbarro pizza joint.

"Yo Dex, man, what the fuck is up with dude? Why you bring him in on this shit?"

"Chill yo, he's cool. I've known that nigga for a minute now and he always comes correct."

"Well I ain't never seen his ass before or heard you talk about him."

"I don't talk about all the niggas I do business with. I tell you about the hoes I get down with and that's about it."

"And where the hell did you get the whip?"

"I was wondering when you was going to ask about that shit, nigga. I bought it off my man Nate's uncle. I gave him the Rolex in exchange for the car and a G. He said he would give me the loot when we got back and do all the paperwork to get the car switched over to my name."

"I thought you was going to lay low on that jewelry and shit for a minute."

"I said I would lay low about pawning it or selling it to somebody who was going to pawn it, but I know dude is going to keep that shit for himself, so I'm not worried. He's a baller. He already got three other whips, so he could afford to give up one, especially since he got a phat-ass platinum Rollie to flash on his wrist."

"True! It ain't shit for him to give up a Honda to get iced out."

"Yeah! So that's why I tell your ass to stop sweating the small stuff and to stay cool. Herb is cool and he don't be running his mouth all like that."

Me and Dex was looking in his direction while we were talking about him in the line to get a Cinnabon. Now that Dex had told me a little something about dude I wasn't that against him rolling with us. If Dex said he was crew, that was cool. He was the kind of cat you kept away from your girl though.

He was about six-three or a little taller, brown-skinned and with cornrows, and he looked aight. He looked like one of them cats that be up in *Vibe* modeling FUBU and Sean John and shit. He probably could have been a model in one of them ghetto rags but he had this big-ass birthmark on his cheek that was in the shape of Africa. He was a pretty boy but the thug in that nigga came through too. He looked like he would turn gangsta in a heartbeat and bust a nigga's jaw up if he had to. Dex told me that he could ball too and that he was close to getting a scholarship to Temple back in the day, but his grades were fucked-up.

We made one more stop after the Maryland House to get gas and to drain the monster. The next time we stopped that car was in the parking lot of the Carolina Duke Motor Inn in Durham. I've stayed in better but it was straight for a little motel in country-ass North Carolina. It was all that three Philly cats on a mission needed.

We were in the room for about half an hour when the phone rang at quarter to five. Dex started scribbling down some shit on the back of an envelope and then he hung up the phone.

"It's on, fellas. We got our first gig tonight at eleven."

9. I'll never figure out how motherfuckers can just sit back and watch other men fuck their wives. That's crazy. I don't think my sex life could ever get that boring where I would call in three black cats from Illadelphia to knock my woman off.

That's all I could think about the first half hour or so. That shit had me tripping. We rolled up in their spot closer to eleven thirty since we got lost on confusing-ass country roads. It was like ten motherfucking miles between each traffic light. I felt sorry for cats who live down that piece and got no car.

Their crib was off the hook. It looked like something out of a magazine and it was all on one level. That was the only thing that fucked it up. There was no basement or upstairs. Everything was all spread out on one floor. They had a thing for red, because every damn thing was red. The carpet, the couch, the walls. It was kind of phat.

The wife's titties was sitting up at attention and she was sexy as shit. She looked like Pamela Anderson or some other souped-up white girl on Baywatch. Her shit didn't look fake at all though. They looked as real as the wad of hundreds that her fat-ass husband waved in our faces when we rolled in. Long blond hair, thick black-girl lips, and the ass was all right. She told us to call her Goldie. For the kind of cheese they was paying I would've called that bitch Big Foot if she wanted me to.

"Hey fellas, thanks for coming."

Her husband looked like a younger version of that dude Archie Bunker from that TV show. He talked like him too and had the same blue eyes. The only thing is that dude couldn't have hated black people like Archie did on TV. Not the way he was grinning when his wife got slayed that night.

We talked a lot of small talk for a while. Nothing really. Archie talked shit about the Lakers whipping our asses in the play-offs while Dex kept trying to change the subject. Cuz loves the Sixers. He is one of them cats who gets into a fight at the bar if somebody says some ill shit about Iverson or any of the niggas on the squad.

Goldie just sat back and took in the scene while the boys talked about sports. She just sipped on her glass of Moët and smiled at us like she was about to have us for dinner. She was wearing a pair of pink silk shorts that were so short and up her ass that they looked like a thong. The skimpy tank top that she rocked was the same color and material but was a little bit see-through. Her nipples was poking through that shirt like rocks underneath a bed sheet. She was ready, and the more her husband talked the more her ass squirmed around in that plush red love seat and she licked her lips.

Eventually Archie stopped yapping and invited us into their bedroom. It wasn't as dramatic as the living room but was tight. They had a king-size bed with at least five huge pillows on it. It looked like something out of a cheesy-ass Sears catalog or something. I expected it to be whips and chains and all kinds of dildos in there, but it was just regular. Archie gave Dex an envelope with the money in it. Cuz ripped it open and counted the loot real quick before he gave me and Herb this real crazy-ass look.

"Yo man, this is $600 more than what you promised. Normally I would keep my mouth shut when it comes to extra cheese, but I know there has to be a catch."

Archie just laughed after Dex said that. He got up from the edge of the bed where he was sitting and walked over to his closet. He opened the door and picked up a digital camcorder that was on the floor next to his cheap-ass shoes.

"I put in an extra six because I was wondering if you fellas wouldn't mind me taping you in action. If you don't feel comfortable with that then I'll just help myself to that extra cash."

"I'm cool with that if my partners are," Dex said before Archie could finish talking.

I looked at Dex like he had lost his fucking mind. That nigga was getting greedy and I wasn't about to have no part in that shit. Herb was nodding his head too like he was with it, so I knew I was in for a battle. Archie must've thought we was some dumb-ass niggers from up north who would do any damn thing for a dime.

He was at least right for two out of three of us, but I wasn't with that shit. I didn't know his ass well enough to be doing shit on camera. Doing it for Tony was one thing. He was a cool-ass nigga, and I know that he was looking out for us. He was hooking us up with more than one job and only taped us so that he could use it against the cats he was trying to get his money from. So of course I told Archie fuck no, and Dex and Herb were pissed.

We argued for a few minutes, and then Archie came up with a solution that I was happy with and that Dex and Herb were only halfway happy with. Archie said that he would give us the same amount of loot if only Dex and Herb fucked on camera. He was so pressed to get them loot-happy niggas on tape that he didn't care if wifey only got it on with two brothas.

I took my cut and then took a seat on a chair in their bedroom so that the games could begin. They looked kind of salty that I didn't have to do shit, but they got over it when they saw they were getting a couple hundred extra to do what they came to do in the first place.

It was some major fucking going on in that joint that night. First Dex and the boaw Herb took all their shit off and posed for the camera like they were ghetto-ass Chippendales. Then they got BJ's from Goldie while Archie taped it all on his brand-spanking-new camcorder. She would have jammed both of their dicks in her mouth at the same time if she could. I know it. She was going to work on Herb and Dex like they was the last two jawns on earth. Man!

She was deep throating the boaw Herb like it wasn't nothing. Standing shoulder-to-shoulder with Dex, she made him look like his ass barely went through puberty. Every time she would come back to Dex she would try to act like a real porno star and try to get it all in, but she would start gagging. I gotta give her credit for trying though. Of course cuz was loving it. He knew that his shit looked like it belonged on a donkey and he had this cocky look on his face the whole time. I was sitting there cracking up. All you have to do is turn on a camera and niggas start acting like they're in Hollywood. They was talking shit and moaning all loud and spanking her white ass like they were going to be on the Playboy channel.

Dex put on a rubber and started to hit it from the back like a champ while she ate Herb's gun. Dex was lightin' that ass up and she would stop doing Herb and scream and moan like an animal. Archie was loving it. I knew that country-ass pervert had a woody in his brown gabardine slacks.

The money I made working for Tony was sweet, but that was

the sweetest cash I ever made in my life. All I had to do was sit there and watch my cousin and some boaw I hardly knew smash some blond-haired bimbo, as they say in the movies. It was sweet.

10. After the boys nailed Goldie to the wall, me, Dex, and Herb said peace and headed out to this twenty-four-hour soul food diner called Pan-Pan. It was a buffet, so we tore that shit up. Macaroni and cheese, smothered chicken, greens, peach cobbler, and this stuffed crab shit that was off the hook.

Somewhere between our second and third plates these bangin' jawns came in the restaurant. There were about four or five schools down in that one area, so we knew from the gate that they was in college. They sat at the table right across from us. It was tight as hell in that restaurant, so they might as well have been on our laps. It was four of them but it was easy to eliminate which one wouldn't get no play, because the shortest one was tore up. She had a thick neck and looked a little bit like Evander Holyfield.

I got on the thick brown-skinned honey who had cornrows going straight back in her hair. Her lips were thick and sexy and her skin was perfect. She had a little bit of makeup on but I could still tell that there was nothing bad being covered up. Her arms were cut a little bit like she worked out but she wasn't too diesel and bodybuilder-looking. She said her name was Onyx. I asked her if it was her rap name or her real name and she busted out laughing. She told me I had some nerve to crack on her name after I told her mine.

I could tell that I had her open by the way she was blushing. She was so sexy, I wanted to smear that peach cobbler all over her titties and in between her thighs and just lick until every grain of cinnamon and sugar was gone. Damn! I had no idea that it was so much more to her.

Onyx had an accent so I assumed she was from down there, but she said that she was from Texas. She went to Duke and was studying to be a lawyer. None of them were in summer school. She said her and the girls stayed in Durham that summer because it was easy to find a job to save up for the fall semester. All I knew about Duke was that their basketball team was the shit. I guess you had to have your shit together to get in there if you weren't on a basketball scholarship.

Dex hollered at a chick named Denise while Herb made small talk with Rita. I could tell that Herb wasn't really feeling her all like that.

When Onyx asked why we were down there from Philly I told her that we were just blowing through Durham to handle some business, and she didn't ask no more questions. Her conversation blew my mind. She was no chickenhead. She was the kind of jawn I could sit with and talk to for hours. She didn't even curse.

When it was time to roll I played real Big Willie–style and wrote her home number on the edge of a hundred-dollar bill. She acted like she didn't notice, but I saw her eyes light up when I pulled out that knot.

I paid for her buffet when I went to the register and gave the hostess the receipt to give to Onyx. I wrote the motel phone number and our room number on the back of the receipt.

The rest of our trip was real straight in Durham until the shit

hit the fan with our money. The second couple was pretty boring. They didn't want to tape it. This redneck-looking dude paid
us to do the usual to his wife while he watched from the corner
of the bedroom whacking off. Neither one of them was anything
to look at. He paid us in cash before we left and that was that.

The third couple was off the hook. I was in shock when we
rolled up in that piece because they was black. I didn't know that
black people got into freaky shit like that too. They both looked
normal, in their late thirties or early forties, I guess. She was
bangin'. This chick would have made Pam Grier suck her teeth
and roll her eyes if she passed her on the street. Her tatas were
firm and full and didn't sag at all for her to be her age and her
body was the deal. She was toned and smooth like one of them
women in *Essence* magazine in one of them damn naked ads for
cocoa butter. I couldn't tell if she had implants, but they looked
all natural.

The husband picked up the pace halfway through the session.

While Herb was putting his pants back on, the husband got
buck wild and stripped out of his clothes and got in the bed and
started to fuck the shit out of his wife while me and Dex sucked
on her titties.

Dude was diesel like he was in the WWF, and he still rocked a
box haircut like it was the eighties. Me and Dex was tripping
later on when we talked about that cat because we both said he
looked like the only black army man they used to sell back when
we was young boaws. We called him the black G.I. Joe. He sat
there as long as he could before watching all that bonin' got the
best of him. He really didn't need us there because he was handling his wife and he was almost as hung as Dex. I guess they
just needed some city boaws to come set it off in there. Plus, that
nigga could barely stay hard. She was screaming like it was the
end of the world and gripping the back of our heads while we

sucked on her big black nipples. Me and cuz both had scratches on the backs of our necks.

I could kind of see why he needed a little help when we left, because all of us were worn out. That woman was a beast. I hope that I can find a wife one day with a sex drive like that. If I do, I know damn well I wouldn't share it with nobody.

They gave us the green and we was out.

As soon as we got back to the hotel I checked the messages and saw that Onyx had called. She invited us to come over to her apartment and chill for movie night. We were all with it, especially since we didn't plan on driving back to Philly until the next day.

We changed our gear and drove over to her apartment at about midnight. Onyx, Rita, and Denise were casually dressed like they had all just come from working out. I expected them to be all dolled up but they were real laid-back. They were a world of difference from the Philly chicks I had messed with.

We watched *The Wood* and *The Best Man* on Onyx's DVD player. When the other four fell asleep at around four in the morning me and Onyx checked out *Whatever Happened to Baby Jane?* I had peeped it a while back and she said it was one of her favorites. We knew the rest of them niggas wouldn't have liked it, so we waited until they were all knocked out.

I know I didn't know her all that well at that point but we definitely connected up in that piece. She only let me kiss her once on the cheek. No freaky shit or nothing. She wasn't even trying to slip me tongue. She was a classy jawn.

I woke Dex and Herb up at around quarter to seven so that we could go back to the hotel to get our shit and hit the road. I was feeling kind of good at that point since I had met a honey that I could see myself driving down 95 south to go and see every now and then. And then the bricks hit all of us.

All of the money that we didn't have in our pockets was gone. Somebody got all three of us for our private stashes. We had about $350 on us but the rest was gone. [I stashed all of my loot in a small side pocket on my bag and only took $40 with me.] We was mad as shit. Herb went right over to the front desk and made a big-ass scene. Me and Dex had to keep him from snatching the fat red-faced man from behind the counter and busting his ass.

"Yo, one of your fucking workers got me and my boys for our money and that shit had better turn up real quick!"

The motel dude told us that no cleaning people had been there since we left the night before but we wasn't trying to hear that shit. When I saw Dex reaching for the burner he had stashed in his waist I knew it was time to roll out of there before it got ugly. We were already wanted in Philly and we didn't need any more drama, especially with guns, or our asses would really be done.

As hard as it was, I knew that we would have to just take it as a loss. It was killing me, trying to figure out how we got taken for our loot. The only people who knew where we were staying were the jawns we met and the three couples who we came to see.

The jobs knew what motel we were at, but none of us could remember whether or not we told them exactly which room we were staying in. Herb blamed it on the jawns while he was slamming shit into his overnight bag. He figured that they told us to come over the apartment so that they could send some cats in to rob us. I wasn't trying to hear that shit, and that's when me and Herb were about to go to war there in room 326. If it wasn't for Dex we would have strangled each other to death.

"Yo, them jawns got us for our loot and you's a dickhead if you don't see it. If you wasn't trying to floss and flashing money all up in that bitch's face at the diner, then they wouldn't have known we had cash like that."

"What! You trying to blame this shit on me, nigga? Them jawns didn't have shit to do with this!"

"How the fuck you know that? Your nose is so open over that ho that you can't fucking see straight. Why can't you get it through your head that they might have got us. We don't know nobody else down there. You expect me to believe that it's a co-incidence that we got robbed like that?"

I stormed out of the room and walked around the parking lot of the motel to cool off. I wanted to knock Herb's head the fuck off. I knew Onyx and her girls didn't get down like that. I was from the streets and I was used to snakes. You would have to get up early in the morning to pull the wool over my fucking eyes. I knew that I wasn't that easy. If somebody was right under my nose stealing money from me I would smell that shit in a heart-beat. Herb didn't know what the fuck he was talking about, simple and plain.

I got a bag of chips and a Pepsi from the vending machine before I went back up into the room. Both of them niggas had packed by then and they were ready to roll. I just stood there and looked around the room before I got my stuff together and headed to the car. None of us said anything to each other when we got in the ride.

A few minutes passed before Dex broke the silence.

"Yo cuz, you wanna ride over there and ask them bitches if they know anything about our money being gone?"

"Yo, I really don't think they had anything to do with it. What are we going to ask them if we do go over there? How are we go-ing to bring that shit up?"

Herb butted in and added his two cents like anybody was fucking talking to him.

"Yo, I say we roll over to that jawn's crib and slap them broads up until they tell where the clowns are that robbed us."

"That's not going to jump off, bruh," I said. "Ain't nobody getting slapped up, because they didn't have anything to do with that shit."

Dex pulled into the Texaco station across from the motel and turned the radio down.

"Listen Herb, I think my cousin is right. I think one them junkie motherfuckers who was staying at the motel broke into our room and got us, or either the security guard or somebody there at the motel. I think we might have to just suck it up and go back to Philly without the money."

Herb was irked but it wasn't shit he could do about it. Same with all of us.

None of us had much to say to each other on the way back to Philly. Dex blasted his Jigga CD and Herb just stared out the window, nodding his head. I just stretched out on the backseat, closed my eyes, and tried not to think about it. A good few hours of sleep always makes me think better. All I needed was a nap to clear my head and figure out why the fuck everything was going wrong in my life.

11. I chilled for a whole week once we got back to the crib.

I ain't call nobody. I ain't hang out on the block. Nothing. I just stayed my black ass in the house and laid low.

It was kind of boring at first. All I did was sleep, eat, and then sleep some more. Dex didn't call me at all that week and I was cool with that. Just when I thought I was about to lose my mind on that Thursday I went downstairs and chilled with my mom. We were real close at one time, but when I started getting caught up in all our little "get money" schemes I hardly talked to her.

My mom is active in the church and all that jazz, and everybody in the neighborhood treats her like she's their mom too. She ain't dated that much since Pop got killed when I was young. The streets say my dad was trying to rob the corner store when we used to live down in South Philly. My mom told me that he would never do nothing like that. Deep down I think that she just told me that to spare my feelings or some shit. It don't matter to me anyway. He's dead just the same and the Korean motherfucker who smoked him didn't have to serve one day in jail.

I don't know how my mom did it but she managed to handle me and my rotten-ass sister. My uncles helped out every now and then, but for the most part Mom held us down. She put in mad hours down at that nursing home just to make sure that we were taken care of.

She's mad cool, even though she's always reading her Bible and telling me that I need to come to church. One thing though, she never trips out on me and tries to judge me like a lot of other church folks that I know. I like to call them Holy Rollers because they shout on Sunday morning and roll out to the hot spot on Sunday night.

I was getting so caught up that I hardly ever stayed my ass in the house and rapped to my mom the way I used to. I can pretty much talk to her about anything, but the shit we were into was too damn much to be dropping on her ears. I just kept it to myself.

She has this thing for *The Golden Girls*. The shit comes on like five times a day on Lifetime or one of the cable channels, and she watches it every damn time. When she's not at home she sets the VCR on the downstairs TV to tape. I know that she has seen every fucking episode at least ten times, but that doesn't stop her from watching it every day anyway. Going to church every Sunday and watching *The Golden Girls* is all she needs to be happy.

I didn't have shit else to do so that day I decided to go downstairs and watch it with her. I have to admit, that shit is funny. It was way funnier than I thought it would be. The tall one with the deep voice had me cracking the fuck up. She used to play on *Maude* too. Those faces she makes remind me of one of those mean-ass ushers who used to cut me and my sister the nasty eye every time we laughed in church.

Anyway, I forget why my mother wasn't home the next day but I decided to watch the show again without her. I would have never thought that a show about four old chicks would open up my eyes and help me to figure out what the fuck was going on in my life.

The episode I saw that Friday was about them broads going away to something like a mystery weekend where they stayed at a hotel and had to figure out who the killer was on a fake-ass murder scenario. They did the same thing on *The Jeffersons*. The tall chick with the deep voice figured out who done it. The one who used to play on *Maude*.

Anyway, I was just sitting there watching when it all became clear to me. It just slapped me right upside my head. I ran up the steps and threw on some jean shorts, a Sixers jersey, and my Tims and I was out.

I remember that day so clear because it was the day that everything all started to fall into place. It was a little bit of brains and whole lot of luck that helped it all come together.

I walked for about twenty minutes until I was almost out of North Philly and closer to downtown. I ran up in one of them pizza joints on Spring Garden Street and got a couple dollars' worth of change for the phone booth.

I walked out to the sidewalk and juggled that change back and forth in my hands until I got enough nerve to drop thirty-five cents into the phone and make that call. I think I knew before I even made the call to tell the truth I just had to hear somebody else say out loud what I was thinking.

First I called information to get the number to the police headquarters down at Eighth and Race. After I got the main number to the Roundhouse I walked back into the pizza joint and got a vanilla cream soda and a bag of chips. I was stalling. I knew what I had to do but I was just on some other ol' shit that day.

I hustled my ass back out to the phone booth and called the main number. Some female cop put me through to the homicide department, and that's when I started asking questions.

Before I asked one question, though, I told them that I may have information about Tony Salvatore's death. I knew that would get the cop's attention, and I knew that he would give me what I needed.

The first thing I asked Officer Simmons was what was the description of the suspects in the case. He paused for a few seconds. I could hear him shuffling papers, trying to hurry up and find the sheet on Tony's murder.

He told me that the two people who were wanted for questioning were two black men in their mid to late twenties. He said that they were both over six feet and of medium complexion.

What the fuck was that? That sounded like every other nigga from South Philly to Wynnefield. I was frustrated at first because Officer Simmons's description was no fucking help.

I moved on to the next question. I asked him when were these two people last seen at the scene of the crime. He told me he didn't want to answer that over the phone. He said that he wanted me to come down to the Roundhouse and speak with someone in person. Whatever. I wasn't trying to hear that shit. I was getting ready to bang on that fool because I knew that I had been on the phone way too long, and them clowns was probably trying to trace where I was at so that they could run up on me and drag me in for questioning. Before I could get the phone away from my ear and hang it the hell up, I heard the cop tell me to hold up.

"I almost missed this morsel of information," he said. There was a long pause, too damn long, and then he cleared his throat. "One of the young men that we would like to question has a birthmark on the right side of his face. Do you know anyone who fits. . ."

I slammed down the phone before he could even finish the sentence. I had already heard too much. I knew it. I fucking knew it.

Dex was wanted alright, but I wasn't wanted with that motherfucker.

Whoever gave the cops that description saw him and Herb

down in South Philly at Tony's house. It had to be before me and him rolled up in Tony's spot and saw his dead body.

Shit was all starting to make sense at that point. The more I think about it the more I think about Dex being so damn calm when me and him went down to South Philly that day. He was way too fucking calm. It was almost like he knew that Tony was going to be dead when we rolled up in that piece. I was freaking the fuck out and he was shook too, but it wasn't the same.

I should've known something was up. I mean, just the fact that Dex was pressed to get down to South Philly to see Tony on the day when the Sixers were playing the Lakers in the fucking NBA finals. He was the biggest damn Sixers fan. His ass should have been glued to the TV. That nigga didn't leave his house one day during the regular season games that were on TV, and he made it to most of the home games down at the First Union Center. And on the day of the biggest fucking game for the Sixers since 1983, he was killing himself to get down there to see Tony. I should've known right there.

After I hung up on the cop, I walked back home going up little streets and zigzagging all over North just in case the cops had traced the call and were trying to find out who the anonymous caller was.

My mind was racing like crazy. I knew that my cousin Dex was shady with niggas in the streets, but I was starting to think that he was slimier than I knew.

And even though the cop wasn't giving up all the info over the phone, I knew that if he answered my question he would have told me that the suspects were seen at Tony's spot way before that day. My cousin, even if it was only my play cousin, was a fucking snake.

By the time I got back to my crib I had a headache. My mom was home by then and she was sitting downstairs watching her tape of *The Golden Girls*. It was the same episode I was watching before I rolled out.

It got me to thinking about why I stormed out of there in the first place. I had a gut feeling all of a sudden that Dex knew way more about Tony getting popped than he was saying. But the show made me think that Dex or Herb or both of them motherfuckers got me for my loot when I was down in North Carolina.

The jawn who plays the slut on *The Golden Girls* had a murder rap pinned on her in that episode. The chick who used to play Maude got her off because she figured out that some other old lady was the killer. The killer slipped up by saying too much. She claimed she was never in the room where the murder took place but she described something that was in the room that she would've never seen if she wasn't in the room. I think it was some lingerie on the bed or something like that.

It's funny how the human brain works, because when I saw that shit I just flash-backed to that hotel room and the day we went to see Onyx and her girls. When we rolled out to go see the girls, Dex was fiddling with his plastic hotel key in his hands while we walked to the car. I could see it in my head. But when we got back to the room I remember his key was sitting right on top of the television. I was the first one to walk in the room and I remember it sitting there, right next to an empty bag of Rold Gold pretzels.

I was sure that we only got two room keys because I was the one who dealt with the guy at the front desk when we checked in. I gave one key to Dex and I kept the other one for myself.

So how the fuck did the key beat Dex back to the room, since he had it in his hand before we rolled out? And since Dex never left my sight that whole night, how did he get my cash? Him and Herb were knocked out and I never went to sleep that night, so how did he pull that shit off?

I had a lot of questions running through my head that Friday night. I was damn there in a trance sitting in the living room when the phone rang.

"Wassup, cousin? Me and Meka are rolling down to Bluezette tonight to get a grub. I heard that Friday night's off the hook down there."

"You know I ain't got no loot like that, Dex."

"Come on now, you know I got you, cuz. Call up one of your honeys and invite her. Don't worry about the bill. I got you."

At first I started to make an excuse and blow him off. I didn't even want to be in the same room with him and I really didn't want to be out with Meka, but something told me to just go with the flow and go to Bluezette. The catfish down there is all that and I was hungry as shit.

I was glad I went. If I was ninety percent sure that my cousin was a snake and a liar before I went out that night, the other ten percent came sliding right into my hand underneath the table.

12.   If somebody wrote a book or a movie about all that went down with me in the summer of 2001, that night would be the part where the suspense picked up.

Motherfuckers would be on the edges of their seats, just on the strength of all the twists and turns that were jumping off anyway.

The restaurant was off the hook that night. Honeys was crawling all over the place. I was kind of salty that I brought this girl Dynisha that I was messing with at the time with me up in that piece. I should've rolled up in there solo so that I could holla at some of them jawns over at the bar. The Philly bitches was representin' lovely that night. Most of them was playing it cool and profiling at the bar. Some of them freaks was so busy trying to get Eric Benet's attention that they looked stupid. He was chilling at a table in the corner with a couple of his boaws, I guess. I was waiting for that nigga to holla back at one of them chicks so I could call Halle Berry and rat on his ass. I know I ain't have her number or nothing but I would have found it. I was ready to playa hate the shit out of his ass. I could slap the shit out of Dave Justice for fucking that up. She's a dime. Damn!

Anyway, I was mad that I brought Dynisha, but the good

thing is that she was looking way tighter than Meka that night. Dex's jawn had this long-ass blond weave in her head even though she's a heartbeat darker than Whoopi Goldberg. I hate to see dark-skinned jawns with blond and white hair in their heads. They do that shit for other women because I ain't never heard a nigga say it looked good. Her nails had like ten colors on them, and that's another thing that chicks do for other chicks, because niggas don't care.

Anyway, my jawn looked good as shit. Dynisha was rocking a short black skirt and a halter top with her whole back out. She didn't have one roll or none of them nasty-ass stretch marks. She's normally light-skinned, but her summer tan had her looking like toasted cinnamon all over. Her hair was up in a ponytail and she had on sandals that wrapped all the way up her thick, sexy calves. She was tight.

Bluezette is two stories high and big as shit. All of us got seated at a booth in the blue room on the second floor. We were a few tables down from where Jill Scott and some dude she was eating with was sitting. I was going to holla at her and tell her how dope her album was, but she was tearing her food up and they didn't look like they wanted to be interrupted.

There was some tension at the table. Meka was rolling her eyes at Dynisha before our waitress could bring us our water. I think she was feeling some kind of way there was somebody hotter than her ass. She didn't handle competition too well.

I didn't pay them too much attention, though. I couldn't keep my mind off Dex. This nigga who was sitting right across the table from me grinning all up in my face and calling me "cuz" had it out for me.

We were tight as shit, but after that phone call to the Roundhouse everything changed. It was like I was sitting across the table from the enemy. I made sure I acted normal like nothing was different, but everything was different. I was watching that nigga like a hawk. I peeped the way he drank his water, the way he fumbled with his handkerchief and shit, the way he rubbed Meka on the cheek and licked his lips.

I was waiting for him to slip up some kind of way and give me another clue right then and there, but he wouldn't do that until much later. And man did he fuck up! As good as Dynisha was looking that night I wasn't giving her the time of day. I would handle her later. She was definitely going to catch it later. From the front, the side, the back. Shit, I was trying to invent in my head new positions to get in that ass.

Right after the waitress handed us the menus Dex said that he had to take a piss, and he got up from the table and headed to the bathroom. As soon as he stood up my eyes went straight down to the table, where his cell phone was. He left it right next to his handkerchief. It was one of them new jawns that are real small.

Something told me to pick that shit up and look at it. From the minute I scooped his phone off the table, Meka never took her eyes off me. She was gritting on me from across our booth like I stole something from her ass.

"What are you doing with Dex's phone?"

"You talking to me?" I said. I never looked up at her, though. I just kept my hands moving on his little silver phone.

"You the only one sitting there with a phone in your hand."

"You need to mind your business."

"My man is my business and that's his phone, so that's why I'm asking."

"So Dex is your man now? That's news to me. I wonder if he be telling every fucking body around the way that you're his girl. What you think?"

I knew that would shut her nut ass up. She was quiet for a few seconds before she opened up her trap again.

"I wish he'd hurry up back from the bathroom so we can order."

My fingers were moving fast as shit, and I was scrolling down the phone list that Dex had stored in the phone's memory. He had a lot of names up in it, but most of them looked familiar.

Nate. Alana. Pookie. Vera. Netta. Tarik. Malika. Meka. Niya. Christina.

They were all people that I knew too, so nothing seemed shady about that. But right when Dex was pushing his way through the crowd and walking back to our table I saw a number in the 919 area code with the name Bleu over top of it. Who the fuck is Bleu?

I knew right off that that was the area code for Durham. Dex would never program the number to one of the jobs in his cell phone. Or would he? I never met or heard him talk of nobody named Bleu.

"What you all up in my cellie for, nigga?"

"I was just making sure you got my number programmed up in here," I said. I handed the phone back to Dex. He had a big-ass smirk on his face.

"You know I got your number in my cellie. You're the first damn number I programmed in that jawn."

For a split second it looked like he was getting suspicious, so I said something real quick.

"Yo cuz, I know you have my cellie number, but it got turned off. I was checking to see if you had the house number in there."

"When the hell your phone get cut off?"

"The other day. I just erased it and put the house number in there. It's still the first number on your stored list."

"Oh aight, that's wassup. As long as I can get to you right away. You never know when we might have to make a run down 95 again."

"You know it," I said. I reached across the table and gave Dex some dap. When I slapped his hand it was like I was touching a lizard or some shit. He was cold-blooded. My stomach was turning on the inside. It was balling into a tight knot. I was ready to go up in that nigga's mouth just because. We was supposed to be tight and he had so much going on behind my back.

And Meka. Since I couldn't trust my own damn cousin I definitely couldn't trust her. Her eyes was cutting through me like fucking razors the whole night, but I didn't give a fuck. She was the least of my problems.

We all ordered our food and started to wreck the rolls and cornbread they put in front of us. Meka was still acting funny toward Dynisha but we were so into each other that it didn't matter. It was all good.

That jawn was getting more and more crowded as the night went on. There were a lot of niggas from the Sixers and the Eagles rolling up in there that night. I guess that's why the freaks were up in there like that. They could smell money from a mile away, underneath a pile of burning tires. Duce Staley, Aaron McKie, Eric Snow, and Donovan McNabb were all hanging around the second-floor bar not far from our table.

A few minutes after our food came is when shit really started to jump off. Dex ain't hardly have a mouthful of macaroni and cheese in his mouth when the boaw Herb came rolling up to our table out of nowhere. He was by himself and way underdressed for Bluezette. He was rocking a pair of blue jeans, a white T-shirt and his Tims.

"Yo wassup, y'all. That food look good as shit. Yo Dex, I need to holla at you for a minute. It won't take long."

"How you know I was here, Herb?"

"You told me before you bounced, nigga."

"Oh yeah, that's right. What's up? I'm trying to get my grub on."

"I need to holla at you outside for a couple minutes."

"Aight, I'll be back, y'all."

Dex got up and started to walk away. I was happy for a split second because that would give me a chance to snoop through his cellie again. That didn't last long though. They were a good five steps from the table when Herb asked Dex to use his cell phone. He turned around and scooped it off the table and headed down the stairs and out of sight.

The whole time they were gone it was killing me. I would've killed somebody to know what the fuck they were talking about and why Herb needed to come down there and talk about it. I wanted to know every fucking word that was going back and forth between them niggas just because. I wished I was a fly on the wall outside of that damn restaurant. The crazy part is that my wish came true. Kind of, anyway.

It was like twenty minutes before Dex came back. He wasn't grinning no more. His face looked hard and stressed. I've seen him with that look before. It was the look he got on his face when he was about to go and whip somebody's ass.

"Yo, I'm going to get a doggie bag for my grub. We need to get rolling because I got some business to handle."

"Is everything straight, cuz?"

"Yeah, I'm cool. I just gotta handle something, that's all."

"That's cool with me. I'm finished my food anyway."

Dex didn't even attempt to touch his food. He looked pissed. Whatever Herb told him irked the shit out of that nigga. I almost threw up when Meka started kissing him on his neck and licking his earlobe.

While Meka was starting the foreplay and Dynisha was packing up her leftovers into the container, Dex kicked my foot under the table and grabbed my knee. When I reached down I felt his hand and a few crumpled-up bills. Even though he was a slimy bastard, he made sure he didn't play me in front of them jawns. He knew I was low on cash, but he wanted me to play it off so I didn't look like a total lame.

Like I said before, if I was ninety percent sure that my cousin was a snake and a liar before I went out that night, the other ten percent came sliding right into my hand underneath the table.

It was $170 all together. A twenty, a fifty, and a crumpled C note.

The hundred-dollar bill made my blood boil as soon as I looked at it. When I went to fold the three bills so I could stuff them in my pocket, I looked down and something caught my eye right away.

Right to the left of Benjamin Franklin's big-ass head was something so fucking familiar. My handwriting. It didn't take but a second for me to realize that this was the same hundred I wrote Onyx's number on. The same C note that I put back in my pocket when we left the Pan-Pan diner back in Durham. The same hundred that I stashed in my luggage that went missing before we even left the state of North Carolina.

I wanted to kick Dex in his fucking forehead.

I thought he must be smoking crack or something. Did he need the money that bad that he had to steal from me? I know it wasn't the most legal thing in the world, but I worked hard for that money. Every stroke, every titty I sucked, I earned that shit.

It was definitely on after I saw that. I stashed the hundred in my pocket and pulled out the fifty to pay for me and Dynisha. We rolled right out of there.

Getting that hundred from Dex, which was really mine in the first place, just fucked up my whole night. I didn't think anything else could happen that night. What else could I find out in one night about this bitch-ass nigga I used to consider one of my main niggas and my cousin?

What I had waiting for me at home that night blew the call to the cops and the hundred-dollar bill right out the fucking water. Way out the fucking water.

The blinking red light in the dark set that shit off and changed everything.

13. After Dex dropped us off, me and Dynisha tiptoed across the living room, through the kitchen, and down the basement steps. It was only about twelve thirty, which is early for a Friday night, but my mom was in the house and all of the lights were turned out. I knew that she was up in her room knocked out though. She could hardly keep her eyes open long enough to see the weather on the news half the time.

I was feeling kind of nice. I had busted a tight-ass grub at Bluezette and I had a honey sitting on my mother's plush black leather couch in the basement. I popped *Gladiator* in the DVD player and took off my shirt. She unlaced her sandals and curled up on the couch like she was at her own crib.

Dynisha was trying to act like she wasn't peeping me in the white wife beater, but I could see her scoping me out. The way she was looking at me I could tell that she wanted to rip my white tank top off with her teeth. Shit was definitely about to pop off.

I ran back up to the kitchen and threw some popcorn into the microwave. I wanted her ass to be deep throatin' me before we got halfway through the movie or the bowl of popcorn. Whichever came first.

She had a dope-ass body and she smelled so good, but she

wasn't the kind of girl that I wanted to make my main jawn. When we met a few summers ago she gave up the skins in less than a week. I don't think she's a ho or nothing like that, but on the real that ain't the way you get a nigga like me to give you a ring.

Right when Russell Crowe was about to get his ass eaten the fuck up by the lions in the coliseum, that's when shit started to jump off. I was playing it cool, not acting pressed at all. Dynisha was licking on my earlobe and rubbing her hand all over my chest. I was glad I did like a hundred push-ups that night before I went to the restaurant. My shit was proper and I know she could feel it. She moved her hand down my chest and stomach to my dick, since I was acting like I wasn't paying her any attention. I just kept on throwing back the popcorn and sipping on my glass of raspberry iced tea.

She was rubbing and stroking my shit through my black khakis and I was starting to respond. In like ten motherfucking seconds she was gripping my hard-ass dick and looking at the thick print through my pants. That's when I started talking shit.

"What you gon' do with that?"

She was blushing like I gave her a compliment, but she never let go of the hammer. I knew she was with it.

"I don't know what I'm gon' do with it. You tell me."

I could see she was trying to start a little back-and-forth type thing and I wasn't feeling that, so I just cut to the motherfucking chase. I unzipped my pants and slid them down my legs and kicked them off onto the floor. My jawn was standing at attention through the slit in my boxers. I felt like I was in middle school again. Dynisha had me feeling like I was about to get head for the first time. Damn!

She went to work like the pro I remembered her to be. It was off the hook. She gave me the five-star, two-nights-at-the-Four-Seasons-hotel BJ, even though I only took her ass to Bluezette.

I was trying to tell her that I was about to come, but shit wasn't coming out of my mouth. I could've tried harder to tell her, but whatever. That shit was off the hook when I came because she kept going like a champ. She didn't gag or slow down or nothing. That freak didn't let one single drop hit my mother's couch either. She was the bomb and I didn't even get the panties off yet.

After I was able to get myself together enough to stand up, I told Dynisha that I was going upstairs to get some rubbers. I planned on blazing her ass and I wanted to make sure I was strapped. She went in the basement bathroom to get her shit together and I jetted up the steps to my room.

I don't even have to say that I was feeling good at that point. She hooked me up so thorough that I had totally forgot about bitch-ass Dex and shady-ass Herb. They were the last damn thing on my mind. I would deal with all that later.

I crept up the living room steps and tiptoed past my mother's room. She sleeps like a rock, but I still didn't want to take the chance of waking her up. I opened the door to my room real slow because sometimes it creeks loud as shit. The nightstand to my bed where I keep my Trojans is right by the door, so I didn't even plan on going all the way in my room or turning on the light. My plan was just to scoop a few Magnums out the top drawer and go back downstairs to Dynisha and all that gravy.

That shit didn't happen. I didn't think that anything could take my mind off all the booty waiting for me in the basement. Right after I grabbed the rubbers and closed the drawer and was about to pull my door shut, I glanced across my room and saw the blinking red light in the dark. That set the shit off and changed everything.

It occurred to me then that I didn't check my messages. At first I paused and started not to. I figured that if another honey called, then it didn't matter, because I already had a bad-ass bitch downstairs who had already drank my babies. It wasn't like if a hotter bitch was on the tape that I was going to kick Dynisha out and call up somebody else. Just leave it alone, I was thinking, but naw. I had to check them messages.

I stepped into my room and shut the door behind me. I never turned on the light, because my eyes had adjusted to the dark and I could see everything I needed to see.

I walked across to the answering machine that was sitting on top of my dresser and looked down at the flashing numbers. There were two messages. If I had known that the second one was going to suck the fucking air out of my lungs I would have sat my ass down to listen to it. I hit the play button and slid the volume button down on the side.

The first message was from this Chinese boaw we call Chen. Me and Kam met him when we was at community. He acted black, dressed black, and if you closed your eyes and listened to him talk you would swear it was Nas or one of them other Queens rappers talking. He was like

> Hey wassup boaw, this is Chen. Hit me back when you get a minute. You ain't holla at a nigga in a minute. Have you talked to Kam? I lost his number. Holla at me when you get this. We gotta hit the club. I'm tired of y'all niggas keeping all the black honeys to yourself. Peace.

I was cracking up at Chen's crazy ass. He's a funny dude. That was the last time I laughed like that for a while. The next message started out real crazy. At first all I could hear was a lot of noise. I could hear car horns and something that sounded like a bus. The first thing I thought was that it was a mistake. I had my finger on the delete button but I stopped myself from pushing it when I heard my name. Or at least I thought I heard someone say my name. I put my ear closer to the answering machine and slid the volume button up a little so that I could hear better.

And just like that I could make out Dex's voice. It took a few more seconds for me to realize that he was talking to Herb. I was thinking, why in the hell are they on my machine having a conversation?

The more the message played the more I could hear them talking. They must've been walking away from the noise because I could make out everything they were saying after a minute.

I could feel the veins popping up out the side of my head the more I listened. They were spilling the fucking beans. Them niggas was running that shit down right through the speakers on my answering machine in my dark-ass bedroom. I was already hip to them rats, but that shit just pushed me right over the edge. This was more proof than I ever needed in my whole life. Them niggas was in up to their throats in some real shit and now they was going to pull me in with them.

I was mad as hell, but I remember feeling happy at the same time. I was happy that them niggas was stupid enough to put their whole damn conversation on my machine. I'll never know how that happened, but all I could guess is that Dex hit the talk button by mistake on his cellie and it called my crib. That had to be what happened. Because the call was recorded around the same time that those motherfuckers went outside to talk. The entire message was like five minutes. They were still talking when my machine cut it off or the cell phone ran out of juice. Damn, I wanted to hear what else they were talking about, but on the real I had heard all I needed to hear. Them bitch-ass niggas put their shit out there and now I knew.

But now that I knew, I still didn't know what I was going to do about it. I was amped as shit that night. It was one thirty in the morning and I felt like it was the middle of the day. I was scared because of what I had stumbled into because of my dick. I was sweating like crazy in that room. Getting paid to get ass backfired even more than it had already. If I was going to live to see my twenty-seventh birthday I knew I had to ditch Dex, Herb, and all of North Philly for a minute.

I was so caught up in that tape that I totally forgot that Dynisha was down in the basement waiting to get nailed. I really wasn't thinking about her after I listened to the tape for the second time. I hit the stop button before it could get to the end of the message again and hustled down the steps to the basement.

I know that I was shook, because I wasn't even fazed when I walked down into the basement and Dynisha was butt-ass naked on the couch with her legs cocked the fucked open. She was licking her lips and playing with her nipples. Any other day I would've been in it like Bennett, but I walked right past her ass and hit the power button on the DVD player.

"What the fuck is wrong with you?"

"Ain't nothing wrong with me. Something came up. You gon' have to bounce."

"What nigga? I'm gon' have to bounce? What the hell is on your bird? You think it's sweet like that? You think you just gon' get your dick sucked and then kick me to the curb? That's real fucking trifling and selfish, nigga!"

"Yo, you need to lower your fucking voice for one. My mom is sleep."

"I should wake her up and tell her that her son is a fucking noodle! What, you can't get it up? You probably was up there jerking off all that time trying to get it up again. That's why you sweating like a damn hog."

"Whatever yo, just get dressed and get up out of here. I got somewhere to be. Look, I'm sorry I can't even get into it right now, but I have to go to Delaware to help my boaw out. He needs me."

"Am I supposed to believe that?"

"Look, I don't care if you believe me or not. It's the truth. Now can you get your clothes on, please."

Dynisha jumped off the couch and started throwing her clothes back on like a madwoman. She was pissed. I wanted to nail. Man, I wanted to nail, but I just wasn't in that frame of mind anymore. I don't know what my frame of mind was, but it didn't have nothing to do with getting no ass.

"So how am I supposed to get home?"

"I'll take you. I'll get the keys to my mom's whip and drop you off at your crib."

"I'm not going home tonight. I'm going over to my cousin Angel's house. She live off Stenton Avenue in Oak Lane."

"Aight, I got you. Let's roll."

I threw my clothes back on and grabbed the keys to my mom's Altima off the coffee table in the living room and headed out the door. Dynisha huffed and puffed and sucked her teeth the whole way up the expressway. I didn't care if she had attitude. I didn't care if she didn't get no dick.

I was in the middle of a fucking movie and my life was falling apart. And at that point I didn't know if I was in a movie where the young black guy gets fucked up and left for dead. Or the flick where the black guy just gets offed first.

While she was bitching and moaning, I was just hoping that I would be the nigga that was still around after the credits rolled.

14. By the time I got back to my crib it was around two thirty. I stopped at the Sunoco station and bought a sixty-minute calling card because I didn't want any of the calls I was going to make showing up on my mom's phone bill.

The house was still quiet. I put the keys back on the coffee table and went in the kitchen to get a glass of ginger ale. My stomach was on some ol' other shit.

I was freaked the hell out and scared of Dex all of a sudden. The same boaw that I rolled with ever since I could remember had me looking over my shoulder. The whole ride back down 76, I could hear his voice ringing in my head. The message on my answering machine was playing over and over again. I was so damn shook driving back that every time I saw a Honda Accord I tensed up thinking that it was Dex following me.

I almost banged out when I was getting off at Girard Avenue, when I looked to my left and saw this cat who looked just like that motherfucker. It wasn't him, but damn, it looked like him. Then again, that motherfucker could have looked like Pee Wee Herman for all I knew. It didn't matter that night. Nothing mattered.

I was seeing that boaw, hearing that boaw, and smelling him

too. He wore this Issey Miyake oil that I liked and he was so much in my head I was smelling him.

Once I got to the top of the steps I paused for a minute to make sure my mom was still sleep. I heard something and I figured that since I borrowed her car she had heard me pull up. One time the smokers was trying to break in the passenger-side door and she jumped up right out of her sleep and started screaming for me to call the cops. She had a sixth sense when it came to that Altima, so I was not surprised at all that she was up.

Instead of going in the room to tell her that I borrowed her whip to take Dynisha home, I just kept on creeping back to my room. I pushed open the door and stepped in without flipping on the light switch. The light on my answering machine was blinking again. Who the fuck else called me this late? I was thinking. I almost jumped out of my skin after I pushed the door closed and started to walk across the room toward my dresser.

"Where you been, nigga?"

"What the fuck! Dex, you scared the shit out me! What the hell you doing in here?"

"Chill yo. You act like we don't have keys to each other's cribs and shit."

That nigga was laying across my bed the wrong way with his feet propped up on my pillows. I could hardly see his face but the moonlight made his teeth stand out. His loafers were at the foot of the bed.

"Yo dude, take your hummin'-ass feet off my pillows. I gotta put my head there."

"Now you know my feet don't stink, nigga. You ain't never answer my question. Where you been?"

"Where I been? I been minding my damn business. What's up with you popping in here damn near three in the morning?"

"I figured you would be tearing them guts up right about now. What happened to your honey?"

"Man, I had to take her ass home."

"You ain't get no ass?"

"Naw. Man keep your voice down, you gon' wake my mom up."

"Oh, my bad. I ain't trying to make Aunt Jaime mad at this time in the morning. So why you ain't hit?"

"I don't know, I guess I ain't feel like it."

"Whatever man. I saw how you was looking at that ass to-night. You was looking at it like you wanted to rip that skirt off and spark it up right in the restaurant."

"Well if you thought we was in here getting our freak on, why you come over here then?"

"Man, you act like I don't know you like the back of my hand. You act like you ain't damn there my blood."

"Yeah, yeah, whatever. You just came over here on some ol' cock-blocking shit, that's all. And where the fuck is your car? I didn't see that shit outside."

"Mcka got it. She gon' come and get me in the morning. But naw for real, I figured that if y'all was going to bone her you would take her to the basement where it's all decked out and shit. I know that you wasn't trying to bring her upstairs so your mom could hear."

Me and Dex were going back and forth in my room like everything was cool. It took me a minute before I snapped out of that shit and came back to earth. This was the same nigga who I had made up in my head was now the enemy. I could trust him as far as I could throw Starr Jones's fat ass across the Delaware River.

I was just rapping with Dex and taking my clothes off, trying not to act all corny and shit. I didn't want to let on no kind of way that I knew what I knew and that I heard what I heard. That was the main thing I kept saying to myself. I had to play it cool.

All that shit was tested though when I walked over to the dresser and saw the light flashing. Shit! That's right when I started to get paranoid. I just knew that Dex had listened to my messages. If he heard that shit, why didn't he say something? I glanced at the machine again and saw the number two blinking. I turned on the lamp that sits on top of my dresser and opened the second drawer to get out my pajama pants.

"You ain't gon' check your messages? I know that at least one of them is me on there."

I froze right where I was standing when he said that. I had my hands buried in my boxers and socks and I just kept looking down into the drawer. I didn't know what the fuck to do. I wanted to turn around and just flare on his ass. I saw myself drilling him with like ten haymakers and then running out of that room and into the streets and screaming for 5-0 to just come and lock his crazy ass up.

It seemed like I was standing there with my back to him for like fucking forever but it had to be only a few seconds. I had so many questions going on in my head and I was trying to think of something to say. I didn't want to end up like Tony Salvatore. Why was he doing this shit and when did my cousin turn into a sick, homicidal bastard? What was he trying to prove?

I had to say something.

"What you mean, one of them is from you?"

I pulled the pajama pants out of the drawer and turned around to face him. Dex sat up on the bed and sat on the edge of the bed with this sneaky-ass look on his face.

"What part don't you understand, nigga? Like I said, I know

that one of them jawns on there is from me. Hit play. I want you to listen to it."

"Why don't you just tell me what's on there?"

Dex started laughing. But it wasn't a laugh like, ha-ha funny. It was a laugh like, I know what you know and you know that I know it.

"Whatever, man, just play the message. I want you to hear it. You'll get a killer laugh out of it."

That's when I almost slipped up. I look back on it now and think that if that nigga was just a little bit smarter he would have caught on. I just blurted that shit out.

"Yo man, what if I tell you I heard that shit already."

It was quiet for a few seconds and Dex had this confused look on his face. He didn't look mad, he just looked irked.

"Nigga, how you heard the message when I just left it on there five minutes ago."

"Five minutes ago?"

"Yeah, I called from my cellie when I was sitting out in the car in front of the house. I was calling to see if you were up in here first. What you talking about?"

"Oh, my bad. I don't know what the fuck I'm talking about. I thought you were talking about a message you left earlier today."

I turned around and hit the play button quick before he could say anything else. The first message was from Dynisha.

Hey, this is Nisha. Listen, I hope that you don't think that you just gon' be able to come scoop me whenever you want to get your dick sucked, because that shit is dead. I got needs too and I don't think I will have a problem finding a man who will give me exactly what I need. Call me when you can get it up again!

*It rubs the lotion on its skin or it will get the hose again.
Put the lotion in the basket . . . put the lotion in the basket . . . put the fucking lotion in the basket!! Yo cuz, pick
up. You in there? Pick up . . .*

I started laughing a little bit to play it off for Dex. He left a
message imitating that crazy boaw from *The Silence of the
Lambs*. We always used to imitate that part of the movie where
the fat chick is down in the well with his dog. I know that's supposed to be a horror flick but that shit was hilarious. It was one
of the inside jokes that we kept going. That's what he meant by
killer laugh.

I was about to piss on myself, my nerves was so bad. I played
it off and laughed and told Dex that he was crazy and he
laughed and everything went back to normal. At least for him, I
guess. I knew what the fuck he was into, and what he had
planned next, so shit wasn't funny to me for real. I hit the stop
button.

"Yo man, I'm going to go downstairs and sleep in the basement. This bed was big enough for us both to sleep in when we
was ten but a full-size bed ain't gon' get it now."

"Why didn't you take your black ass home to your own king-
size bed?"

"Man, my mom is tripping. She keep talking all that shit
about me needing to get a job and saying that I need to move out
and all of that, but I ain't ready to roll out just yet. I'm trying to
get some serious cheese first."

He lied just like I expected. He should have come better than
that too. I knew that Aunt Verdele wasn't even thinking about
that nigga at that time of the morning. I'm sure that she was already passed the hell out right next to her best friend, Jack
Daniels.

"Oh aight then, that's cool. There's a blanket down there in the closet."

"Aight bet. Wake me up at like eight if I don't get up on my own. I got some running around I gotta do tomorrow."

I wanted to tell him that I knew already. I wanted to bust his fucking bubble and tell him that I already knew. I knew where he was going and why and what the fuck he was going to get. Instead of trippin', I just played it cool and told him good night.

When he left the room I listened to him walk down the steps and across the living room. I could even hear the basement door creak open too. I remember thinking, damn, I hope my mom can't hear that good, because I know she had to hear me fucking bitches down there. I'd be having them hos screaming.

I took off my clothes and threw on my pajama pants. When it was totally quiet I was tempted to get up and listen to that message again. I talked myself out of it though. I knew that would be stupid with Dex being in the house and all. If he knew that I heard half that conversation he would be looking at me with blood in his eyes. I knew I was his dawg and all, but I knew that he wouldn't think twice about shutting me the fuck up. It's a shame, but I fucking knew it.

I laid down across the bed without pulling the sheets over top of me. It was too damn hot. I laid there and made as much of a plan as I could. I would wait until the morning until Dex left and I would listen to him and Herb on the tape again. I had to hear that shit again. It was too much.

After that I was going to make a few calls. And then I would get the fuck out of Dodge.

15. The first thing I saw when I woke up was Dex's black-ass face. He was standing over top of me and talking with his hot-ass morning breath. He was just rambling and shit.

"Yo cuz, I'm glad I wasn't depending on you to wake me up. It's almost quarter to nine. I heard your phone ring a couple of minutes ago. I think that might have been Meka. I called her last night from your mom's line downstairs and told her to call me on your phone to wake me up because I figured you would be knocked out. My damn cell phone battery is dead and I left the charger in the car. Let me check your answering machine to see if she left . . ."

That woke me up. As soon as I heard him say answering machine I jumped out of the fucking bed so quick I was dizzy. I could not let Dex go anywhere near that play button. I know I looked like a dickhead, but I didn't care. I just started talking off the top of my head and making up excuses.

"Yo man, she ain't leave no message. I would have heard it. . . ."

"Nigga, what you mean you would have heard it? I was just standing over top of you talking for a minute before you even knew I was there."

I was stuck for a minute. I knew he was right. I was a hard sleeper. My mom always said that you had to light dynamite under my nose in order to get me up in the morning, especially if I had a late night. My last resort was to look over at the dresser. The light was not blinking.

"Look nigga, it ain't even got no new messages. If it was her that called, she didn't leave a message. Just call her and see if she called."

"Why you all jumpy and shit? Was you and that freak down there smoking L's last night?"

"Naw man, you know I ain't smoked a blunt in like three years. I don't mess around with that stuff no more. . . . You know how crazy I act when y'all wake me up."

"Whatever man, you don't have to tell me, but you acting like you smoked a lotta weed last night. Your eyes are red as shit and you acting all noid. You better leave that shit alone."

I busted out laughing at Dex's lame-ass joke. Somebody should have given me an Oscar for how I played that off. I just wanted to get his mind off my machine and make him think that everything was cool. I had only dozed off maybe a couple hours before then, because I couldn't sleep.

I kept getting this same vision in my head. I kept picturing Dex coming in to my room and smothering me with a pillow. In the vision I saw Herb standing off in the corner laughing and counting a stack of money. That shit kept running over and over in my head.

Before Dex could pick up my phone to call Meka, a car horn was honking outside the house.

"That's probably her. Let me roll."

"Aight then, cuz," I remember saying. "Holla at me when you get back."

"Aight. I'm gon' call you at around three or four. I may have another gig for us later on tonight. Peace."

If all went well, I wouldn't be around at three or four. I didn't know much of nothing at that point except that I wasn't going to snitch on Dex. I was going to disappear and let him hang himself. He was being so sloppy that I knew all that shit would catch up to him. Especially hanging with a dickhead like Herb.

I was hyped when Dex finally left the house. I was tired and on edge. I ran down the steps and looked out the peephole and made sure that he was really gone. This time I locked the top lock because I knew he didn't have the key for it.

I ran back up the steps skipping two at a time. I wanted to hear that tape without being interrupted. As soon as I got to the top of the stairs I heard my mom's door open.

"Hey mom."

"What are you doing up this early?"

"I just went downstairs to make sure the door was locked. Dex stayed here last night."

"He didn't have one of them nasty little heifers up in here did he?"

"Naw."

"Oh, cause I could have swore I heard a woman's voice last night. Then again I could have been dreaming. I ate some of that sloppy joe and I was drinking Pepsi last night at Bible study. Whenever I eat like that I am destined to have bad dreams."

"Oh, aight then, Mom . . ."

I tried to keep on walking toward my room but she had the raps for some reason that morning.

"Hey baby, since you're up, why don't you go with me down Ninth Street. I need to do some serious shopping and I can't be carrying all of them bags by myself. We need meat and fruit and vegetables. . . . We need everything."

"Mom, can we go later? I ain't hardly get no sleep last night."

"Boy, we gon' be down there and back before you can even blink. Just throw something on. That way we can beat the crowd. You know how it can get down there on Saturday mornings."

"Aight Mom, let me throw something on."

Just that quick my whole damn plan had a monkey wrench thrown in it. I couldn't tell my mom no. Especially since I was the one who ate up all the food in the house in the first place. Damn!

We were dressed and out the door in like twenty minutes. I told her I wanted to drive because I knew that if I was behind the wheel then we would get there and get back. She drives so damn slow. She was only fifty-six and drove like she was in her eighties.

It didn't matter that we got down there early because Ninth Street was packed. Motherfuckers was thick down there like it was the middle of the day. It was mostly old people with their young grandkids who looked like they were forced to come and help shop, just like me.

It was wall-to-wall niggas down there. I know they call it the Italian Market and all but I never see no Italians down there shopping. All I ever see is niggas. I hated going down there because the smell of all that raw chicken and pigs and any damn thing else you could imagine made me want to throw the fuck up.

I was just going along with the flow, following my mom from store to store and carrying them heavy-ass bags. After about half an hour of pushing and shoving through the crazy people, I went outside the House of Pork and leaned up against the wall. It would've been the perfect time to whip out a Newport if I still smoked.

That's when I first noticed the white chick with the shades on. She was standing directly across the street, just staring at me.

And when I thought about it I remembered seeing her in the parking lot where I parked my mom's car. I was on delayed reaction, but after a while I realized that she was following me. And she looked kind of familiar too, but I couldn't remember where I knew her from at first.

I played it real easy. I acted like I didn't even notice her. After a while she was acting like she didn't even care that I saw her. It was almost like she wanted me to see her.

The bags was starting to get heavy, so I told my mom that I was going to take them to the car and come back and meet her near the stand where we get our plums. I walked down Ninth Street until I got to Washington Avenue and crossed the intersection. The parking lot is right in the middle of the block between Ninth and Tenth, so I was walking up the street that way. I looked over my shoulder real quick and saw that the white chick was still coming on strong.

I cut across the parking lot and walked to my mom's car. I opened the trunk and tossed the bags in there but I was looking over my shoulder the whole time. This chick was walking up on me like I wasn't already about to snap on the first motherfucker that flinched.

She was about to catch it.

I slammed the trunk and leaned back on the car and waited for her to approach. For some reason I knew she was harmless. She spoke first.

"Hello, stranger."

"Stranger? Where do I know you from?"

"How soon we forget. I guess you have so much pussy up in your face that it all starts to look alike after a while."

She stepped back like she was auditioning for me and took off her glasses. She was tall, about five foot eight, and had smooth pretty skin. Her hair was long, black, and straight. She had big titties and pretty thick lips for a white girl. She looked like she was about three years older than me, thirty-one at the most. It took me a few seconds before I realized where I knew her from. She was one of the jobs that I fucked for Tony.

Seeing her ass standing in the parking lot on Washington Avenue gave me a flashback. I remember hittin' that shit from the back and she was moaning and looking over her shoulder and licking her lips like she wanted to eat me. I was shocked that she was giving me so much rhythm back then. Especially considering the circumstances. It was always a life-or-death situation for their husbands or boyfriends, so most of the chicks was traumatized just to be there in the first place.

She seemed real nervous standing there in the parking lot, but I knew that she was up in my face for a reason.

"What's your name again?"

"So you forgot my name? That's funny, because I remember everything about you. I remember the scent of your cologne, I remember the way you sucked on my tits until my eyes rolled back into my head, and I remember you putting all nine inches of that delicious cock in my mouth too."

"OK, so you remember. . . ."

We both laughed. The uncomfortable kind of laugh when you don't know what else to do. At that point she was running her finger between my pecs. I had on a white wife beater.

"My name is Tammy."

"So Tammy, why you following me and my mom at the Italian Market, and how did you find me?"

"Well, there are a few reasons that I'm following you around. One, I think you have a great ass. Two, I want to take you to dinner. And three, I have a business proposition for you. And as for how I found you, I'll save the answer to that question for another time."

"Thanks for the compliment. Now what kind of business did you have in mind?"

I just knew that she was going to offer me some money to hit it again. And as broke as I was at that time, I had my mouth all ready to say yes. White girls were never really my thing, but she looked all right and had a tight-ass shot. I was with it. She leaned real close to me and whispered it in a low, sexy voice.

"I want you to kill my husband."

"What?! You got me fucked up with somebody else. That ain't my thing, sweetie!"

I stepped away from her and looked her up and down like she had bumped her fucking head. That bitch went from zero to sixty in like one second flat.

"Oh, come off it already! I know that you and your buddy killed Tony. Everybody knows."

I grabbed her by the wrist and pulled her real close to me. I looked her right in the eyes and asked her what the fuck she was talking about.

"Like I said, don't act all self-righteous with me, because I know what you did."

"What the fuck are you talking about? What did I do?"

"Look, let's stop playing these games. My husband already got the call. I know what you and your partner are into. I don't give a rat's ass about that. I just want that prick of a husband of mine to pay for what he did. And I figured since you guys offed fat-ass Tony so smoothly that slicing up my husband would be a cinch."

I was stunned. I was so fucking mad at myself for letting Dex get me into all that bullshit. What the fuck did she mean, everybody knows? I knew that I didn't do shit, but if this trick was saying that everybody knew, it was only a matter of time before the jakes was hauling my ass down to the Roundhouse.

"Look, I didn't kill nobody and I don't even want to know what your husband did. I don't give a fuck. So you can just take your lily-white ass back over to Jersey to your big house with your two-car garage and your matching Benzes and stay the fuck away from me."

I pushed past her and started walking toward the exit to the parking lot. She grabbed my arm and started begging me to hear her out.

"Listen, I know that this is a lot to hear all at once. I know this. But please hear me out. Meet me at Zanzibar Blue tomorrow night at seven. I can explain all of this better then. Please just come and hear me out. I think you'll be interested to know how all of this affects you."

I just walked away and left her standing there. I didn't even notice my mom was walking toward me with this confused look on her face. Tammy turned and walked away.

"Baby, who was that white girl you were talking to?"

"Nobody, Mom. She was asking where a good place was to get fruit from."

"Fruit? It looked like she was upset. Are you telling your mother a fib?"

"Well Mom, you know I can never keep anything from you. She came up to me and told me that she thought I was handsome and she asked me if I was dating anybody. I guess she got upset when I told her that I wasn't feeling her all like that."

"Hmmm . . . well you know what I say. If she can't use my hot comb, then don't bring her home."

I cracked a weak smile for my mom and then took the bags

out of her hands so I could put them in the trunk. While I was getting in the car, I looked up and saw Tammy peeling out of the lot in a silver four-door Benz. She glanced at me and winked her eye before she turned onto Washington Avenue, and just like that she was out.

She left me hanging. As much as I was acting like I didn't want to deal with Tammy, I knew that I would have to see her ass again.

16. I tossed the last bag of turkey chops and chicken wings into the freezer and jetted out of the kitchen before my mom could ask me to do anything else. I was already way off where I wanted to be by twelve o'clock.

When I walked through the living room to go upstairs my mom was sitting in front of the TV watching *The Golden Girls*. I guess that shit came on on Saturdays too. As soon as I went in my room I closed the door behind me and locked it. I was so ready to hear that tape again, I was about to bust.

Even though I was tired and riled up by all that shit Tammy was talking, I had all this energy when I went in that room. The cord on the answering machine wasn't long enough for me to pull it over to my bed, so the first thing I did was pull the chair from my desk over to my dresser so that I could sit down while I listened to it again. I didn't want to take the chance of blasting that shit so my mom could hear it. She would find out that Dex was a criminal when it was time. I don't think she could have handled it then.

Right when I was about to hit the play button, the phone rang. I started not to answer it, but for some reason I picked it up. It was Dex. He was screaming and cursing and talking so damn loud that I didn't know what the fuck he was talking about. I had to pull the phone away from my ear because that nigga was so amped.

"Yo Dex, chill man! What the hell is wrong with you?"

"Yo man, is Aunt Jaime in the house?"

"Yeah, why? What's up?"

"Man, you need to come outside. I don't want her to see me like this and I need to fucking ask you something. This shit is serious, yo!"

"Where the fuck you at?"

"I'm parked right in front of the house. Come outside!"

I rolled my chair back underneath the desk and flew down the steps.

I looked out the peephole before I opened the door, and I could see Dex standing outside the driver's side of the black Honda pounding his hands on the roof. Herb was sitting in the passenger seat.

When I opened the door, Dex looked at me with this crazy-ass look in his eyes. That nigga looked like he could spit fucking fire if he wanted to.

"Yo, get in the car. We going for a quick ride."

My heart was flipping inside my chest. All I could think was, damn, these niggas know that I got them on tape and they trying to see me about that shit. I wasn't trying to get in the car. Even if they didn't know I knew, I wasn't trying to be in that car with Herb and Dex when the cops rolled up on them. That's the last thing I needed. I shut the door behind me and I lied.

"I gotta help my mom with the groceries and shit, wassup?"

"Well just get in the fucking car then, so we can rap."

I looked in the car real quick at Herb and he seemed heated as shit too. My first thought was that their plans had fallen through for the day and that's why they were so damn stressed on a

Saturday afternoon. But naw. Shit was a little deeper than that. Them motherfuckers were worldwide in the worst way and nobody was smiling.

I got in the back and sat on the driver's side behind Dex who jumped in the car before me and slammed the door. As soon as my ass hit the seat they were both talking over top of each other. I didn't know what the fuck they were talking about. Herb was waving some papers in my face and Dex was trying to talk over top of him.

"Hold up, hold up. First of all, turn down the fucking radio! Now what the hell are y'all niggas talking about!?"

"Listen cuz, this shit is serious. Them motherfuckers got us on the Internet on some ol' gay shit."

"What?"

"Yeah, you heard me. The couple that we did the job for in North Carolina put us up on the Internet on one of them faggot-ass websites!"

It felt like I was swallowing my fucking tongue. I couldn't breathe after I heard him say that shit. I was ready to move to Canada and change my name. I couldn't stay in North Philly with everybody thinking I was sweet. I wasn't ready for that shit.

"What are you talking about, Dex? What couple?"

"The white man that we was calling Archie, and the Pam Anderson–looking chick who had the big titties!"

When he said that I felt relieved as a motherfucker because I remembered that I didn't even fuck her. I thought that I was out of the woods but that shit don't go down that smooth. Dex and Herb were not trying to hear it.

"Look at this shit!"

Herb turned around in his seat and handed me the papers he had in his hand. My jaw dropped.

The first picture was of Dex and Herb with no clothes on just looking at the camera with serious faces. I could tell from the background that they were on Goldie and Archie's bed. In the next one they were kind of facing each other and holding their jawns and smiling.

In another one they were back-to-back and looking at the camera. The fourth picture almost looked exactly like the first one. The last one took the cake. That bastard must have done some kind of photo magic, because it looked ridiculous. The background was real colorful, all psychedelic and shit, and Dex and Herb was facing each other. They was real close to each other and both holding their dicks. If they were one inch closer, their shit would have been touching.

It didn't even look right. Ghetto, coochie-loving Dex all up on another nigga like that. That shit looked crazy. Everybody knew he wasn't sweet, but everybody who was going to be seeing that wouldn't know. They would just think that both of them boaws was like that. Damn! Since I was there when they took the pictures, I knew that no gay shit was jumping off. Them niggas was just bugging out for the camera and happy to be getting an extra two hundred for their work. But if somebody else looked at them jawns they would think that they both was fruity. Thank God I didn't do that shit. Thank God.

I looked down at the bottom of the paper and saw the website address for where the pictures came from. They were definitely on the Internet.

"Yo, how did y'all know these were on the Internet?"

I looked up and that's when I noticed that Dex's knuckles on his right hand were all busted up. Blood was also smeared on the bottom of his white shirt.

"Dex, what the fuck happened to your hands?"

"Cuz, I was around the corner on Twenty-fifth Street rumbling Yanni!"

"The faggot boaw?"

"Yes! That motherfucking clown was telling everybody that me and Herb was on the Internet fucking. I just beat the shit out of that pussy. I went to his house and I dragged his ass out of the house and we whipped his motherfucking faggot ass in the middle of the street!"

"We? Y'all rolled on Yanni?"

"Fuck yeah! That pussy better not ever mention my name again!"

"Who broke that shit up?"

"His mom and his peeps came running out the house crying and screaming and shit and said they was going to call the cops, and that's when we was out."

"So who all did he tell?"

"I don't know. He told enough people though, because Don and them are the ones who gave us the pictures. Fucking Yanni printed them out and gave it to them because they ain't believe that shit when he told them."

I couldn't believe it. So much was happening all at once. I almost felt sorry for Dex but I got over it real quick. I was more worried about me. I was wondering if people were going to start to thinking that I was like that since we were always together. That shit was off the hook.

Herb was just gritting on me the whole time. Ever since I got in the car he was looking at me like he smelled a rotting corpse. That motherfucker had the nerve after what he said about me on that tape. I should've been the one dragging him out the house, taking it to his jaw.

I was thinking about how Yanni's family had called the cops

and I knew that meant shit would be even hotter for Dex and Herb. I didn't want no part of them that day. I was about to bounce because I didn't think that they would make it to the end of the day without getting locked up.

Them niggas knew the pigs was out looking for them. I know they was mad and all, but that wasn't the way to handle it. They could've got any damn body around there to whip Yanni's ass. One of them young boaws could've dropped his ass right quick. They didn't have to be the ones to get their hands dirty if they thought he was trying to play them. They was fucking up again and I didn't want no part of it. I didn't know what else to say, and I wanted to get out of that car, so I was about to just be like, peace. That's when Herb started talking shit and got me hyped.

"I think it's kind of strange how the one time you decided not to get in on the job, that shit winds up on the Internet."

"Yo Herb, what the fuck you trying to say?"

"I don't know. What am I trying to say?"

"It sounds to me like you're talking a whole lot of shit."

"Yeah, well all I know is that I'm on the fucking Internet on a gay website and that shit ain't fucking cool. And your ass just conveniently ain't feel like fucking that day!"

"What the fuck is you talking about? I went there to do the job pussy. I wasn't with getting all on tape for that man like y'all was. That's why I said no. That's all that is to it. Get that shit straight!"

"You ain't feel like taking no pictures 'cause you knew that the shit was gonna be on a faggot-ass website!"

"How the fuck was I supposed to know that shit? You ain't making no motherfucking sense. You must've forgot that Dex was the one who told me about that job. I didn't know them motherfuckers until I went down there with y'all."

Me and Herb was going at it up in there and Dex was all

quiet. That was making me mad, because it was obvious to me that Dex agreed with him. I knew just by him not saying anything that he was on Herb's side; Dex always had something to say. He was never that quiet.

"Cuz, so what? You think I knew that shit too? You think I knew the white dude was going to put y'all on a gay site?"

"Man, I don't know what the fuck to think. . . ."

When he said that I knew that Herb had already convinced him that I knew what he was taping them for. I just followed my gut for once and it proved to be a good move. I should have done that shit more often. I don't know more than the next nigga. I wanted to knock Herb the hell out and shake some sense into my cousin.

I couldn't even get hyped about it though, because I knew my cousin was already a lost cause. I ain't perfect but I knew I didn't deserve to go down like that. As soon as I was ready to argue my point, it hit me that I could give a fuck what them niggas thought. They were the shady ones. Herb and Dex were into shit I couldn't even say out loud.

"Alright, then fuck it. I'm out. I can't fuck with y'all like that no more then."

That's when I reached to open the back door and it wouldn't open. I slid across the backseat to the passenger side and tried that door, and it wouldn't open either. Dex was calm as shit when he started talking again. He didn't even turn around. He just kept looking straight ahead.

"Just chill, cuz, you ain't going nowhere."

"What the fuck is you talking about, Dex? Open the fucking door."

Herb added his two fucking cents and we got into it again.

"He said fucking chill. Just calm down and listen!"

"Who the fuck are you talking to Herb? You don't want it

with me like that, Herb! What nigga? What? I will bust your fucking ass if you don't open this fucking door!"

He turned around and looked at me like he was about to swing, and I was ready. I ain't never rumbled a nigga from the back-seat of a Honda Accord, but I figured there's a first time for everything. I could see me smashing his head through that fucking windshield. I could see it as clear as day in my head. I was heated.

Dex was still calm.

"Look cuz, calm down. I want us to go down there and handle this shit. I want us to go back to North Carolina and take it to that pussy. He's going to pay for this shit."

"What? Go back down North Carolina?"

"Yeah, go back. I want to see Archie about this shit. We went down there and did what he wanted us to. We fucked his wife the way he obviously can't, and he does this ol' nut shit in return. He has to pay."

I knew that Dex was dead serious. I knew what he had done in the past and I knew what he was capable of doing to that perverted white man who reminded us of Archie Bunker. I wanted to get out of that car.

"Did you try and call him and ask him why he did that?"

"It ain't shit to talk about, cuz. Plus, I called down there and their phone is disconnected. We need to go down there and handle this shit in person."

Man! I was stuck. I knew I had to come up with a way to get out of that shit. I was not going back to Durham. Fuck that! I don't want no blood on my hands. I wanted to keep my shit clean. I was thinking fast on my feet. I had to stall them cats.

"Yo Dex, why don't you let me call Onyx and ask her to go to their crib to see if they're still there. That way I can make sure they are there before y'all go."

"That might work, but I don't know why you said y'all. You're rolling with us, nigga."

"Cuz, I'm trying to tell you. I don't even want to get into that shit, because both y'all niggas is mad as hell and who knows what y'all are going to do."

When I said that he looked in the rearview mirror at me and his eyes looked cold. He was definitely gone. That fool was on a mission and his dumb-ass sidekick was on it with him.

"We all in this shit together, cuz. Just because your ass is not up on the Internet for the world to see looking like a cocksucker don't mean that you ain't in this."

"Look, whatever man. I'll make the call when I go in the house and I'll get the ball rolling on this shit, alright?"

Herb came at me again. I was ready to rip his tongue out.

"Dude, how is you gon' call that chick? I thought you told us that you lost her number before we left North Carolina?"

"I did dickhead, and I found it."

"You ain't say nothing about finding that bitch number."

"Why the fuck would I tell you if I did? You got me messed up with one of your boaws. I don't fuck with you like that. Anyway, let me out of the car, Dex. I'll call her and ask her to do that. I'll hit you on your cell when she calls me back, aight?"

"Aight then. I got some serious business to take care of anyway."

I knew about his serious business. I glanced at the clock in the car and saw that it was twenty minutes after twelve. I knew that he was running late for that serious business. The accidental message told it all.

Dex got out of the car and opened my door from the outside. I guess he must've had them kiddy locks on the car. That shit had me shook for a minute. He got back in the car and slammed his door before I could get all the way out. He peeled off doing like sixty as soon as I slammed the door. I just stood in the middle of my block and watched the car until it got to the corner and banged a crazy-ass right and disappeared.

Them niggas was salty as hell. I would've been too though, if somebody had me out there like that and I knew I wasn't a fudge packer. What made it so bad is that Dex hated gay people. He always used to fuck with Yanni and kick his ass when we was young boaws. I guess Yanni just had to show motherfuckers them pictures to get back at Dex. I guess cuz had that coming.

I went back in the house and my mom was still watching her show. She didn't have a clue about what was going on all around her, and I wanted to keep it that way. I loved her so much. Even if she *thought* I was doing anything that wasn't sanctified, she would be hurt.

I hustled up the steps and went back to my room. I closed the door behind me and locked it. Listening to the answering machine was the last thing on my mind. I had to call Onyx. I wanted to holla at her anyway but I didn't have the number until Dex gave it back to me without even knowing it. There was something that I liked about her.

I pulled the calling card out of my dresser and the Benjamin out of my wallet so that I could make the call. I memorized her number that time though. I had a feeling I would be using it a lot.

17. When Onyx finally called back I was asleep. Not getting sleep the night before really kicked in on me all of a sudden. I was trying to wait for her to call me back, but I dozed off after just laying there staring at my ceiling for half an hour. I was just laying there trying to figure out how I was going to get out of all that mess.

I couldn't help but keep thinking of my fucking life as a book or movie. That shit is funny now, but I was really sitting in that damn room thinking damn, if this shit was a book, would it be the middle, or near the end? I kept thinking, is some shit about to jump off to make it the end for all of us?

I knew that Dex was playing hardball but that dickhead Herb was the one who was going to get all of us locked up or shot. That pretty boy, thug-acting cat was bound to fuck up one way or another. I just knew I ain't want to have no part of it when he did. For real.

When I got out of the bed to check the messages it was about two forty-five. She sounded like she was smiling real hard and shit when she was talking. I could tell she was on my dick.

Hey you, this is Onyx. I got your message. I hope all is well with you. I thought that you forgot about me. Well anyway, I'll give you a call back in a few minutes. You said you would be there all day, so I figured you probably couldn't get back to the phone in time.

Hey, it's me again. You notice that I never say your name when I call because I don't even want to sprain my tongue trying to pronounce it. Anyway, give me a call when you get this. I'll be here until at least six o'clock.

I was so happy that she called me back that quick. I could tell that she really wasn't used to dealing with city boaws like me. I wasn't a thug or nothing like that, but I could tell she was feeling the East Coast flavor. I know a whole lot of cats who love to keep it gangsta, but that's not really my style.

I went to the bathroom and brushed my teeth first. That was something I didn't do since the night before. I was so damn sleepy that I just wanted to go back to sleep, but I was looking forward to rapping with Onyx.

I pulled out the calling card again and gave her a holla. She sounded more country than I'd remembered when she answered the phone. I almost laughed in her ear.

"Hello, can I speak to Onyx?"

"This is she. Who's calling?"

"It's the Philly boaw you love to call and leave messages for."

"Oh here you go. . . . You're a trip."

"I can hear you smiling through the phone, girl."

"Anyway . . . so how have you been? I thought that you had spent that hundred-dollar bill or something and forgot to get my number off of it."

"Naw, I wouldn't spend that jawn if it was the last C note on this planet."

"Whatever . . . You probably spent it on one of your many lady friends."

"Come on now. I told you I don't be out there like that. I just keep to myself and keep my eyes open for 'the one.' "

"The one . . . Oh, that's funny."

"So what were you doing when I called you, Ms. Onyx?"

"Do you really want to know?"

"That's why I asked."

"Actually I was sitting here reading my Bible."

"Naw, really?"

"Really. Southern girls need a little Jesus in their lives too. Is that a problem?"

"Ain't nothing wrong with that. I just didn't expect you to say that, that's all."

It was quiet after that because I didn't know what to think. I was feeling her but I wasn't ready to be putting in long distance money and going through all of the changes of talking to a church girl. I knew she would be playing a whole lot of games and I wasn't with it.

But then I thought of all the freaks that I met in church when we used to live down in South Philly. They was off the hook. I got most of my play when I was a young buck by going to church. I thought about Serena Jackson, the soprano chick who used to sing the solos every time the youth choir sang. And then I thought about how she used to make me hit high notes when she dropped to her knees, and not to pray. My mom thought that I liked coming to church because I was getting something from hearing the Word. If she only knew. Serena was my salvation. She was two years older than me and always willing to share her wisdom with me in the wardrobe room every other Sunday on the third floor.

I didn't even care that Onyx was reading her Bible. Good for her. I figured that I would do my Christian duty by making her scream for God sooner or later. I said something to break the tension.

"So are you on the choir down there at Duke?"

"Actually I am not. I would love to get more involved on campus, but right now my priority is getting out of here on time. My parents don't have it like that, ya know? That would be tight to death if I could take my time and do as I please, but I have to get that degree."

"I can dig it. Maybe if I hang around you long enough you'll inspire me to go back to school and get my paper too."

"Hey, all things are possible for those who believe. With Christ anything is possible."

Those words were stuck in my head for a long time after that. I knew that God could make things happen for a nigga. I used to pray all the time. On the real, I used to like going to church. Even if Serena Jackson wasn't there. I was so stressed when I was going through all that shit with Dex and Herb that I thought about praying. But then I felt guilty because I never got on my knees except for when I wanted something. My mom always used to tell me that I need to count my blessings and pray even when everything is tight, but I didn't listen to her all the time. I knew she was right, but I didn't listen. The last time I went to church on the regular was right after I graduated from high school back in '92.

After that I played church on the same days as everybody else. I came through on Easter and Christmas and I brought in the new year with my mom before I stepped off and went to the spot with my boys.

Before I knew it I had dogged the rest of the calling card talking to Onyx. I felt like a damn spaz because she had to call me back after it cut us off right in the middle of her telling me about what it was like growing up in Texas.

I made up some mess about my long distance just getting cut off, but I think she knew I was talking shit. I couldn't tell her I could only use calling cards because I was too damn paranoid about somebody coming behind me and tracing my calls one day. I was thinking like a criminal on a bad cop show. I watched enough TV to know what cops did and what they didn't.

I hated lying to Onyx. It was normally so easy for me to game a bitch up, but she made me feel guilty for not putting all my cards on the table for her. Maybe I felt bad because she was sitting on the other end of the line with a Bible in her lap. Or maybe Herb was right. Maybe she had me open and I didn't even know it.

Dex called three times on the other line to ask me if I had talked to her yet, but I lied and said that I didn't. I told him that I called Onyx but that she didn't call me back yet.

He was vexed as a motherfucker. It sounded like he was ready to hop in the whip and drive to North Carolina right then and there. I kept blowing him off and clicking back over to holla at Onyx. I didn't rap on the phone that much with chicks because they mostly don't talk about shit. Onyx was on some other ol' shit. Even though she was saved and all, that's not all she talked about.

We talked about movies a lot because we both were into that. The older the better. She promised to rent *To Kill a Mockingbird* the next time I came down. I pictured her sitting there with her braids looking all good, but I didn't feel the same way I feel about most chicks when I talked to them. The more we talked the less I felt like I wanted to hit it and be out like I normally did. It was hard for me to even picture her naked.

Onyx talked a lot about music, and not just the gospel stuff. She liked gospel music as much as the next one, but she talked a lot about her regular music. She kept carrying on about some dude named Donny Hathaway. She told me that I needed to check him out. I heard of him before but couldn't think of one song that he sang except for the one that the radio stations ran every five minutes around Christmastime.

By the time we hung up, I knew that I couldn't get her involved in all that shit down in Durham. I never brought up Archie or Goldie. If she knew what I really was down in Durham for, she would never talk to me again. Onyx wasn't the kind of chick that would hang around with a cat who had sex for money. I knew right off that she wouldn't have been with that. I told her that I would call her the next day and that we would pick up where we left off. It was like a quarter after five when we hung up. The time flew by quick.

I made up my mind right then and there to just tell Dex that I wasn't going. I planned on lying to him and saying that I never talked to Onyx. I knew that it was no way that I was getting in the car with Dex and Herb. Them niggas would just have to suck it up and work it out on their own. They blew that thought right off the hinges when they came at me on some ol' foul shit. I should've known that Dex would get his way. I should've seen that shit coming.

In the meantime I had to get myself ready to meet up with Tammy the next day. I didn't want no part of killing her old man, but I was so damn pressed to know what the word on the street was on me, that I had to meet with her at Zanzibar Blue.

I thought the meeting would be the highlight of my Sunday. It's crazy how the big brown envelope kicked me in the ass harder than anything else.

18. I woke up the next morning at around eight. Well, to tell the truth, I was blasted out of my sleep by my mom's stereo.

She plays this Daryl Coley gospel CD every Sunday morning. Normally I would have just rolled over and went back to sleep, but I couldn't. I was up for the day. I started to get up and get dressed so I could go to church with her, but I didn't want to send her into shock.

Even though it was eleven hours before my meeting with Tammy, I got up and picked out what I wanted to wear that night. I wanted my shit to be tight. Not so much because of Tammy. I could give a flying yak's ass what she thought about me. It's just that Zanzibar is a pretty classy jawn. I went there once before then and I knew that any nigga that tried to come up in there with jeans and a white wife beater on would get played at the door.

I pulled out a pair of black dress pants and a dark orange Kenneth Cole short-sleeve shirt, and threw them over the back of my desk chair.

I remember it being hot as hell that early in the morning. I don't have an air conditioner in my room, so I waited until my mom left, then went in her room. I got ass-naked and stretched out on her bed after I put the AC on full blast.

I was just laying there, zoning out. I tried not to think about pyscho-ass Dex. I tried not to think about breaking Herb the hell up in a one-on-one. I tried not to think about what Tammy said, that everybody knew I was a killer. And I tried not to think about how my cash got stolen down in North Carolina.

I tried, but that shit ain't work.

Everything was on my mind at once. I knew I would need like five Tylenol before nine o'clock if I would keep sweatin' all that shit. So I just got up and put on a pair of boxers and went downstairs to make something to eat.

I made pancakes and sausage that morning. Before I could get finished cooking I looked up and saw Dex rolling through the front door. The first thing I noticed was that he was wearing the same thing he had on the day before. He strolled right up in my crib and didn't shut the door behind him.

"Wassup cuz?"

"Wassup Dex? Yo, shut the door."

"Hold up. Herb left something in the car, he's coming in too."

"What?!"

"Come on now, don't start tripping."

"Trippin'? That nigga is not coming up in my fucking crib! What the fuck is wrong with you, man?"

"Cuz, just hear me out. I know y'all ain't roadies or nothing but we need to talk about some things real quick. It ain't gon' take that long."

"You don't hear me. I don't fuck with that nigga like that!"

"Cuz, please. It ain't gon' take but like ten minutes."

"Ten minutes and he better not get out of line, or I'm gon' see his ass . . . I ain't in the backseat now."

"Aight man, aight. Just chill. . . . Here he comes."

When Herb came in the house he mumbled wassup and sat his nut ass down on the couch. He was holding a big-ass brown envelope. I just gave him the nod. I didn't even open up my mouth. Dex sat right next to him and picked up the remote and turned on the videos.

I didn't give a fuck that morning. I already knew them niggas was heated over all that shit with Yanni, but I just didn't give a fuck. I just started talking off the top of my head.

"I'm surprised that y'all are hanging with each other out in public today."

"Why you say that, cuz?"

"I mean with all that shit that went down with the Internet and the pictures, I figured y'all would be playing it low right about now."

"I don't give a fuck what them niggas around the corner think. If they think I'm sweet I dare them to step to me on that shit or say something to me about some gay shit. I'll leave all of them niggas on that corner looking like Swiss cheese if they get out of line!"

"Well I know you don't care what they think, but what about what the honeys think? You know that shit is gon' get back to all the chicks too, because that's who Yanni hangs with the most around there."

"Man, fuck them bitches too. I know I don't get down like that, so if they start talking shit, fuck them too! It ain't like I ain't fuck half them bitches already anyway, so fuck it!"

I could tell I was getting Dex mad. Herb was just sitting there not talking. He was salty that I was making light of that shit but he couldn't sound off like he wanted, since he was in my crib. I was tearing up my pancakes and sausage and clowning them niggas.

At first I felt bad when I heard how Archie put them out there like that, but I was getting a kick out of making jokes about them motherfuckers. They was the snakes, not me. They was the ones who would throw me to the lions in a heartbeat. The only reason I think they didn't toss me to the killer cats is because they didn't figure out how to at that point. Just when I was having fun messing with Dex, dickhead opened up his mouth.

"Yo, can I use your bathrooom?"

"Naw dude, it's out of service."

"What? What you mean, it's out of service?"

"It's out of service."

"Yo, if you don't want me to use your bathroom, that's all you gotta say."

"Aight then, I don't want you to use my bathroom."

Dex just covered his face with both of his hands and shook his head.

I don't know why he was so pressed for me and that nigga to be cool. He wasn't pressed to let me in on his big money scheme or to tell me what the hell went down with Tony. He was stabbing me in the fucking back all around the board and he wanted me to be cool with this clown he rolled with. That shit wasn't happening. Dex cut the TV off with the remote and tossed it back on the coffee table.

"Listen cuz. Let's get down to business. So did shorty call you back?"

"Yeah, she called me back."

"So what's the deal? Did you tell her to go to Archie's crib to see if him and his wife was still there."

"Naw cuz. I ain't even talk to her about that shit."

"What? I thought that was the whole point of you calling her ass up yesterday. Why you ain't say nothing to her about it?"

"Man. I don't even want to get her involved with that shit."

"Involved in what? All you had to do was make up a lie and

tell her they was your friends and their phone was cut off and you wanted her to check on them. You acting like she your bitch or something, cuz."

"Naw it ain't even like that. I told y'all yesterday that I ain't want nothing to do with none of that shit."

"No, it's not like that, cuz. It's just that you been actin' so shady lately that it's like I can't trust you. We supposed to be like blood."

I wanted to slap Dex upside his head with a brick. That nigga was in the middle of my living room and putting on the performance of his life. Denzel ain't have nothing on Dex that day. He was trippin'.

What really set that shit off is when I told him that him and Herb's ten minutes was up. It was too hot in the living room to be getting into it with them cats. I thought that I would just get rid of them and chill for the rest of the day.

Dex had different plans. Or really I think it was Herb who had different plans, because I know it was his idea to drop that ton of bricks on me. Dex started getting louder and louder the more he talked, and I was just sitting on the other couch staring at his ass getting all hyped up.

I guess he could tell I didn't care by the expression on my face, so he dropped the bomb on me. I never thought he would stoop as low as he did that day, but then again I don' know why. My mother always told me to never hang around with a thief, because nine times out of ten that thief is also a liar, and maybe much worse. Damn, she was right!

Herb has this cocky-ass look on his face when Dex started to break down how they were going to blackmail me into taking the trip with them to Durham. I wanted to hawk spit in his face and rub it in with my size-twelve Tims.

"I hate to do this, cuz, but I'm gon' have to play hardball now."

"What the fuck you mean, hardball?"

"If you don't roll with us when we go to Durham tomorrow, I'm gon' make sure Aunt Jaime gets a copy of this."

Dex took the big brown envelope out of Herb's hand and tossed it at me across the coffee table. As soon as I caught it I could tell it was a VCR tape inside.

"What the fuck is this?"

"It's a Tony Salvatore special, starring you."

"What the fuck you mean, starring me? How did you get a copy of one of Tony's tapes?"

"He let me borrow it one day before he was killed, so that I could see how I looked doing it on tape."

I was fucked-up for a couple of reasons. I couldn't believe that Dex was playing me like that. I trusted Tony, so it wasn't a big deal when he taped me and Dex nailing the jobs. I knew he had to tape us fucking them broads because that was the only way he could blackmail their husbands and boyfriends. Now that shit was happening to me.

I never even took the tape out of the envelope. I was trying to play it cool. I figured if I acted like I didn't care, he would just say that he was playing and him and Herb would go on their way. Them niggas was serious as three blocked arteries though. They was for real.

"Come on nigga, you gotta be kidding me, right? You gon' send my mom a tape of me fucking a job?"

"No, I'm not. You know why? Because you're going to go down there with us so I don't have to."

"That's some shady-ass shit, Dex. You know what that would do to my mom if she saw something like that?"

I tried to call his bluff, but he was ready. I told him that he knew how close me and my mom was and that I would just sit down and tell her what I did. I told him that I would come clean and admit it to her before he could send her any damn tape. Now!

He wasn't trying to hear that shit. He came one better.

"Yo, that's cool. You can tell Aunt Jaime all you want, but if you do that then I'll just take it one next step and send it to her church. Now you know and I know that that would be embarrassing as hell. She would be devastated. You want all them people on her choir to see her son bonin' a white chick?"

He had me on that one. I didn't want my mom to have to go through that. And I knew as holy as them folks was supposed to be at her church, that they would all talk shit about her behind her back and start acting funny.

I wasn't having that. I knew Dex was serious.

"Alright man, call me tonight at like ten and I'll let you know what I'm going to do."

"Ten it is. Come on, Herb."

When they left I made sure I locked the top lock and flew up the steps to my room. I ripped open the envelope and popped the tape in my VCR. It was fuzzy for a few seconds, but when the picture cleared up I could see myself as clear as day.

I was fucking the shit out of this job in a bathroom at one them hotels. I couldn't remember when or where I made the tape, but it was definitely me. I had the jawn sitting up on the edge of the sink and I was standing in front of her, hittin' it. She had her head cocked back and she was moaning all crazy. It looked like she was loving it.

Damn! That shit wasn't turning me on though. It made me sick to my stomach. All I could think was that there were more than a dozen other tapes out there somewhere, and Dex and Herb knew where they were. Them damn tapes were making their pockets fat as hell too. Shit!

I made up my mind that I was going to Durham. I pulled the tape out of the VCR, went downstairs to the basement, and smashed it with a hammer. At least I would get to see Onyx. Something good had to come out of that trip.

I sat around the house mad for the rest of the day. My mind was still going though. I was salty as shit that Dex had the upper hand, but I was working on a plan. I just wasn't sure that my plan was going to work. If it didn't, my ass would wind up dead or in jail. And I kept thinking that I couldn't let that happen, because then that would be a typical nigga ending for a book or movie about all the shit going down with me in the summer of 2001.

19. Tammy was sitting at the bar drinking a glass of wine when I rolled up at Zanzibar Blue. She was rocking one of them red Chinese-looking dresses and her hair was pinned up. It looked like she had chopsticks in her hair.

She already stood out like a sore thumb since she was one of the only white chicks up in there and she was sitting by herself. Her face was all made up like she was about to go and take pictures for a magazine or some shit. That bitch was definitely dressed to impress.

I walked up to the bar and sat on the stool next to her without looking at her. I was mad uncomfortable at first because it was all these fine-ass sistas up in there. And when I sat down next to that white chick all eyes were on me. Them bitches was sucking their teeth and rolling their fucking eyes at me like I stole something from them.

I guess they figured, here we go again. Another handsome, single brotha with a white girl. If they only knew. If I wasn't there on business I would have been all up in their grills trying to holla. I made a note to myself that I would definitely have to come back up in there on another Sunday night.

It was pretty crowded that night. This cat named Frank

McComb was in the restaurant part singing. That nigga was blowing too, because the crowd was all into it. I was feeling the scene, but I was just mad as shit that I had to come off thirty ones to get in there. The chick on the door said that there was a cover charge to get in whenever there was a singer there. Just when I was wishing Tammy had picked a cheaper place for us to meet she slid a small white envelope across the bar and tucked it underneath my hand.

I peeked inside and saw a single fifty-dollar bill.

"What's this for?"

"Sorry about the cover charge. I should have checked to see if an act was performing before I told you to come here. I would have called to change the location, but I don't have your number."

"Oh, you know where I live and how to follow me through the city and shit, but you don't know my digits?"

"Yes, is that hard to believe?"

"Yeah. So how did you find me?"

"Can we hold off on the questions for a while?"

"That sounds like another question to me, Tammy. Is it? Look, I don't have time for games. I came here because I want answers, and in order to get answers I have to ask questions."

"How very true."

"So what's the deal?"

"Well I will say this. People talk. You have such an unusual name, and the fact is I remember your partner—Dex is it?— mentioning Twenty-fourth Street back when I met the two of you, and I just got in my Benz and started driving around and asking questions."

"How did you find out my name?"

"I pay attention. Now I know you fucked my brains out and all but that doesn't mean I was totally brain-dead when Tony called you into the other room the time we were together. I was a journalism major before I married money and dropped out of school. I have a good memory, and you, my friend, have an impossible name to forget."

Tammy had her shit together that night. She didn't seem as paranoid and jumpy as when we were down on Ninth Street. I wanted to get down to business. I got the bartender's attention and ordered a coke.

"You're not getting rum in that?"

"Naw, don't assume because I fuck for money that I'm a drunk too."

"A little rum in your coke doesn't make you a drunk."

"I'll pass just the same. I don't drink."

"Interesting . . . very interesting."

She didn't seem like she was pressed for time. I think she was enjoying all the attention and our casual conversation. Those black women were cutting her nasty looks and bumping into her bar stool on purpose. She didn't seem fazed by that shit. Tammy was in her own world.

I was constantly looking around us to see who was nearby. Everyone was paying attention because of the jungle fever shit, but nobody was trying to listen to us.

"First of all, please forgive me for being so forward with you in the parking lot the other day. I was really upset and I just wanted you to know that I meant business."

"Well I got the fucking picture. So what is this about everybody knowing that I'm . . . well, you know. Because that shit is not true."

"I have reason to believe otherwise. My husband told me for a fact that he talked to Dex and he had a guy with him, and I know that you two were together back when we hooked up at the Marriott."

"Well when you go home you need to ask your old man what

Dex's partner looked like, because it wasn't fucking me. Ask him, you'll see."

"What he looked like?"

"Yeah, ask your old man if Dex's partner has a big-ass birthmark on his face and see what he tells you."

"A birthmark?"

"Yeah, a birthmark. And when he tells you yeah like I know he will, make sure you remember that I don't even have a freckle on my face."

"Hmmm . . ."

She just stared at me for a while. I guess she was trying to figure if I was bullshitting her or not. I think it was starting to sink in that I wasn't a killer. I was a lot of things, but I wasn't a fucking killer.

"You wanna order something off the bar menu?"

"Naw, I'm straight."

My mom had cooked when she got back from church. The pot roast, rice, greens, and cornbread had me straight.

"So why do you want your husband whacked?"

"You say it so matter of factly."

"Well that's how you said it to me in the parking lot."

"I guess you're right. . . . Hmm, where do I begin? Let's just say that I made the ultimate sacrifice for him while he was screwing around on me."

"What do you mean?"

"Well, you probably know this already, but Larry has a gambling problem. He would go into the hole so bad in Atlantic City that it would almost take us under. We fought all the time about it. I told him that he needed to get help and he just ignored me and said that he was just having a bad streak."

"Oh yeah."

"Yeah. Well anyway, to make a long story short, Larry met

Tony somehow and he started borrowing money from Tony. When he couldn't pay it back Tony laid it down."

"He laid it down?"

"Yeah, you know the rest. He gave Larry a few weeks to come up with the cash. I think he owed sixty grand all together. Tony said if he didn't come up with it in that time then he would make sure that he was floating in the Schuylkill River. Or there was another option."

"And what was the option?"

"You were the option, silly. Tony said that he would give my husband an extension if he got me to have sex on tape with a black guy. He said that if I did it he would have three more months to get the money together."

I was sitting there taking all of this shit in. I knew the basics of Tony's business with me and Dex. Tammy assumed that we were put down with all of the details but we really weren't. I never asked Tony too many questions. I just did what I was paid to do and I was out. I figured the less I knew the better off I would be. Yeah, looking back, Tammy definitely thought I was more involved in the whole game than I was.

"So why do you want him killed? Because he made you fuck me?"

"No, of course not. I did that for my husband because I love him and I didn't want him to get hurt. I had the option to not do it. I could've simply abandoned him and moved far away but I didn't. I went through with it because I wanted to. Making me fuck you was one of the best things my husband ever did. That wasn't the problem at all."

"So what was the problem?"

"In short, I found out that he had the money. The cheap bastard just didn't want to pay it because he wouldn't have had any extra money to gamble with. That son-of-a-bitch would rather sacrifice his wife than just pay up. And to make matters worse, I found out that the prick is fucking his receptionist."

"Damn. You got it bad, lady."

"Yeah, and he traipsed off and took her to Vegas around the time that he asked me to be with you guys. He told me he had to go out of town on business, when he really was screwing that bimbo. How could he?"

Just as she finished running down her sob story the crowd in the restaurant started clapping and screaming for the singer.

"Listen. I was wondering if you would like to go upstairs a little later on. I have a room at the Bellevue and I don't have to check out until tomorrow. It would be a waste if I didn't get any good use out of that room."

"And what does that have to do with me?"

She just looked at me like she was embarrassed that I didn't jump all on her weak offer for some ass. I didn't go there to fuck Tammy. I just wanted to find out as much information as I could.

I figured I was in the dark long enough. Everybody around me seemed to know what was happening. I guess it could have been worse though. Tony seemed like he was in control of everything and that motherfucker still got canceled.

Tammy drank the rest of her wine and looked me in the eye. I could see that she was stressed out and mad horny at the same time. She reached into her pocketbook and pulled out another envelope. This one was a little bigger and it was sealed.

"This my chocolate friend, may change your mind about joining me in room 2017."

"You think your chump change is going to make me come upstairs and dig you out?"

"Oooh, I like the way that sounds, and if you consider $600 chump change then you know something that I don't."

I ripped the envelope open and pulled out the cash. I counted it twice. It was six crisp hundred-dollar bills like she got them straight from the bank. I piled the loot in front of me on the bar and put my glass on top of it.

"If I come up there and fuck the shit out of you, that don't mean I'm gon' kill your husband. I'm no fucking murderer."

"Oh, I understand that. One doesn't have anything to do with the other."

"I'll fuck you under one condition."

She leaned close to me and put her hand on my leg.

"And what is that condition?"

"You can't tell Dex that you talked to me. And I'm serious as a fucking heart attack. I mean that shit. Matter fact, don't tell nobody that you talked to me."

"I understand that. I won't tell a soul about our meeting. But I will have you know that I do plan on contacting him to kill Larry."

"Are you sure you want to do that? You can't take that shit back when it's done and besides Dex don't need no more trouble."

"Look, me and my husband have a very healthy life insurance policy and I know that if I don't get him he'll get me before I can blink. And the sad thing is, that bastard would be perched at a craps table in Vegas with that bitch on his arm before the flowers on my grave wilted. I'm going to get him before he gets me."

"Oh well, it seems like you made up your mind, but I really wish you would use somebody else other than Dex."

"I think he's the man for the job. If Tony is any indication . . ."

I didn't respond. I picked up my glass and shook the last little bit of ice into my mouth and picked up the six bills. I told Tammy to get up from the bar and go upstairs to the room. I rolled out about five minutes later because I didn't want anybody to see me with her.

I didn't want no jungle fever rep messing up my flow with the honeys. That thing was strictly business. After I tore up the hotel room to make sure there were no hidden cameras or shit in that jawn, I tore up her ass like a champ.

I left her ass twisted and wrapped up in them king-size sheets and went back to my own crazy-ass drama.

20. The drive to North Carolina for the second time was the worst. Dex's dumb ass was so pressed to leave at seven in the morning. I told him that we were going to get stuck in traffic.

But he thinks he knows every damn thing. It took us like twelve hours to get down there because of the Philly rush hour in the morning and the Virginia traffic in the afternoon.

I knew it but he ain't want to listen to me. Even if we were only in that car for two hours that day it would have been too much. There was tension like a motherfucker in that Honda. I didn't want to be with them niggas. Herb wanted to knock my head off just because, and Dex was acting all weird because he knew that he was out of line when he said he was going to send that tape to my mom's church. I was heated at that shit and I knew I was going to make him pay for it. He fucked up when he brought my mom into it.

We stopped for gas and to get food, but I ain't really have shit to say to them. I would take a leak, go to Roy Rogers or Burger King or wherever and get my food and go back to the car. I had no rap for them cats.

I waited until we were like an hour from Durham before I told them that I wasn't staying with them niggas. They tried to act like they had a problem with it but I told them cats that they were lucky I came along for the ride and not to push it.

I called Onyx the night before and told her I would be down there for the day. She asked a lot of questions at first. She wanted to know why I was coming down there again, and why I was only staying for a short time.

At first I got hyped when she told me that her roommates went out of town for the week. I thought the trip was gon' be worth it after all. But then she busted my bubble when she said that I could sleep on the couch bed. I was salty as shit but I was cool with that. I would rather sleep on her couch bed than be all up in Herb and Dex's face like everything was cool.

It was about eight when we got there, and we were all tired as shit. Dex and Herb checked into the Super 8 motel that was right down the road from where we all stayed before and hopped back in the car. Them niggas weren't wasting no time. They wanted to see Archie and they wanted to see him right then and there.

We drove the same damn winding roads until we ended up in front of the house. It was one of them country-ass cribs where the neighbors were at least half a Philly block away on both sides. There was nothing across from the house but grass and more damn grass. All the lights were out and the red Navigator and the black Camry that was there before was gone.

Dex turned off the car and Herb hopped out first. He ran up on the porch and looked into the dark living room. I could see from the car that there were no curtains. He ran back to the car and told us that the same furniture was still in there and it looked like they still lived there. Dex got out of the car and went to look in their mailbox that was right near the road. It had only two pieces of mail in there, so he assumed that somebody was coming home every day to pick it up.

"So what do you niggas plan on doing when or if they come home?"

At first they both ignored my question. I should've asked before I left Philly, but I knew it was going to be bad and I knew that I would change my mind and then he would send the tape and then and then and then . . . I asked the question again.

"Yo Dex, what if dude and his wife come home right now? What are you going to do?"

"I'm going to make him wish he never bought that camcorder."

"So what that mean? . . . You slap the dude up a little bit?"

"Naw, I'm trying to do something serious."

That's when I figured I would start talking some sense into his ass.

"Yo Dex, don't even think about smokin' his ass."

"Why not?"

"If you do that what purpose will it serve? OK, let's say you pull out the burner and knock off the dude and his wife. The pictures are still going to be on the Internet and they'll be dead, and then the cops will be looking for you, and then you'll be in jail."

Of course Herb told Dex to ignore me.

"Hey yo, fuck that! That's the chance we gon' have to take. Your ass ain't up there on the computer lookin' like a mo. You talking a whole lot of shit for somebody that ain't up on everybody's computer on some sweet shit."

"I know that shit. And I also know a little bit about the Internet, motherfucker, and I know that if those pictures are on one site, then chances are they're on another one too."

"What the fuck you talking about?"

"If dude sold them to one site, then who says he didn't sell them to another? And on the Internet, they steal pictures. You know how many times I been on the Internet looking at smut and saw the same jawn three, four times on another site? The same ass, the same titties, the same pictures all on totally different sites. So on the real he don't even have to sell them to nobody else for them to use them on their site. Y'all ass could be on ten different sites by now. Herb, you don't even know how to log on to a computer, nigga, so you wouldn't know that."

"Oh you went to community for a couple of years and now you supposed to be a fucking Einstein or some shit. Come on!"

Dex was quiet, so I knew I was getting through to him. Herb on the other hand just kept yapping but wasn't saying anything.

"Cuz, you might be right."

"I know I'm right. Now, I'm not saying don't bust that pussy in his fucking mouth, but definitely don't do nothing that's going to land your ass in the electric chair."

"How can I find out what websites those pictures are on?"

"I have no idea. Just tell dude that if you see them pictures again on the net then you're gonna come back down here and toast his ass."

"Man, but how I'm gon' know if they out there on other sites? I don't be on my mom's computer all like that."

"Well you gon' have to get up on there to see. You and Herb are going to have to do that."

We sat there in the quiet for a long time. Every now and then a car would drive by, but Archie and his big-titty wife were nowhere to be seen. After a while Dex and Herb got hungry, so we bounced. They dropped me off at Onyx's and they went to Pan-Pan to get something to eat.

They told me that they would come back to get me the next night so we could take another trip back to the house. I was cool with that because it gave me the whole day to chill with Onyx. And man, what a fucking Tuesday.

She kept her word on that couch bed shit. When I walked up in her crib, the extra blanket and pillow was already sitting on the arm of the couch. I guess she wanted me to know from the gate that she was serious.

Any other time I would have been irked if a bitch acted all stingy with the ass, but I was so happy to get away from them two characters that I would've slept on a bed of nails if I had to.

We stayed up late, talking and watching movies. We watched *Misery* and *Arlington Road*. Before I fell asleep she pulled out all her Donny Hathaway CD's and let me get a load of that cat. Some of the songs sounded familiar, but I was tired as hell so I was knocked out before even one CD finished. I didn't even get a kiss.

The next day we got up mad early and went over to Duke's stadium to run. Onyx was an exercise freak and couldn't go more than two days without working out. I was feeling that about her because every nigga wants a woman that tries to keep her body tight. We ran a few miles on the track and then went on the in-field to stretch. It was about seven in the morning, so we were the only ones out there.

"Brotha, I didn't think you would be able to hang that long."

"What, you trying to play me? I got skills, girl. I used to kill them cats on the track when I was in high school."

"You ran track in high school?"

"Yup, I was the truth too. I ran the 800 in like one minute and fifty-six seconds when I was in the tenth grade."

"What? You ran around the track twice in less than two minutes?"

"Yeah. I did it a couple of times. Once in the city champs and once on the four-by-eight at the Penn Relays."

"You ran at the Penn Relays? I have a couple girlfriends down here from up north who told me that they're tight to death. I want to go so bad one day."

"I go every year but the tenth grade is the last time I actually went inside of Franklin Field."

"What do you mean, you go every year but you haven't been inside the stadium?"

"Let's just say I got for the show. The Penn Relays brings all the honeys out. It's like the Greek picnic or a big festival or something. There's always just as many people outside as there are in there watching the meet."

"Oh I see, you just go down there to get your pimp on."

"I'm not a pimp. I just enjoy looking at beautiful women. That's why I'm staring at you right now."

"Anyway . . . why did you stop running in the tenth grade if you were so good?"

"Man, I was tired of running. My mom put me in track when I was like eleven and I think I was burnt out. It started not to be as fun anymore. It was cool when I used to go way out to West Oak Lane to run for the Wildcats. I still have my little blue and white uniform. It was cool back then, but when I got into high school I was into all kinds of other stuff."

"Like what?"

"Here you go. Am I on the witness stand right now? Is this how you gon' be with the people in court when you're a lawyer?"

"You better believe it. I'm gonna interrogate and investigate until they can't stand me no more."

"I can believe it."

"But anyway, you never answered my question. Now what kind of stuff did you get into? And remember, you're under oath."

"I mean, nothing really. The typical stuff that young boaws get into. Girls, standing on the corners, acting like we know everything. Is that juicy enough for you?"

"I'll get more juice out of you later."

We was really vibing that day. I don't never let a jawn get all up in my business like that. I just met her really, but she just made me feel so chill. It was like I knew I could trust her right off the bat. We talked while we stretched for another thirty minutes and then we were out.

We went back to her crib and took showers. She said she was going to take me out for a day on the town, but on the real there wasn't much to do down there. We went to get some grub from one of the all-you-can-eat lunch jawns and then went to the movies. We saw *Jurassic Park III* and it was the worst. We were cheering for the fucking dinosaurs after a while. It was wack but we had a good time because so much shit was making us laugh.

There was a white dude in the empty-ass movie theater who was sitting a couple rows behind us. He was just as pissed as us at that wack-ass movie. He kept screaming the same damn thing at the screen, and it was killing us.

"C'mahn! Die already, fuckers!"

That was our running joke for the rest of the time I was down there.

After the movies we went to one of the corny-ass malls and walked around for a few hours. There wasn't shit to do that would impress me, but I was cool just chilling with Onyx.

Everything was straight. It was a perfect day. I wasn't thinking about Dex or Herb or Archie or the Internet or none of that shit.

I damn near choked on a mouthful of Cracker Jacks when we were driving home. A word on the top of a lounge caught my attention and snapped me back into my crazy-ass reality.

21. Onyx looked at me like I was crazy when I screamed at her to pull the car over to the curb and park. She was asking me a million questions, but I just ignored her at first.

I just kept looking at the mirror on the passenger side of the car at the sign to that bar. When I saw that large neon sign, it just stood out right away. It stood out I guess because of the way it was spelled. If it was spelled the regular way I probably would have never noticed. The "e" was in front of the "u" though, and that made me notice it. I saw it with my own eyes: b-l-e-u.

That is the same way it was spelled in Dex's cell phone when I looked at it in Bluezette. It was the same damn way. I knew that something or somebody was in there that I needed to see.

I told Onyx to stay in the car. She asked me a million more questions, and I just kept telling her that I would only be a few minutes. I didn't understand why she was so irked at first.

"Why are you so preoccupied with going to a strip bar?"

"Is that what that is?"

"You have to do better than that. Don't act like you didn't know that."

"Yo really, I didn't. I just need to go in there though, to see something."

"Don't you mean see someone? Like Bambi or Cinnamon or Passion?"

"Naw, come on, really. Just trust me on this for a minute. I will explain everything to you when I come back to the car."

"If you're not back in ten minutes I'm leaving."

I told her to give me fifteen minutes to be on the safe side, and then I hopped out of her purple Neon. My stomach was all knotted up when I walked up to the door. I don't know what the fuck I was going there for. I just knew that I needed to go inside. I knew that if I didn't I would regret that shit all the way back to Philly and when I was home.

When I rolled up in the spot there were only about ten men in there. I guess that was normal since it still wasn't all the way dark outside. This busted-ass white girl was up there swinging around the pole and popping her flat ass but nobody was paying attention.

This diesel-ass white cat stepped in front of me real quick and told me that it was a ten-dollar charge. I told him that I wasn't staying, that I just wanted to look around a little bit. He wasn't trying to hear that shit though, and we got into an argument. Right when it looked like he was about to grip my black ass up and toss me out on the sidewalk, this white chick came out of nowhere and told him to let me in.

I looked her up and down real quick. I never saw that bitch a day in my life. She looked like poor white trash or something though. She wasn't nothing to look at. Stringy blond hair, skinny legs and arms. I couldn't believe that cats paid to see her naked.

She caught me off guard after he stepped off and she started talking to me.

"You're Dex's friend, right?"

"What? How do you know me? Have I met you before?"

"No, you've never met me, but I know that bastard. I'm Nancy."

"How do you know Dex?"

"Is he here with you too? Where is he? He owes me money."

"What? Slow down. How do you know him?"

"Is he coming in here? Where is he?"

"Look lady, I don't know where Dex is."

"Oh, so you came down by yourself this time?"

"What are you talking about?"

"Look, I know more than you think. . . . Forget it."

"So what's the deal?"

"Look, I've already been screwed by Dex. Nothing comes free from now on."

"You have something to tell me?"

"I'm not saying another word until I see some green. He owes me two hundred big ones."

I went into my pocket and pulled out a hundred. Normally I would never do shit like that, but I just knew that what she told me was going to be worth it. I waved it in front of her nose like she was a dog and it was a piece of meat.

"OK, here's the green. Now what's the deal?"

She snatched it out of my hand and tucked it into her bra. That's when she started to look around like she was all nervous. She was whispering so low that I could hardly hear her over the country-ass music in that jawn.

"Listen, I did something for Dex and he said he was going to pay me, but he never did. That's the second time he didn't come through when he said he would."

"What did you do for him?"

"Look, he pissed me off, so now I don't care. Just don't tell him I told you."

"OK, I won't. What did you do?"

"I went to your motel room the last time you guys were down here and I took the money."

"What! You took my fucking money!"

"Calm down before they throw you outta here. Yes I took the money. Dex told me to do it and he said he would give me two hundred dollars. I haven't heard from that bastard ever since. And the number he gave me is to a Chinese take-out joint up in Philadelphia."

I had so many questions for that white girl. I was throwing them at her quick because I knew Onyx was getting mad waiting in the car for me.

"How did you get the money? How did you get in the room?"

"I had the key and Dex told me where to look to get your money and the other guy's."

"How did you get the key? So Herb wasn't in on this too?"

"I don't think the other guy was in on it, because I took his money too. Dex dropped the key in the parking lot like he told me he would."

"What do you mean he dropped it in the parking lot?"

That's when Nancy started to run it down. She was spilling out all that shit on my rat-ass cousin. She told me how she was sitting in the parking lot of the motel in her car when me, Dex, and Herb left for Onyx's crib.

He told her that he was going to drop the plastic hotel key on the ground as he was getting into the car. Nancy told me that when we pulled out she got out of her car, scooped the key off the ground, and let herself into our room.

Dex told her where all our money would be when he called her on his cell phone earlier that day. He told her to get all of it and stuff it into the small inside pocket of his luggage. I couldn't believe that I was robbed before my ass even made it over to Onyx's. That bitch was in and out in like twenty minutes. Before she left, she put the motel key on top of the TV like he told her.

That way it would seem like he forgot his key and I was the only other one with a key.

I finally knew how Dex's key beat his ass back to the room.

"Why didn't you take your cut when you had it in your hands?"

"Dex told me that he needed every dime because some goon was going to kill him if he didn't pay up on a debt he had up north."

"And you believed that?"

"I shouldn't have, but I did. I haven't seen nor heard from that moron since then, and that was weeks ago. He said I would get my cash in a few days. Please don't tell him I told you all this."

"I won't say nothing. You don't tell him you told me either. You don't want to know what he'll do to you if you do. Matter of fact, don't even tell him we met."

I looked her dead in the eye so she would know I wasn't fucking around. It looked like she wanted to cry. I gave her an extra twenty because I felt sorry for her. It looked like she was on drugs. I didn't even ask her how she met Dex or how many times he had been down south. My mind was on Onyx back in her car. I thanked Nancy for giving up the info and then I bounced.

Onyx was still waiting there for me, but she was heated. I knew it would take a lot of smooth talking to get her in a good mood again. She hardly talked to me the whole way back to her crib. She blasted some gospel tape and acted like I wasn't even in the car.

When we got back to the apartment she had an attitude with me. She sat on the other end of the couch and just flipped through the channels with the remote. When she finally started talking again of course she went right back to asking all the damn questions.

"What was that all about? You couldn't control yourself?"

"What do you mean, I couldn't control myself?

"You had to run up in that booty club and see some flesh?"

"Naw Onyx, it's not even like that. I had to handle some business. There was somebody up in there who I really needed to talk to."

"So I guess you really had to see her take off her bra and I guess you really had to tuck a twenty-dollar bill in her G-string."

"You know it was only white girls up in there right? I told you, I don't get down like that."

"What's that supposed to mean?"

"White girls are not my type all like that."

"So you do go to strip bars to see black girls?"

"Yeah . . . I mean no . . . I mean, I have been before but it's not like I go on the regular."

"What do you mean, on the regular?"

"Look, I ain't one of them perverts that goes and spends all his money getting lap dances from a stripper jawn, if that's what you think."

"So who did you have to talk to in there? When we first pulled up outside the place you acted like you didn't know it was a strip club, and then all of a sudden you were acting like your best friend was up in there. How do you explain that?"

I paused a long time before I started to answer her question. I wanted to tell her everything. I wanted to tell her about Dex and Herb and what they were into. I wanted to tell her how I was so caught up in all that shit, but I knew she would've called my ass a cab right away. I wanted to, but I couldn't.

"Look, it's deep right now. That's all I can say. I think I can trust you enough to tell you what's going on one day, but it's so much right now. I just don't want to pull all that shit—excuse me—I don't want to pull all of that stuff on you."

"Is it that deep?"

"Yes. I swear to God it's that deep."

"Don't swear. You don't have to even go there."

"My bad. I know I shouldn't swear, but you see what I'm saying?"

"I guess. I just don't want to get my feelings all wrapped up in a man who turns out to be a crook or something. You don't sell drugs do you?"

"What? Drugs? Why I gotta be a drug dealer just because I'm from Philly and I wear Tims in the summer. No, I don't sell no drugs."

I felt good because I knew I was telling her the truth. I sold weed for a minute but that was way back in the day. Now if she would've asked me if I ever fucked people's wives on tape for money, then I would have been lying if I said no. She didn't ask that though. She just asked about drugs, and that wasn't my thing, so I was telling the truth.

After a few minutes she stopped with all the damn questions. She was still acting kind of funny towards me though. Like when we were out at the track she was mad comfortable with me. I could tell I had her open. She was listening to me like I was standing up on stage with a microphone or some shit. But after I stopped at Bleu she was acting like we were cool but still didn't trust me all the way.

Onyx popped *Independence Day* in the DVD player and we watched most of it without talking. Halfway through the movie Dex called and said that him and Herb were on their way to pick me up so we could take another trip out to Archie's.

They got there in like twenty minutes and I met them outside in the parking lot. I didn't want either one of them motherfuckers around Onyx. All of a sudden I felt real protective of her and I didn't want them getting nowhere near her. Later on we found out the hard way exactly why I felt that way.

22.   I hopped in the car without saying nothing to either one of them niggas. The only reason I felt like I had to go along at that point was to make sure they didn't do anything crazy, like blow Archie's head the fuck off.

I just looked at Herb and gritted on his nut ass. I didn't want to be around him at all. I felt like I couldn't blink for one minute around him. I knew without a doubt that Herb would put my ass six feet deep if I gave him the chance. He was sitting back waiting for me to slip up so that he could take me out. I knew he would have to outsmart me in order to kill my ass, and I wasn't going to let that happen.

We drove back to Archie and Goldie's, and that time they were home. Lights were on all throughout that motherfucker. Dex turned the lights off on the Honda before we could even pull all the way off the road. Both of their cars were parked in the driveway.

Deep down I was hoping they weren't going to be home. I was hoping they were on vacation or something and that Dex and Herb would just let that shit go and get their asses back home. We all jumped out the whip and started to walk toward the house. I grabbed Dex's arm when we were walking across the grass.

"Yo Dex, remember what I said. Don't do no dumb shit."

"Aight, I'm cool."

I knew that both of them had guns. I didn't even bother to ask. I wasn't packing heat though. The little piece of bullshit gun that I had was back in North Philly wrapped up in one of my old T-shirts in a sneaker box.

Dex tiptoed across the porch and reached out and grabbed the doorknob. It was open. I guess that was some down-south shit, because we lock our shit up in North Philly.

He opened the door and we all crept up in that jawn. I was the last one in, so I shut the door and locked it behind me. Nobody was in the living room, but we could hear voices. It sounded like a few motherfuckers up in the bedroom. As soon as we started walking through the living room, Dex and Herb pulled out their burners. I knew it.

Herb was the first one to get to the bedroom door. None of them heard us at first. Archie was sitting with his back to the door and the camcorder in his hand. His wife Goldie and these other two chicks were getting it on in the middle of the bed. One of the girls was Chinese or Japanese and the other one was black. They was sixty-ninin' each other while Goldie was spanking the black jawn on the ass with a paddle. That shit was crazy.

I was only looking at them for about three seconds when Herb just snapped. He ran in the room and started screaming. Archie damn near had a heart attack when he realized that we were in the house. The first thing he saw when he whipped his fat head around was Herb's gun all up in his grill.

"Dear God!"

"Don't be calling on God now, pussy. You done fucked up!"

Herb raised his hand with the gun and just smashed it across Archie's forehead. His ass flew out of the chair and dropped to the floor. The women started screaming like somebody was killing their asses. I remember being glad that they didn't have no next-door neighbors. If that shit happened in my row house in North Philly, both of my neighbors would have heard every damn thing.

When Archie looked up, all of this blood was running down his forehead and his face. It looked so red because his face was so fucking white. Dex pushed into the room and aimed his gun at Goldie.

"All y'all bitches, shut the fuck up. Nobody is going to get hurt if y'all just calm the fuck down!"

"Please don't hurt us! Please don't hurt us!"

Goldie was breathing all hard and crying and the other two jawns shut up like Dex said. They just hugged up real close on each other in the other corner of the bed and was shaking.

"Like I said, ain't nobody going to get smoked unless y'all do something to make us pissed."

Herb yanked Archie up off the floor and tossed him in the bed next to his wife. I sat down in the chair where Archie was sitting and just watched.

"I guess you're wondering why we're back down in North Carolina and why my man Herb just busted you in your fucking head. But then again, you probably already know."

"Please . . . don't hurt my wife. Please, I'll give you whatever you want. Please don't hurt her."

"Shut the fuck up! Ain't nobody thinking about your trick-ass wife. We came down here because you played us and put them pictures you took on the Internet on a fucking gay website!"

"What? A gay website? I have no idea what you're talking about. . . ."

"Keep on playing dumb with me, man, and I'm going to put a lump on the other side of your forehead! Now why did you play us like that?"

"I-I-I sold one of my contacts a few of the pictures I took of you guys but I never gave them to any gay site."

"Then how the fuck did they get on there?"

Before he could answer the question Herb stepped in front of Archie and sucker punched his ass out of nowhere. He caught that boaw with a hammer. His whole shit just flipped back like his head was about to fall off. He grabbed his mouth and balled up on the bed next to his wife. She started getting all dramatic and shit like she was about to faint.

"I'm going to ask you again. How did me and Herb's pictures get on a faggot website? And if you even think about lying, Herb is going to break your fucking jaw the next time."

Archie sat back up on the bed and wiped the blood off his face with the bottom of his polo shirt. He was trying to calm himself down.

"Listen, I sold the pictures to a triple X site that I do business with, but I don't know anything about a gay site. My contact must have double-crossed me and sold them to another site without me knowing about it. I swear to God I didn't know anything about that."

Herb took the pictures of him and Dex out of his pocket and threw them at Archie. He looked through them one at a time while his wife looked over his shoulder. Dex was just pacing back and forth in front of the bed like he was trying to figure out if dude was telling the truth or not. Herb was standing there looking like he wanted to smash dude in the face again.

"I want you to get that motherfucker on the phone right now and tell him to take that shit off the computer. Call his ass right now!"

"Hand me my planner from the nightstand honey. Now he may not be home but . . ."

"He better be home if you know what's best for your ass!"

Archie was hitting those numbers on his cordless fast as shit. He had to break some kind of world record for dialing a phone number. He damn sure didn't want no more of Herb. His contact picked up the phone kind of quick.

"Yeah Bruce, I have some very upset people over here right now. . . . What does it have to do with you? I'll tell you, you damn prick. The pictures of the black guys and my wife that I sold to you showed up on a gay website. . . . We had a deal. They were only to be used exclusively on the interracial sex site. . . . What?! . . . What? . . . What?! You gotta be kidding me!"

"What the fuck is he saying?"

"Hold on Bruce . . . He said that the company that runs the triple X interracial site also owns the gay site. It's the same damn company and the contract I signed said that they could use the images on any of their sites."

"Is he still going to be talking that dumb shit when we start cutting you and your wife's toes and fingers off up in this piece. Does he know that the black guys in those pictures are crazy as shit!?"

"You heard that Bruce? This is extremely important. You have to get those pictures off of there."

Dex snatched the phone out of Archie's hand and started to yell at the dude on the other end.

"Listen motherfucker, your friend and his wife are about to get the shit beat out of them if you don't get up on that Internet and take the pictures of us off of there. Better yet, I'm going to torture them until they tell me where the fuck you are so me and my squad can come track you down."

Dex paused for a while. The dude Bruce on the other end must have been running his mouth, because Dex was quiet.

"Aight, here's the deal. I'll give you until seven tomorrow morning to get that shit off of all them sites. I don't want there to be no pictures of me and my boaw on none of them fucking sites. You got that? Now y'all can test me if y'all want!"

Dex hung up the phone and started acting like he was the fucking leader. He made the two freaks put their clothes back on. He told them that they couldn't leave the house until after we were long gone. Goldie put her clothes back on too. They had a bathroom in their bedroom, so Herb went in there and wet a washcloth so that Archie could clean his face.

While he was cleaning the cut on his head, Herb took it one step further and started to accuse Archie of stealing our money from the motel the first time we went down there. I wanted to tell his nut ass that his partner had dicked him, but I wasn't on his side. He was so fucking smart he was stupid.

It was a long way off from seven and I didn't feel like sitting up in that house with them motherfuckers all night. I wanted to be with Onyx. I had some serious ass kissing to do.

Dex pulled me to the side and told me that him and Herb had already checked out of their motel and that they had all their shit in the trunk of the car. He said they wanted to be out as soon as the dude called back and told them that their pictures were off that site. They wanted to check the computer at Archie's house before we hit the road. Dex told the two jawns to stay too, so they wouldn't run and snitch to the cops.

I decided to go back to Onyx's crib to get my stuff and chill with her. I planned on just coming back at seven in the morning. There was no reason for me to be there. I was like, fuck it. I did my part.

For some reason I was feeling kind of bold, so I told Archie that I was going to take his Lincoln Navigator. It ain't like he was going nowhere any time soon that day. He looked at me like I was crazy.

"What do you need my truck for? How far are you going?"

"I'm only going about twenty minutes away. Don't worry man, I ain't gon' do shit to your truck. I just want to see what it's like to push one of them jawns. I'll be back in a few hours."

"Why don't you use my wife's car? It has a full tank of gas."

"Did you not just hear me? I want to whip that Navigator. I done drove a Camry a million times already."

"OK, just please be careful. Please be very careful. . . ."

Why is it so damn easy to look back and see that something you did was stupid as shit? That was one of those things. I should have just took his wife's car. Taking the truck opened a can of worms I was ready to close and throw in the damn river.

Archie had a whole lot of shit with him.

23. I didn't go straight to Onyx's crib. I was having too much fun whipping that truck. His system was the shit, but I had to play the radio since the only CD's he had in there were country music. The biggest truck that I had ever been in before that was a Pathfinder, so I was really feeling that jawn. I went up and down the highway a few times just to see how it drove.

The driver's seat was so high up on that chumpee that I felt like I was sitting on top of the world. That shit didn't last long though. Because if I was sitting on top of the world, Onyx sure enough knocked my ass right back down into the bottom of the gutter before I left her crib that morning.

When I showed up at her apartment she answered the door rubbing her eyes. The television and the stereo were on. I could tell that she was sitting in the living room waiting for me and she fell asleep. It was after two o'clock.

I sat next to her on the couch and started to rub her face with the back of my hand. I felt like I was in a cheesy-ass chick flick, because I never do shit like that. She was in a better mood than before I left with Dex and Herb.

"So what's the deal, sweetheart?"

"What's the deal? It's two in the morning. Where you been?"

"I had to go with my cousin to handle some business."

"You been handling a lot of business since you been down here and I still have no idea what you do or where you go."

"Trust me, it's no big deal."

"If you say so. You know the only reason I put up with you is because I get a good vibe from you. Although you are very evasive when I try to talk to you about certain things, I still have a good feeling about your spirit. I guess what I'm trying to say is that I can see the God in you."

She caught me way off guard with that. She said she saw the God in me. I didn't know what that meant. I ain't no damn satan worshipper, but nobody ever told me nothing like that. Nobody ever associated me with God in my whole life. She was on some other stuff.

"Girl, I think you're still a little sleepy. What you talking about?"

"See, I don't want to make you uncomfortable or nothing like that, but it's just an observation I made. Although you're very street and Philly and all I can just see that you have a good spirit. God is going to use you one day."

She was cheesing all hard, like somebody was about to take her picture. Her smile was dope. It was the kind of smile that was going to get her in a motherfucking Colgate commercial one day.

"I don't know what to say. I guess thank you."

"Anyway, I don't want to freak you out or have you thinking I'm about to go into a sermon. Let's just enjoy the rest of the night. Hey, I want you to hear something."

She went over to her stereo and popped in a CD. She played Donny Hathaway again. I thought his voice was dope, but most of the songs she played made me feel sad. It gave me goosebumps, and that don't ever happen when I listen to music. I remember thinking that he sounded a little like the boaw who sang at Zanzibar Blue when I met Tammy.

"So what do you think?"

"This is tight. I could see myself listening to this."

"Well good, because I made you a tape to take with you."

"That's wassup. You taped one of his albums?"

"Actually, I kind of just put my favorites all on there. There aren't that many songs by him because he died young."

"Really. Somebody smoked him?"

"No, he wasn't shot. They say it was suicide."

"Damn."

I remember thinking at that very moment that I would probably do the same thing if I got locked up for all the shit we were into. I just knew that I would rather die than sit up in jail for the rest of my life. I knew that if we got caught and the jury said the "G" word, then I was going to hang myself in my prison cell the first night. I was dead serious. Just the thought of one of them sex-starved clowns like on *Oz* pinning me down and fucking me in the ass was enough to make me do it.

Me and Onyx rapped a lot that night. She told me about why she wanted to be a lawyer and how everybody in her family kept telling her to just drop out and become a singer.

She sang and acted in all her high school plays and nobody in her family was trying to hear that law school shit. Their ghetto asses wanted to see her on Showtime at the Apollo more than they wanted to see her in the courtroom.

She was a character though. She kept me laughing and even though she was all country and shit she could relate to a lot of the stories I told her about Philly.

Before I got up to get my shit together, we watched *The Princess Bride*. I know that shit is a kiddy movie and all, but Andre the Giant was up in there and I used to be a big wrestling fan when I was a young boaw. Onyx was down too. She knew all about the old-school characters that I used to watch, like Junk-yard Dog, Hillbilly Jim, Jimmy "Superfly" Snuka, and Rowdy Roddy Piper. I was really digging that jawn. I hadn't ever met a bitch who knew about the feud between Hulk Hogan and Andre the Giant at WrestleMania III. She was the shit.

After I threw my stuff into my overnight bag, it was five fifteen. Onyx was still wide awake and talking and shit, but I was tired. I was ready to drive back over to Archie's and get back on the road to Philly.

I was just hoping that those motherfuckers took the pictures off the Internet so we could roll out. Me and Onyx said peace to each other. I hugged her and kissed her on the cheek and was ready to be out. I ain't even try to rub on her titties. She wanted to walk me out to the parking lot though. I said no at first, but she was all hyped about it since she wasn't going to see me for a minute. I said fuck it. She was on the first floor of the complex anyway, so it wasn't like we had far to walk to the truck. It was still dark outside.

We were so busy rapping that when we got to the truck and I stopped to open the door, she just looked at me like I was crazy. She probably thought that I drove Dex's black Honda.

"This is what you drove here?"

"Yeah."

"Whose truck is this?"

"A friend of mine let me borrow it."

"This Navigator is tight to death. I love the color."

"That cherry red is tight, ain't it."

She started to walk around the truck to check it out after I opened the door to throw my bag on the passenger seat. I felt good for a hot minute because she seemed impressed that I was pushing a whip that was so murder. That shit ain't last long though.

She got quiet when she walked to the back of the truck. After a few seconds she came flying back to the front of the truck where I was standing, with her arms folded all tight. I didn't even notice the mad-ass look on her face, because I was so caught up in her nipples. They was hard as shit and poking through the pajama tank top.

"Hey, you said your friend let you hold this truck. You know William?"

"William?"

"Yes! I knew this truck looked familiar. This is William Larchwood's truck, isn't it?"

I paused for a minute to think about it and I remembered him introducing himself as Bill. I guess William Larchwood was his real name. I called myself playing it off real smooth, but looking back I know I had to look like a dickhead.

"Oh yeah, this is Bill's truck. You threw me off when you said William."

"You call him Bill? Where do you know him from?"

"On the real I don't even call him Bill. I call him Archie because he looks like the dude who used to play on *All in the Family*."

"Oh I see. He does sort of look like him. That's so ironic."

"Why you say that?"

"Because he looks like the actor—what's his name, Caroll O'Connor?"

"I don't know what his real name is, everybody just knows him as Archie. Why did you say it's ironic? You heard he's prejudice or some shit? Don't tell me that my man Bill hates black people."

She looked at me kind of funny, like I had dog shit on my face or something. And that's when she dropped the bomb on me.

"Prejudice? No. I said it's ironic because that actor played a cop on that show, *In the Heat of the Night,* and William Larchwood is a cop."

"What you mean, he's a cop?"

"Stop playing with me, boy. You're driving his car around and claim to be friends with the man and you didn't know that he's a police sergeant. He's one of the most decorated police officials in Durham. I see him all the time when I go to the courthouse for school stuff."

At first she thought I was joking with her, but Onyx figured out kind of quick that I ain't know that shit. My whole damn body felt light, like I was about to float away. I had an instant headache. It never would have crossed my mind in a million fucking years that perverted-ass Archie was a cop. And a sergeant at that.

None of us ever asked what our jobs did for a living. It was none of our business. That shit had me thinking. The dude who we called black G.I. Joe was probably the fucking mayor or some shit. That box-headed motherfucker probably had a phat-ass office up in city hall. Damn! I was shook as hell. Dex and Herb was back over at the house holding a fucking police sergeant and his wife hostage and ain't even know it.

I knew that even if they took the pictures off the Internet and we rolled out of there that morning we probably wouldn't make it out of the city alive. Especially since Herb clocked that bastard in the head with his burner.

All of this shit was running through my head, and Onyx was just standing there looking at me like she was staring at a monster.

"What is going on?"

"Look Onyx, we need to go back into your apartment. I can't talk about this out here."

I was looking around the parking lot like a dope fiend. I was on edge like a motherfucker, but I was ready to tell her what was going on. At least most of what was going on anyway. As soon as I grabbed her arm so that we could go back to her crib a bright light came across the parking lot. A fucking cop car rolled right up on us while we were standing there. I whispered under my breath to Onyx.

"Just be cool. I got this."

Two white cops got out of the squad car and started walking over to us. The door to the truck was wide open.

"Hello officers, can I help you?"

"Yes. Do you know who this truck belongs to boy?"

"Yes I do. It belongs to Bill Larchwood."

The worse shit was going through my mind at that point. At first I was thinking that maybe Archie or Bill or whatever the fuck his name was had escaped from the house and told the other cops that he had been held hostage by two coons from up north. I pictured Dex and Herb getting shot in the back as they tried to escape. And now the pigs were coming for me. I just hoped they didn't shoot Onyx too. That's all I was thinking. Don't shoot her too.

"So why are you standing there with the door to his vehicle open?"

"He said that I could borrow his truck, sir."

"Oh is that so? Sergeant Larchwood let you borrow his brand-new Lincoln Navigator?"

"Yes."

"We'll see about that. Shut the door to the truck and give me your license."

I pushed the door closed and reached into my pocket to get

my wallet. I was moving slow as hell though. I didn't want to make sudden moves and give them a reason to blow my head off. I pulled the license out of my wallet and handed it to the one cop. The other dude just stood back closer to the car. Officer Willoughby looked down at my license.

"Is this your real name?

"Yes."

"OK, I'm going to give the sergeant a call. You just stand right there and don't move."

I could hardly breathe because I didn't know what the fuck was going to happen. I just knew it wasn't going to be good. While we were standing there waiting I didn't say nothing to Onyx. I knew that she was scared and I knew nothing I said would make any sense right then anyway, so I just shut up and waited.

Like ten minutes passed before both of them got out of the car and walked over. They didn't have their guns pulled out, so that was a good thing. Both of them had serious-ass faces though. The other cop's name was Officer Hill.

"We talked to the sergeant and he confirmed that he knew you. He also wanted us to pass along a message."

"Yeah, what's the message?"

"He said to hurry back because the pictures are gone and to bring him a two-liter Pepsi and a bag of barbecue potato chips."

"That's all."

"Yeah, that's all."

"Thanks, officer."

The cop handed me back my license and made a lame joke about my name. I heard them all already so I didn't pay him no mind. I just cracked a phony-ass smile and thanked God I didn't get shot by them two redneck cops. I looked at Onyx and told her to go back to her apartment.

"I have to leave right now. I promise I will call you as soon as I can and I'll tell you everything. I know you have a lot of questions, but so do I."

She hugged me real tight and then she was out. I felt so bad because I know she was feeling me and I was giving her every reason to just leave my black ass alone. I hopped in the truck and peeled out of the parking lot like a race car driver. I wanted to get out of North Carolina before anything else could happen.

When I got back to Archie's it was still dark outside. All of the lights were on in the house and I could see Herb standing in the living room window looking out at me.

He had the raps as soon as I stepped foot in the house. The two freak jawns were sitting on the living room couch. He was talking to me like we were cool. I think he was so damn happy that they got what they wanted that he forgot he hated me for a minute.

"Yo, they took the pictures down off all them sites."

"For real?"

"Yeah. And Archie gave us a couple dollars for all this shit he put us through."

"Are they still in the room."

"Yeah, them freaks still in there. Me and Dex got bored with these two and made them finish what they started while we watched. It was off the chain."

"Really. Yo, are y'all ready? I have to get back to Philly."

"What you in a rush for?"

"I just got shit to do, nigga."

I walked past Herb and went into the bedroom. Everybody looked tired as shit. Dex didn't even have the gun out no more. I guess Archie knew he wasn't going to shoot him.

"Wassup Dex?"

"Yo cuz. They took the pictures off the site."

Archie was staring at me but I refused to look him in the eye. It was obvious that Dex and Herb didn't know, because they were acting too cool. I think they would have jetted out of there and left my ass if they found out that Archie was a pig.

When I finally did look at him I just gave him this look like, you don't have to worry about me ratting you out. I didn't want to make our trip any more hectic than it had to be. I just wanted to roll out of there. I gave him back his keys to the truck and that was it. I didn't say shit to Archie. He kept staring at me though.

"That's cool. Are you ready to roll, Dex?"

"Yeah, me and Herb was waiting for you."

"OK, I'm ready."

Dex told the two freak jawns that they could leave but that they had to wait until fifteen minutes after we rolled. They were bawling and shit when we first rolled up in there, but at that point they were chilling. I guess they figured out they wasn't going to get smoked, so they was cool.

When Dex and Herb walked out of the house I made up a lie about having to use the bathroom and ran back in the house to talk to Archie. We walked back into the kitchen. His eyes were bloodshot red and he looked stressed. You could tell that his ass had been through it. He was a top cop and all but he ain't really want it with three black cats from up north.

"I hear you found out what I do for a living."

"Yes I did, Sergeant Larchwood."

"Listen. Please don't go and . . ."

"Look man, you don't have to worry about me saying shit to nobody. Just make sure those pictures stay off the Internet. I don't have the time to be coming down here for no bullshit."

"They won't be put back on the net and that's a promise."

"Look, I could give a fuck about your promises. I just want

you to think about what would happen if the police department found out what your ass was into."

"Listen, give me your address and I'll send you a little something."

"I don't think so. I don't know you well enough for that. But here's what I'll do. I'll give you a call and let you know when and where to send it."

"That'll be fine."

I wrote his number down on the back of a matchbook and then I bounced. I was so relieved after we got on the expressway and was on the way back to Philly. I was relieved to be alive and relieved that the fucking cops wouldn't be tracking us down to shoot us.

24. I was so happy to be back in North Philly. I threw my bag on the floor in my bedroom and just fell out across my bed. I was sick of them niggas and sick of being paranoid all the damn time.

Dex pissed me the hell off when he dropped me off at my house that night. Before I got out of the car he told me that the tape of me nailing the white chick that he gave me was the only copy. I wanted to spit in his face because I knew he was lying. I guess that was his way of trying to make me feel like I could trust him and that he wouldn't do anything to backstab me. I knew that he would have really sent that tape to my mom's church if I didn't go with them.

I was ready to just go down to the Roundhouse and rat on Dex and Herb. I know it isn't cool to snitch, but I was sick of them niggas. They were so fucking sloppy that I thought the cops would've scooped their asses by then, but for whatever reason they were luckier than a motherfucker.

I just laid there on my bed and tried to not think about them. There was so much other shit that I needed to be doing. When me and Onyx went to the mall I dropped like thirty-five dollars on one of them little tape recorders that the newspaper reporters always have in the movies.

I pulled it out of the box and went through my desk drawer for some batteries. After I put them in the recorder and tested it a few times to see if it worked, I went over to the answering machine and played the message with Herb and Dex. I wanted to erase it off the machine so nobody else could hear it but I wanted to have a copy of it for myself.

My mom wasn't home so I turned up the volume all the way on the answering machine and hit the record button on my tape recorder.

"So what the hell are you saying, Herb?"

"Dex, just listen. We gotta make sure we lay real low. My man Boo told me that he been seeing these white guys rolling though your block."

"White boys?"

"Yeah Dex. They was in a black Escalade, all rimmed up and everything. They asked one of the corner boys which house was yours and shit."

"Was they 5-0?"

"The boaw who I talked to said that he don't think they was."

"Look, we gotta go over Jersey and pick up the loot from the Jewish cat tomorrow morning. The quicker we get all the cash from these clowns the quicker we can be out."

"How much did he owe Tony?"

"I think like forty grand."

"Damn, that means he gon' have to give us twenty tomorrow and he'll be straight. That's wassup."

"And don't forget we have to go to Delaware by one o'clock to hit up the two cats down there."

"Yeah, they owe twenty and thirty grand so we'll walk away with twenty-five out of there."

"We racking up this weekend and them motherfuckers is getting a break since we only asking them for half of what they owed, dude."

"Hell yeah . . ."

"Yo who the hell is that freak in there with your cousin?"

"I don't know, some bitch named Dynisha. I think he used to mess with her back in the day."

"For real. I would tear that ass up. She look good as shit."

"Yeah, whatever Herb. My food is getting cold in there. You need anything else?"

"You know what I was going to ask you too? What's up with your cousin? You think he's on to this shit? I think he been acting kinda shady."

"Who, cuz? Hell naw. That motherfucker is just happy to get a few dollars every now and then. He don't have a clue."

"Do he know what we did to Tony?"

"Nigga, I said hell no."

"No, I'm just saying, he always looking at me like he know something."

"Trust me, his ass don't know nothing. I'm a genius, re-member. Why you think we fucked Tony up so gruesome like that? I knew that the news and shit would start talking that ol' Mafia shit because that seemed like something they would do . . . the acid, the potato peeler . . . Nah mean? That shit is off the chain."

"True . . . true . . ."

"Do you read the paper? The Daily News and Inquirer got they—quote unquote—Mafia reporters writing about that shit every day. Ain't nobody even thinking about us. They think Tony got whacked like on the Sopranos or *some shit. Kitty Caparella write a different story every day about what her sources have been saying about what happened. They're way the fuck off and I hope they stay off."*

"Fuck yeah . . . So why you think the cops was asking around about us?"

"They only want to talk to us because one of them nosy-ass neighbors on Tony's block probably told them that we used to go to his crib . . . They gotta look into everything because they figure we might know. But you know that."

"Yeah, but yo, if your cousin starts acting shady or some shit, I'm gon' fuck that pussy up. . . ."

"Chill man, it ain't even gon' be all that. I can trust him."

"If you could trust his ass so damn much, why didn't you get him to help us kill Tony, huh? Why didn't you put him down with the scam we got going against these motherfuckers who still owe Tony loot?"

"Herb listen, I know that nigga better than anybody else and he ain't built for shit like this. He's a hustler just like me, but that nigga would've panicked if I asked him to help me kill Tony. He was about to pass the fuck out in his crib when we went that day and he was already dead. He was breaking the fuck down like he was about throw up and pass out and shit. Why you laughing, Herb?"

"He's a bitch. I'm glad you ain't tell him about that shit. That means more cheese for me . . . and I'm trying to get a Benz truck by September."

"That's wassup . . . I want a silver E-Class. . . . But listen, I gotta get back in there and eat my food. . . ."

"Oh yeah. I had to tell you too that I got a call from the white boaw who lives off Roosevelt Boulevard and he said he ain't gon' have our money on Sunday, and then he starts getting all hyped up and talking shit."

"You talking about dude who flies the helicopters?"

"Yeah . . . the boaw was like, I know why I'm paying y'all anyway, he was like, Tony is dead so he shouldn't have to pay off his debt. I told that pussy that we was only making him pay half so he should be grateful."

"Then what he say?"

"Then he started getting real bold and was like y'all greedy niggers will get the money when he gets ready to pay it."

"Did you tell him that you ass-fucked his wife and that we got it on tape?"

"Yeah."

"And then what he say?"

"He acted like he didn't care if we mailed out the tape to her job."

"He's trying to see if we're bluffing. . . . Fuck that shit, we're going over to his house right now and seeing about that pussy. Let me go back in there and tell them that I have to roll. Once I drop them off I'm gon' come by your house to scoop you so that we can go see this clown."

"Aight bet . . . I'll be in the house."

"Aight, oh yeah and remember we have to make sure that . . ."

The message cut off at that point and I hit stop on the tape recorder. I hit the delete button on the answering machine and hid the tape recorder in the bottom drawer of my desk underneath a stack of papers.

I knew I was going to need that tape one day, but I didn't know it was going to keep my ass from getting killed the way it did.

25. If the summer of 2001 was a book this is the part where the chickenhead bitch would start to show her ass.

I knew from the gate that Meka was going to be trouble. I told Dex that I didn't like her and he just blew me off and said that she was cool. I was pissed at first, but the more I thought about it the more I could see how he would think she was cool. They were both fucking snakes. But eventually snakes always outsnake each other.

The shit all started when Meka went on a rampage after she heard about all the shit about Herb and Dex on the gay website.

The way I think it went down was that the gay boaw Yanni told Peanut and Peanut told Rahmir and Rahmir told Boo and Boo told Juanita and Juanita told Meka that Dex and Herb was fruity. Juanita only told Meka to be smart, since she liked Dex first and was trying to holla at him, but Meka went behind her back and started messing with Dex first.

I heard that Juanita was loving that shit. My boaw Quan who told me all this said that she had a big-ass smile on her face when she told Meka that Dex and Herb was on the Internet all greased up and naked next to each other. Of course she exaggerated that shit and had them doing more than just posing next to each other, just to get Meka heated.

Meka flipped on Juanita and they was in the street rumbling. As much as I hate that bitch, I have to give her props though. Quan said that Meka took the guns to Juanita. He said that Meka wore her ass out in the middle of Opal Street over that shit. She was salty as hell. She walked around acting like she was the shit all the time and now everybody was playing her over Dex.

After they fought, Meka went over to Dex's crib to ask him if all the shit that people in the street was saying was true. He wasn't there, but Aunt Verdele let her in anyway. From what Dex told me she was chilling up in his room waiting for him to come back, when she started to look through all his shit. That's when she saw the five pictures of Dex and Herb and had a fit. When that nigga came back home she started to flip on his ass.

Now that's when I got into all of that shit.

After Meka screamed on Dex he broke down and started telling her everything. I know he didn't want to tell her that he fucked white bitches for money, but at that point it was better than having her think he was a flaming faggot. I guess Dex figured he could take a chance by telling her what we were into. He was so busy trying to clear his name that he didn't think about how risky it was telling a clucker like Meka all of that information.

He never told her that he killed Tony but he told her that he was the one who paid us. Dex also told her that Tony was the one who got killed in South Philly and was all over the news. I don't know why he even told her that much. I guess she still didn't believe him all like that, so he brought her around my crib so that I could back his story up. I wanted to lie and act like I didn't know shit that he was talking about, just to make Dex look like a flaming dickhead but I didn't.

We were all sitting in my living room and she was flipping out for like an hour, but then she calmed down. I told her what I thought her ass should know. I didn't mention names or places or prices. I just backed up his story. They eventually left and I was happy. I thought that was all the shit I would have to put up with that day, but man was I wrong.

Like four hours later two detectives were standing at the bottom of my steps looking up at me. My mom let them in. They said they wanted to talk to me down at the Roundhouse concerning a homicide investigation. They never mentioned Tony's name though.

My mom was having a fit. She was all shaking and shit and about to break down, but I just played it off and told her that it wasn't a big deal. I acted like I wasn't about to shit a brick just so she would calm the hell down.

I knew that the pigs coming to my crib had something to do with Meka. It was so obvious to me. Dex had just told her that we knew his ass and just that quick they were at my door. Her gold-digging ass probably found out that there was a reward and turned us in. Damn!

I was pissed as shit but I just stayed cool.

They took me down to the Roundhouse in a regular detective car. It wasn't the regular jawn with the flashing lights on top of it. That made me feel a little bit better. I didn't even get a chance to call Dex before I left the house.

When we got down to the Roundhouse they took me up to this room on the third floor of the building. They didn't mention anything about Dex or Herb the whole way down there and I didn't bring their names up either. I was going to just play it by ear.

The one who did all the talking was white and tall. He looked like Bill Clinton but a better-looking version. His name was Detective McBreen. His partner was this tall black cat who reminded me of my high-school principal. He was brown-skinned and tall and had a big-ass bald head. He just sat there most of the time gritting on me. I guess he was trying to intimidate me but I wasn't paying Detective Young no fucking mind. I just kept telling myself that I wasn't a murderer, so I didn't have shit to worry about.

"Are you familiar with Tony Salvatore?"

That caught me off guard. I started to say no, but then I thought that if they had a picture of me coming out of his house then they would know I was lying. And then I thought that if they asked me if I killed him and I said no, they would think I was bullshitting about that too.

"Yeah I knew Tony."

"What was your relationship with Mr. Salvatore?"

"We didn't have no relationship. I just knew him."

"Where did you meet him?"

"I don't remember."

"What do you mean you don't remember?"

"I don't remember where I met him. I meet a lot of people every day."

"What are you, a politician or bus driver? What the hell do you mean you meet a lot of people every day? What do you do for a living?"

"I am currently unemployed."

"So let me get this straight. You live at home with your mother and you don't have a job but you meet a lot of people every day. What are you, a drug dealer? Do you hustle?"

"No, I'm not no drug dealer. What, just because I'm under thirty and black and unemployed I gotta be hustling?"

"Not at all. I just asked because you're not making much sense."

"How am I not making sense? You asked a question and I gave you an answer."

"Yes, but I'm not sure I buy your answer."

After he said that, Detective Young got up from the table and went and poured a cup of coffee.

"Hey Ricky, can you pour me a cup too?"

"No problem."

Detective McBreen turned back around and faced me. He was quiet for a little while. He just kept rolling a chewed-up pencil back and forth in front of him on the table.

"So we have established that you knew Mr. Salvatore but that you can't recall where you met him. Do you at least remember the last time you saw him alive?"

"I don't know. Maybe it was down Ninth Street. I go shopping with my mother down there some time. Yeah, I guess that was the last time I saw Tony."

"The Italian Market?"

"Yeah."

"Was he alone?"

"Yes. Why am I being questioned about Tony? As you can see we weren't that tight, so I'm sure there are like a million other people y'all could be talking to."

"Actually his neighbors said that the last time they saw him alive he was with two young black guys in their mid to late twenties."

"And? What does that have to do with me?"

"Well, we got a tip this afternoon from someone who believes that one of those young men was you."

"What?!"

"Yes. So now we have *you* at the scene of the crime, and all we have to do is figure out the motive and . . ."

"No wait, back up! You don't have me at the scene of shit. You need to tell whoever tipped you off that they're wrong."

"Is that so?"

"Yes that's so. How y'all just gon' believe some random-ass person who calls up here saying that they know some shit. Who the fuck was it that called and gave y'all my name?"

"We cannot divulge that information."

"Oh I see, y'all can't divulge that information but y'all can come to my house and upset my mother on some ol' shit I don't have nothing to do with. Y'all motherfuckers is trippin'!"

I was hyped as shit in that room. I was trying to stay cool, but I wanted them pigs to feel me when I said I ain't have shit to do with Tony getting killed.

Detective Young put his coffee down on the table and pulled his chair up real close to the table. He was sitting directly across the table from me. He put his elbows on the table and folded his hands together.

"Listen brotha . . ."

"Don't brotha me! You sitting up there acting like you believe this shit!"

"Like I said, listen! We're just doing our jobs. We want to make this as easy and simple as possible. OK, you say you weren't at Tony's but maybe you know who was there."

"Am I the only person who was brought in for questioning?"

"Why do you ask that? Is there someone else you know who we should be talking to?"

"I am just asking to be asking. Because if I am the only person y'all are talking to, I think that's fucked-up that y'all are wasting y'all time and the real killer is out there somewhere probably killing somebody else."

"Oh really!"

"Yes, really. Now what was that description again? It sounds kind of generic to me. It sounds like every nigga I know."

"We already told you the description. Two black men in their mid to late twenties, both wearing velour sweatsuits."

"Is that all?"

"What are you getting at?"

"You need to check your suspect sheet on this case again or something because if that's all you got you gon' have to interview every black man in Philly."

Detective Young grunted and snatched the folder from the middle of the table. He flung it open and snatched out the piece of paper that was on top of the stack. The other one was just tapping his fingers on the table and staring at me like he was trying to read my mind.

The black detective stared at me for a few seconds and then looked back down at the sheet of paper a couple of times before he said something.

"It says here that one of the suspects had some sort of birthmark on his face. Did you know that?"

"Like I said, I don't know shit."

"Then why did you keep asking about the description?"

"Because I knew it had to be more to it than that. I hate seeing that shit on the news. Two black men wanted, in their twenties and six feet tall. That's damn near everybody and that shit ain't cool, because then y'all start to harass everybody."

"Anyway, just because you don't have a birthmark doesn't mean you're off the hook just yet. How can we be so sure that you're not the other person who our witness last saw coming out of Tony's house?"

"You can be sure because I'm telling you that it wasn't me. Man, you know what? Forget this. I'm not saying shit else until I get a lawyer, because y'all just gon' twist my words around later on and I know I ain't no killer. I ain't saying shit else."

That caught both of them clowns off-guard because they both looked irked as shit. They wanted me to sit there all damn night spilling my guts until I confessed to something that I didn't do. I was not trying to play their cop games.

"OK, you are free to leave but you make sure that you stay close. Don't go skipping town on us here. Keep your ass in Philly."

"I don't have no reason to run. I ain't do shit."

I got up from my chair and left and neither one of them cats offered me a ride back home. I didn't want to be sitting up in that car with them anyway.

I walked home that night. I walked all the way back to my house and it was the best walk I ever fucking had because I got my head straight.

26. When I got home that night I had three messages on my machine. My Chinese boaw Chen from South Philly called, the jawn Dynisha, and Onyx.

I called Onyx back first since she sounded so hyped on the machine. She told me that she was going to have a few days off work and that she wanted to come to Philly to see me.

That news was right on time, because I was in a pissy mood. I wanted to see her again real bad. I told her that she could stay with me, but she said she was going to stay at the Marriott. One of her friends had the hookup, so she only had to pay like twenty-five ones a night to stay at the one at Twelfth and Market. Plus, she said she ain't want my mom to think she was a hoochie.

She might've been right on that one. My mom always warned me about them chicks who don't have no hang-ups about me digging their ass out on the couch and then sending them on their way.

When we talked Onyx said that she was going to roll into town on Thursday and that she had to leave by Saturday night. That was cool with me. I just wanted to see her again. Before we hung up she asked me if I had listened to the Donny Hathaway tape that she made me, and I felt kind of bad because I didn't. I told her that I would before she got there though.

We talked a little while more, mostly about nothing. She never asked me about Archie though. I figured she was waiting to see me face-to-face to get the scoop on what was going on with Bill Larchwood. When we hung up the phone that night I felt much better.

And then I started thinking about all the shit that me and Dex did with Tony. I was feeling stupid for getting into that mess, but it was hard not to. It was a sweet deal. Not to make excuses or nothing, but I don't know too many niggas that would *not* be with smashing a few jawns for some cash. It was almost like being a porn star, except our shit wasn't on the shelves at West Coast Video. And it's not like I was selling drugs in the street. What we did was on the down low and I thought nobody would ever find out about it.

All that night I kept going through all of the jobs that me and Dex hit when we was working for Tony. The craziest night of all was with the Puerto Rican chick who me and Dex nailed at this little motel out on Roosevelt Boulevard that everybody takes their jawns to.

I guess Tony was feeling kind of crazy and booked us in a room with a caveman theme. I guess he wanted to know what it would be like if Fred and Barney fucked Wilma.

This jawn made Jennifer Lopez look like Buster Douglas. She was the hottest job that me and Dex ever nailed. She had a crazy body and face. I couldn't believe that her husband was going to let somebody hit that shit. I would've skipped town with my wife and changed our names if she looked that damn good. There's no way that I would have let another man get a taste of that just because I owed a lot of cash. Never.

I think her name was Dawn, but I'm not sure. I do remember

that she came out of the bathroom dressed in this Bedrock-looking outfit that just barely covered her body. She was tight and I remember she didn't seem all nervous like a lot of the other jobs. It was almost like she was looking forward to getting down with me and Dex.

Dex was so hyped over that bitch that he ate her pussy, and that was something that we definitely never did with the jobs. They were there to please us. Tony always told us to make it seem like we were smutting them jawns so that their husbands would be real mad. I guess he figured no man would want everybody to see his wife getting nailed like that. I know I wouldn't.

I remember that while Dex was eating her out, she was giving me a BJ at the same time. When he was done that nigga jumped up and put on a rubber so damn quick I thought he was going to pull a muscle. He was so damn anxious to hit it but I ain't gon' front because so was I.

We tag-teamed it from the front, doggie style, and we let her ride us. That bitch-fuck game was off the hook. It was like she had done something like that before. She was taking everything we gave and throwing it back at us. She was a heavyweight.

The funny part was when she started to mess Dex's ego and she told him that he wasn't the biggest that she had ever been with. That just made him work extra hard.

Dex was real cocky with that. When we was young boaws he had all the young jawns open because he was hung like that. It was like the summer before ninth grade and me, Dex, and our boaw Darryl were at Dex's house and that fool came walking through the living room with his jawn out.

He was showing off, I guess, because it was a little bit longer than the ruler he was holding in his hand right next to it. He got off on that shit.

A nigga like me can't get caught up in that shit. I guess some chicks are really into size, but I always felt like it don't matter, because I never got any complaints. The night we nailed the Puerto Rican jawn was a good example, because when we were done she just wanted to talk to me. I could tell that Dex was kind of salty, because he was going all out to impress her but she ain't seem that pressed.

The more I laid there that night and thought about the sex episodes with Tony, it made me want to get the tapes back. I could not have my snake-ass cousin blackmailing me every time he felt like it. And what pissed me off even more is that Herb and Dex was getting major coins and I wasn't getting one fucking dime.

I got madder the more I sat there and thought about it. I was heated. I knew it was time to set that shit off. I got up and called Dex's house phone and he wasn't there. I left a message and told him to call me when he got in. I called downstairs to his mom's line and there was no answer there either. I jumped up and ran out the door. I had a key to his crib and it was time to use it.

It took me like twenty minutes to walk around Dex's house. When I got there all of the lights were out. It looked like nobody was home. I looked around and there was only a few kids at the other end of the block playing. It's North Philly though, so I know somebody else had to see my ass go in that house. Eyes were always watching around there.

Once I got in I locked the door behind me and ran up the steps to Dex's bedroom. It looked like a hurricane had hit it. Clothes were all over the floor and there weren't any sheets on his bed. It smelled like sour milk and wood chips. That nigga was trifling.

I pulled the chain on his lamp and started to look around for the tapes. I looked in his dresser, under the bed, in between the mattress and boxspring, in his closet, every fucking where. I could not find those damn tapes. I stood there and I thought about where else they could possibly be. I know he didn't trust Meka or Herb enough to give the tapes to them, so they had to be in the house. But where?

I was about to give up and leave when I had a blast from the past. I turned off the light and ran down the steps, through the living room, and into the basement. I tried to flip on the light switch, but it wasn't working. I felt my way down the steps into the basement and stumbled across the floor to the TV. Their basement didn't have a small window like mine.

I hit the power button so that I could have a little bit of light to see with, and then I went to work. When me and Dex were young we used to sneak and watch porno movies like every other young boaw. We did it all the time in his mom's basement.

I don't know where Dex got all them tapes from but he would keep them jawns coming. At first we only had one. I think it was called, *Those Young Girls,* and it only had white people. And then one day that nigga just called me and was like, "Yo, I got two more tapes and this time they got black people."

We was hyped as hell. We watched them every time Aunt Verdele left the house. By the time I was in seventh grade and he was in eighth, we had like twelve tapes. Everybody wanted to be our friend.

So I thought back and remembered how Dex would hide the tapes so his mother would never find them. The bottom of the wall in the far corner of the room opened up like a small door. It didn't have a handle or a knob or nothing. You just had to get a grip on the edge and pry it open. The smaller your hands were, the easier it was to get that jawn open. The space inside wasn't that big, but it was big enough for us to stuff our tapes in, and a couple dirty magazines. I have no idea why it was there or what it was used for before they moved in. And I don't know how Dex found that shit, but his mom never knew about it. He stashed all our smut tapes in there back in the day, and I had a strong feeling the tapes that Tony made were there too.

I got down on my knees and crawled into the corner. I could hardly see, so I was basically just feeling with my hands until I got a grip on the edge of the little door. It took me a few minutes, but I got it open. I reached inside of the hole and I could feel the tapes right away.

I pulled one out to make sure that it was what I was looking for. I walked over to the television to use the light and saw Tony's handwriting right away. He scribbled the names Dawson and Feldman on the front of the tape in red ink. Bingo.

I hustled my ass back over there and dropped down to my knees again. I pulled out all the tapes one at a time. There were thirteen altogether, and from what I could see there were at least two jobs on each one. All of a sudden I was nervous as hell. There was a big plastic Gap bag near the television, so I grabbed it and dumped all the tapes in there.

I turned off the television and headed up the steps. I was sweating, I was so damn nervous. I had the tapes, but now what? I wanted to break them motherfuckers up right away but I knew that would make too much noise and take too much time and make too much of a mess. I decided that I was going to destroy them when I got home.

I walked over to the front door and looked out the peephole and it seemed cool. I didn't see anybody.

Looking back though, I wish I could've been like Spider-Man. I remember I used to watch it when I was little and he would have some shit called Spidey-sense where he could tell that something bad was about to happen. If I'd had Spidey-sense I would've turned my ass around and run out the backdoor.

But since I didn't have no motherfucking super powers, I was caught off guard.

27. I walked out of the house and locked the door and acted real cool like nothing was out of order. The same kids were playing down the street and Dex and Aunt Verdele were nowhere to be seen.

I was like three doors down from Dex's house when shit jumped off. All I remember is hearing the car doors slam and whipping around real quick to see them niggas coming at me. It was three guys and a girl. The only one I recognized was Yanni. The two dudes and the girl looked familiar but I don't know who the hell they were. The boaw who was walking in front of all of them stepped to me first. He was like six-three and diesel like he lifted weights all day, every day. He had on a white wife beater, a pair of jean shorts, and black Tims. He looked mad as shit.

My first instinct was to run back to the house, but all of them were in my way back to the door. I don't know if those niggas had heat or what, I just knew that something was about to go down.

"Yo dude, you rolled on my cousin?"

"What? Naw, I don't know what you talking about."

I knew that he probably meant Yanni, but I wasn't trying to

take my eye off the muscle dude for nothing. That's when Yanni started going off and shit.

"You know what the fuck he talking about, bitch! Your cousin Dex and Herb and you jumped me in front of my house."

"What? Yanni, what the fuck you talking about? You know I wasn't there!"

"Whatever pussy, you roll with him so you gon' have to get your ass whipped too. Whip his ass, Pooch!"

Before I could even react the boaw Pooch just sucker punched the shit out of me. He caught me dead in the mouth. I staggered back a few steps and stumbled into the steps of a house. All I could think was, don't fall, but I couldn't help going down. The string from the Gap bag was all twisted around my wrist and I was trying to keep my eyes on the Pooch dude.

After I fell on the step he ran up to me and just started throwing hammers at me. I was blocking my head with one hand and trying to get the bag off with the other. That shit wasn't happening though. After a few seconds I just started throwing blows back at that nigga, with the bag on my arm. We were locking that shit up.

I grabbed his throat with one hand and used the hand with the bag to push myself up off the step. Once I was up on my two feet I just started going at his fucking head, but he was swinging back just as hard. Pooch grabbed me by my shirt and spun me out into the street. When he did that, the string to the bag broke and some of the tapes flew out of the bag and into the middle of the street.

I couldn't stop to pick them up though, because dude was really trying to fuck me up. He was fighting me like I spit in his mom's face or some shit. When the bag was off my arm, I stepped back and threw my hands up. I was hyped by then because now

I knew it was about to be a straight-up rumble. He threw his shit up too and we just started locking it up again.

Flaming-ass Yanni was in the middle of the street screaming at the top of his lungs.

"Whip his fucking ass, Pooch! Whip his ass!"

I was mad that he had got the first hit in and caught me off guard, so I was fighting mad at that point. My mouth was all busted and blood was all over my white T-shirt.

At that point, there was mad people running out of their houses and looking out the windows at the fight. It was summertime in North Philly, and them cats loved to see a rumble. At first I was giving dude a run for his money. Then he just started turning into some Tyson shit.

He caught me on my jaw and knocked me back onto the hood of this parked car. He tried to jump on me, but I kicked the shit out of him in the stomach and sent his ass flying back. That just made his ass even more mad, because then he really started to snap. He was all over me after that.

He was starting to get over, but what made it worse is that the other boaw who got out of the car with them just came out of nowhere and stole me with a right hook. I was already getting fucked up by the boaw Pooch and then that happened. I stepped back and then turned to rumble the other one, but Pooch just kept coming at me too. As soon as I let down my guard with him, he tackled me and I fell in the middle of the street. Them niggas were on me like a pack of wolves. Both of them had on Tims and they was kicking me in my back and ribs. Yanni jumped in it too and was trying to kick me in the face, but I was just blocking my face with my hands. I can still hear his sweet-ass screaming.

"Stomp that bitch! Stomp his fucking ass. Yeah bitch, and tell your cousin his ass is next. . . ."

After I was on the ground getting the shit kicked out of me for like more than ten seconds, these three older guys that live on the block started to break the fight up. Two of them grabbed Pooch and the other one grabbed Yanni. The other boaw who jumped in the fight grabbed my collar and just started dragging me up the street. My whole back was getting scraped up nasty as shit. I don't know what the fuck he was trying to do but my whole shirt just ripped right off. It lay shredded and bloody in the middle of street. He kicked me one more time and then he let me go.

I was so fucked-up but I had enough energy to jump up off the ground as soon as he walked away. I didn't want to feel them taking the boots to my ass again.

After that they all walked through the crowd of newsy-ass niggas and got back in the squatter-ass ride they came in. They pulled off real slow like nothing happened.

Even though it wasn't my block and I didn't really know those people, I was so fucking embarrassed. I know I got rolled on and all, but I felt like a lame. I ain't never had my ass whipped like that until that day. Them niggas did me real dirty.

I was standing there in the middle of the street with no shirt on and a busted mouth. My body was sore, and the bad part was I knew that shit was going to hurt even more later on. This old lady who looked like Rosa Parks came up to me and was just staring before she said anything.

"Honey, you want me to call the cops?"

"Naw, I'm cool. . . ."

"Sweetheart, you're not cool. You need to see a doctor. Them boys was kicking all over you."

"Naw really, I'm cool. . . ."

"You don't even have a shirt. How far do you live from here?"

"I'm fine. I'm going to just go to my cousin's house and get a shirt."

I pointed to Dex's door.

"Oh, you related to Verdele?"

"Yeah."

"Oooh, she gon' be mad as hell when she hear about this."

I didn't even respond to that. I just reached in my pocket for the keys and started to walk toward the house. That's when I remembered the tapes were all over the street. That was the reason I came.

Most of the tapes were still in the ripped Gap bag but there were about six of them scattered in the street and underneath a parked car. I scooped them up real quick and stuffed them inside the bag.

I walked back to the house trying not to look any of them niggas in the face. I let myself back in the house and locked the door.

I ran upstairs and went inside the bathroom so I could look in the mirror. My shit looked swollen already and it was still bleeding. I had a lump on my forehead too. Damn! I went back downstairs to the kitchen and got some ice out of the freezer. I put some ice cubes in a few wet paper towels and just held it up against my mouth.

I was just standing there in the kitchen trying to keep my hand from shaking. I was so fucking mad that I wanted to go and get my burner and just go blaze them motherfuckers. They came at me over some shit that I have nothing to do with. Somebody was going to pay for that shit. I wasn't going to rest until one of them motherfuckers was at least crippled.

As soon as I walked back into the living room I could hear somebody outside the door. After a few seconds I realized that it was Aunt Verdele coming in. I snatched up the bag of tapes real quick and ran across the living room to the leather couch. I reached over the back of the couch and dropped the bag behind there. Then I jammed it underneath far enough so that nobody could see it.

I turned around and sat on the couch just in time.

"Hey Aunt Verdele. . . ."

"Boy, what happened to you?"

"I just got rolled on."

"I heard. My neighbors just told me. Who was they?"

"I don't know them boaws. I seen one of the boaws before, but I don't know who the main ones was who I was fighting."

"Oh, this shit is crazy. Where's Dexter?"

"I haven't talked to Dex. I came around here to see if he was home and I got rolled on."

"Oh baby, let me get some more ice. . . ."

"Naw, I'm cool. Can you give me a ride home?"

"Of course. Let me get my mace just in case them niggas come back and try to act up. Ain't nobody gon' be fucking with my nephew."

She got her can of mace, I got a T-shirt out of Dex's room, and then we were out. I just left the bag underneath the couch.

28. When I woke up the next morning my shit was fucked up.

It felt like somebody had just beat me over every inch of my body with a metal bat. My mouth was sore and my back was stinging. It was raw from where the boaw had dragged me.

When I came in the night before, my mom rubbed this stuff on my back and gave me an ice pack for my face. She was crying and telling me to call the police, but I said I didn't want to. Then she was asking me all these questions about the detectives. I just told her they was asking me questions about something I didn't know nothing about and left it at that.

I was laying there that day feeling salty as hell because I got my ass beat and I still didn't get the tapes like I set out to. I went through all of that, and the goods was underneath the couch in Dex's living room.

I looked at my answering machine and there were no messages. I was surprised that Dex didn't call me by then. I called his cell phone after his mom dropped me off but there was no answer. I didn't know where he was at.

I got out of bed at around nine o'clock and went down the hall to the bathroom. My stomach got weak when I first looked in the mirror at myself. I just looked swole as hell and my left eye was a little bit shut.

Them motherfuckers put that shit on me. It was cool though, because I had it in my head already that my revenge was gon' be even more off the hook. Them clowns gon' pay.

I ran back to my room to get the phone, and it was my man Chen from down South Philly.

"Wassup nigga, where you been?"

"What the deal, Chen?"

"Nothing man. I'm chilling."

"Ai yo, what I tell you about calling me nigga? You're Chinese remember? You don't have that right."

"Whatever nigga, I'm black. I ain't no fucking Chinese."

"Aight then, just don't be talking all that nigga shit around no other black people. You know I don't care, but the next nigga might bust a cap in your ass."

"Whatever man. I might be black but I'll still get all Jackie Chan on a nigga."

Chen is cool as shit. He reminds me of one of those people that come on Jenny Jones who are white or Puerto Rican but act black. I started to call the show one day and tell them about Chen, but then I changed my mind. I didn't want him to play himself on TV.

He looked straight-up Chinese. Nothing about his ass looked black except for his collection of Sean John and Enyce gear. His wardrobe looked like it could be in *Vibe* or *The Source*. He was definitely urban. I would never give him the "ghetto" title, because he wasn't broke enough.

His people had businesses in South Philly and they kept his ass laced. He had a '99 Lexus with rims, and he loved flossing. I always knew when Chen was rolling up on my block because he would always be blasting Biggie or Jay-Z. He was an honorary nigga if nothing else and he was my dawg because when it came down to it, he helped to save my ass when I needed him.

"So wassup, man?"

"No, I should say, wassup with you? I finally talked to our boy Kam and he told me that you did some ol' foul shit."

"What? He said that?"

"Yeah man. He said your cousin or somebody went up to Penn State and beat his girl's guts up and y'all walked in on it."

"Damn."

"Is that true?"

"Yeah, it's true, but I ain't have shit to do with it. Dex just lost his fucking mind, that's all."

"Yeah, well I heard that Kam beat his ass down and then kicked y'all out his house."

"I felt bad about that shit. I did."

"Well the next time you come down South Philly, don't bring that nigga with you. I don't want to have to bust his ass for trying to holla at my girl."

I wanted to tell Chen that Dex wasn't thinking about his flat-ass girl, but I just laughed and played it off. I was happy to talk to that boaw. It was a distraction from the beat-down I took.

He called me because he wanted me to go with him to First Fridays. I had been there a couple times and it was tight. I loved going with Chen, because more than ninety-five percent of the people at the party were black. He always stood out, but he didn't care, because he thinks he's so gangsta.

I told him that I got rolled on the night before and that I would go if my shit wasn't as swole-looking by Friday night. He was ready to jump in his whip and come to North Philly to see them fools. Chen was a soldier. I told him to chill until I asked around and found out who were the other two boaws with Yanni. I wanted to have a plan first.

Dex didn't call me back or answer any of his phones the rest of the day. I was thinking that the cops might have picked him up for questioning too and kept him for some reason. I didn't know what to think. He always called me back. Especially since he got that cell phone. Something was wrong.

Even Aunt Verdele didn't hear from that nigga. And I know she was dying to tell him that I got jumped in front of the house. Everytime I talked to her she was ready to go out there and go to war. She might've been damn near fifty but she loved to fight. I know she would've jumped in that shit if she walked up on them rolling on me. She just drank too damn much though. I know that shit got to Dex, but he tried to act like he didn't care.

I had Herb's number too, but I refused to call that nut. I would rather Dex just call me up when he was ready before I called that pussy and asked.

I spent most of that day with the ice pack on my face and popping Tylenol. I took so damn many that I was getting immune to it. It was like candy to my body. My shit was fucked up.

I was salty as hell and I was mad. All I had on my mind was revenge. I wanted revenge against Herb and Dex for all the shit they did to me. I wanted revenge on Yanni and his crew for fucking me up.

My mom saw how heated I was and she kept telling me to call the police and let them handle it. She knew I wasn't going to let that shit slide. She said she could tell by the look in my eye that I was filled with rage. She was right.

She told me to pray about it. Take it all to God, she said. On the real though, I was too mad to talk to God. What would I look like praying, as heated as I was? I always thought you were supposed to holla at God when you were calm and able to think about what you were talking to him about.

The way I felt at the time, God didn't want to hear what I was saying. Besides, I looked at it like I was in control of my own destiny at that point.

I prayed to God that my father didn't die when the crazy Korean shot him, but he did. I prayed to God that my hamstring wasn't permanently damaged when I pulled it at the city champs in tenth grade, but it was. And I prayed that the cops would lock Herb and Dex up before they pulled me under with them, but they were still running the streets.

When I was laying in my bed that night listening to WDAS, a song came on by this chick named Regina Belle. Onyx always said that good music speaks to your soul, because you can feel it.

Well Regina Belle was speaking to my soul that night, because the words of one of the songs they played by her rang in my head until I fell asleep. It was like the words of the song were plucked right out my fucking head. It was the way I felt.

and I don't even pray anymore at night because I don't think that anyone hears, all that is heard when it's late at night are my tears, all my tears, so many tears.

29. It was like ten after six when Onyx called me from her cell phone and told me that she was out in front of my house. I went outside and she was sitting behind the wheel of her Neon looking so damn good. She was smiling at me like I had a diamond necklace for her.

My eye was cool at that point, but you could still tell that I had been smashed in the mouth. I knew that she was going to say something. The smile left her face fast as shit.

"Jesus! What happened to your lip?"

"Nothing. I just got into a little scuffle the other night."

"A little scuffle? With who?"

"Some cats around here tried to stick me up when I was coming from the store . . . but I'm cool."

"Aww, baby. It looks like it hurts."

"It's cool. You know I'm a trooper, so I'll bounce back. You looking good. Did you have any trouble finding your way here?"

"Not at all. I got door-to-door directions from off the Internet."

"That's wassup. Yo, why don't you come in the house so that you can meet my mom and I can throw some stuff in a bag."

"That would be nice."

When I walked in the house with Onyx my mom was sitting on the couch in the living room watching *The Golden Girls* and drinking a glass of ice tea. It was hot as hell that day.

Now, normally my mom would just give a phony smile and speak to my company and go back to doing whatever she was doing. I had been through so many jawns over the years that I guess she didn't even use the energy to get to know them. Because nine times out of ten I would just drop them and be on to the next bitch.

I can't even explain it, but my mom just instantly liked Onyx or something. Onyx walked right over to her and reached out her hand when she came in.

"Hello. How are you, Mrs. Arthur? I'm Onyx."

"Well, it's nice to meet you, Onyx. Please have a seat. How was your drive?"

"It was fine. The expressway was a little congested when I got close to Philadelphia, but other than that it was a good drive. As long as a I have my music I'm fine."

"Oh yeah. What kind of music do you listen to?"

"I love all kinds of music. Your son can attest to that. On the way here though I mostly listened to India Arie, Kenny Lattimore and Karen Clark Sheard."

"What you know about Karen Clark Sheard?"

"Oh I love her. Her music really moves me."

I went into the kitchen to get Onyx something to drink, but I was listening to every word they said. That was the longest my mother ever held a conversation with any of my jawns. I couldn't believe that shit.

And what made it even harder to believe for me is that *The Golden Girls* was on. She ain't never talk to anybody when her show was on. She didn't even answer the phone unless a commercial was playing between six and seven o'clock during the week. And here Onyx was talking to her like they went way back.

I could see why my mom was feeling her. It was just something about her. She had this glow about her that made everybody stare at her. It wasn't because she dressed with her tits and ass hanging out or shit like that. I don't know what it was. Whatever it was, you just couldn't ignore her. After I gave Onyx her tea, I went upstairs to get my shit together. I just threw some clothes into a duffel bag and grabbed my toothbrush and deodorant from the bathroom.

I checked the bottom drawer of my desk to make sure the tape was still there, and it was. I was so paranoid about that tape. I knew my mom wasn't going to look through my room and find it, but I didn't put nothing past Dex.

While I was tossing my socks and underwear into the bag I pushed my door open so that I could listen to Onyx and my mom talking. They were still rapping about music and church and living down south. They definitely hit it off with each other.

I gave them a few more minutes to talk and then I came downstairs to the living room. Of course my mom had to pull out the embarrassing pictures of when I was ten and show them to Onyx. She had jokes but I wasn't mad at her. I was just glad that she brought her sexy ass to Philly.

"You didn't tell me that you had a thing for tights."

"Man, I did not want to be Robin Hood for Halloween. She made me do it."

"Whatever, you was working it!"

"Aight, aight. I'm ready when you are."

"Guess what?"

"What?"

"Me and your mother are in the same sorority."

"For real?"

"Yes! She's my soror."

"I didn't know you was in a sorority."

"Yeah dummy. I pledged my sophomore year."

"How did you know my mom was in it?"

"How can you look at all of these beautiful giraffes around the living room and ask that. I knew she was in Delta Zeta Alpha as soon as I looked up on her mantelpiece"

"So what, y'all gon' start doing them crazy steps and making them loud irritating noises now?"

"Stop playing, boy. We let the Deltas and AKAs handle the loud irritating noises."

They both busted out laughing but I didn't get it. That college shit was over my head sometimes. I gave my mom the number of the hotel in case she needed to get in touch with me, and then we was out. I was so ready to be alone with Onyx.

By the time we got checked in and went up to the room, it was close to seven thirty. Even though I was right downtown in Center City it felt like I was off in the Bahamas somewhere.

I didn't want to see or hear from anybody. I just wanted to chill with Onyx and see if something was going to jump off. She had told me back in Durham that she wasn't a virgin but was trying to save herself for her husband. She said she was a born-again virgin.

So I took it like, whenever the last nigga pulled up out of that ass, she shut the door and locked it. It was like the coochie was on the injured list. I knew that if I stroked it and touched it good enough, it would recover. It had two days to get it suited up and back in the game.

I took her out to eat at the Hard Rock Cafe across the street from the hotel. We had a good time at dinner. I could tell she was so happy to be in Philly. When she went to the bathroom I played a practical joke on her and I told the waiters that it was her birthday. Like fifteen minutes later they ran out and made her stand on her chair. Then they sang this goofy-ass song to her and gave her a small cake.

The look on her face was funny as hell. She had no idea what was going on, but she went along for the ride. When we left Hard Rock we laughed all the way back to the room.

Onyx was just what I needed at that time in my life.

She had me so distracted that I wasn't even thinking about the fact that Dex hadn't called me back since I got jumped. I was irked because I know his mom and every damn body else on his block had to tell him what happened. Oh well, I was with Onyx and we was chilling, so none of that shit mattered. I would deal with all them clowns later.

We just watched movies on cable and chilled once we got back to the room. There was only one king-size bed in that piece, so I figured that was half the battle. If there was two jawns in there I know she would've made me sleep in the other one. Now she didn't have a choice.

Everything was cool until I got up from the bed to get a pair of basketball shorts and a tank top out of my bag to sleep in. I freaked her the hell out when I took my shirt off. I totally forgot that my back was all fucked up.

"Oh my God!"

"What?"

"Your back! That looks so painful."

"Don't worry, it's cool."

"Cool? It looks like someone tried to skin your behind. Did this happen when you were attacked also?"

"Yeah."

"What did you have that they wanted? Did they take your money?"

"Naw, they ain't get cash from me at all."

"That's crazy. Sugar, you look like you been through it. I have exactly what you need to make you feel better."

I looked at her when she said that and gave her this sexy smile to let her know that I was going to tear that cat up.

"No, not that! Get your mind out of the gutter!"

"What? I ain't say nothing."

"You ain't have to say it dirty."

She got up and started looking through her suitcase. She pulled out a bottle of bubble bath.

"I'm going to draw you a bath. You need to soak and relax yourself."

"That sounds good. Are you going to get in there with me?"

"No silly, it's all about you tonight."

"Well I want it to be all about us."

"You're simple, boy."

The bubble bath was ready in like fifteen minutes. She called me into the bathroom and told me to get in. I made sure that I stripped down out of my boxers when she was looking right at me. I wasn't hard but I saw her take a quick peek at my shit. She was trying so hard to act like she wasn't pressed. She left the bathroom.

I sat down in the tub and it stung my back a little at first, but then it started to feel good as shit. The bubble bath was the vanilla kind and it had me feeling nice. After a few minutes I forgot Onyx was even in the other room. I was ready to go to sleep in that jawn.

She knocked on the door and came back like ten minutes later. She had on these long-sleeve red silk pajamas that showed just how thick that ass was. That girl had major gravy, but she wasn't showing no skin. She sat on the edge of the tub and squeezed the washcloth out over my head. Then she dipped her hand into the water and started to rub my back.

It was so many bubbles in the tub that it kept her from seeing how that shit made me hard. I wanted to rip them damn pajamas off her ass and pull her in the bathtub with me. I played it easy though, because that wasn't the way to go with her. She was not the type of jawn that would get off like that.

She started talking to me in this low sexy voice.

"Does this feel good?"

"You know it do, girl, so why you ask?"

"I just wanted to make sure that you were enjoying your bath."

"I am."

It was quiet for a while. I just laid back and enjoyed that shit. Her hands were all over my body in that water but not where I wanted them to. She rubbed everything but the gun.

"So . . . I think you have some explaining to do."

"What are you talking about?"

"You know what I'm talking about. You told me back in North Carolina that you would tell me what was going on with you. I think now is as good a time as any."

"You're right. Just let me get out of the tub first. Hand me a towel."

She went back into the room while I dried off. Mad shit was racing through my head.

I didn't want to lie to Onyx, but I was thinking that the truth would make her run out of room 1326 screaming and hollering. Every bone in my body told me that I could trust her but I was scared. I didn't know what I was going to say.

I thought about just telling her half the story, but then I knew she would have so many questions that the rest would come out eventually. I threw a fresh pair of boxers on, brushed my teeth, and turned the bathroom light out.

I walked back out into the room. Onyx was sitting in the middle of the bed Indian style with a serious look on her face. I knew right then and there that it was time to put that shit on the line.

30.   Onyx was still there when I woke up the next day. That was way more than I expected. She was right next to me in that king-size bed at the Marriott with her legs wrapped around me.

I thought she would have been dressed and halfway down 95 south by the time I opened up my eyes. I laid a lot of heavy shit on her the night before, and I was expecting her to get as far away from me as possible.

She didn't bounce though. She was right there where I could feel her skin and smell the Victoria's Secret lotion that she put on before she went to sleep.

Her head was on my chest and my arms was wrapped around her. I don't even remember how we got like that, but I know we didn't bone. I fucked the mood up for that when I started to run all that shit down to her.

She cried a couple of times, but she never left the room while I was talking. She didn't get up to use the bathroom until after I told her everything.

It was real tense up in that piece but I felt a hundred percent better after I told her that. I told her about the jobs and Tony and Dex and Herb's schemes for a couple of reasons.

One, I needed to get that shit off my chest and I felt I could trust Onyx. Two, I figured if I got killed or some shit then at least she could tell my mom that I wasn't no murderer. I wanted at least one other person to know the truth.

I couldn't tell her exactly why Dex killed Tony though. I couldn't tell her what he planned to do after he had collected all the money from the men who owed Tony either. At that point I didn't know none of that shit. I would find all that out later.

We got up and got dressed for breakfast. She was acting her normal self but wasn't talking as much. She said she wanted to see a little more of Philly, so we walked over to Eighteenth and Walnut to go to the IHOP.

I don't know if she wasn't talking because she was so caught up in window shopping or if she really didn't know what to say to me. I was still in shock at that point that I told her all that shit. I was just hoping she wouldn't stab me in the back.

When we got to IHOP, both of us was mad hungry, so we busted a big-ass grub. I think all she needed was a fat-ass plate of grits, cheese eggs, pancakes, and turkey sausage to loosen up her mouth, because she was soon back to her normal self. I love a jawn that can throw down. I hate when I take a bitch out and they be acting all cute like they don't eat. Onyx wasn't like that. She reached onto my plate like three times to steal apple pieces from my waffle. The more I hung with that chick the more I saw how much we had in common. Yeah, she was about to be a lawyer in a few years and all, but we was clicking.

I already knew that she was a big wrestling fan back in the day, and that was enough to make her my main jawn. Most bitches don't get into that kind of stuff. Then, while we was eating, we realized that both of us had the same favorite show. When I was a young boaw my favorite shit was *The Six Million Dollar Man* and *The Bionic Woman*. I never missed an episode. I used to watch that shit so much I thought I was bionic just like

Steve Austin and Jaime Sommers. They were definitely the shit. Onyx knew every single episode just like me.

She took that shit one step further though. She told me that when she was a young buck she broke her arm after she jumped off the roof of her house. We laughed so fucking hard because I told her that I was going to do the same thing until Dex talked me out of it. I would've broken more than my arm, because I lived on the fourteenth floor of the projects down Thirteenth Street. That whole morning I kept thinking she would be the perfect jawn if she was giving up the ass. Damn!

After we ate, I took her to Penn's Landing so we could sit on the water and chill. It was early for it to be so crowded down there. When we first got there I checked my messages. There wasn't shit on there from Dex. I didn't know what was up with that nigga.

"So what are you thinking, Ms. Onyx? What do you think about all of that stuff that I told you?"

She took a deep breath and just stared out at the speedboats flying by down the river.

"I don't know where to begin. I mean the biggest thing—and I said this last night—you need to go to the authorities and tell them everything. But you have this thing about ratting out your friends."

"Exactly."

"I think that's so ironic, especially considering all of the stuff that they are doing to you and everything you're going through because of them."

"I know that Herb and Dex are snakes. I know this. It's just that in the street you don't snitch. You just don't do it."

"OK, I understand. Let's say that these two go to the police before you do and they say that you killed Tony. Then what?"

"Well they can try that shit if they want to, but I have proof."

"You better hope that tape holds up in a court of law. There are different laws in different states, but that's only one thing. The other thing that is very tough for me to swallow is that you slept with all of those women. That is the thing that takes me back the most."

"Why you say that?"

"Do you realize what that is?"

"Come on now, I know boaws around my way who slept with just as many if not more women. Is it because I got paid that you have a problem with it?"

"Oh no, the money has nothing to do with it. I'm speaking from a spiritual point of view. Do you realize that you have taken a part of each of those women and it's with you right now?"

"What, you think I caught something? I wore a rubber every time I nailed."

"No, it's not so much that, although that is definitely a concern of mine. It doesn't really matter that you wore protection. Having sex is the most intensely intimate thing you can do with someone. Even if it's for money or done out of lust, it still means a lot."

"I hear what you're saying but I don't think that's the case with me. I just looked at it like it was work, nah mean? I got paid and that was that. I don't want none of them women, I don't need them, that's it."

"You're not getting what I'm trying to tell you. I don't know . . ."

"What? Tell me what you're thinking."

"OK, here it is. You know that I think you're a cool guy. I am starting to really get feelings for you, but everything I stand for is telling me to pick up my things and run. I don't know why I'm still here."

That comment kind of hit me right square between my fucking

eyes. She kept her cool for the rest of the conversation but I started getting hyped.

"What do you mean? You think I'm a bad person since I don't go to church and read the Bible every day like you. You think I'm a sinner?"

"We all are sinners. Every single one of us."

"So you consider yourself a sinner too?"

"Of course."

"What kind of sins do you do?"

"What do you mean? Where do I begin? Come on, you should know better than that. Just because I'm saved doesn't mean that I don't got issues too."

"So what kind of issues you got? Do you dance at the go-go bar at night or drink at the bar every other night? What kind of stuff you into, Onyx?"

"Come on now. You know I don't do any of those things. Why are you getting so worked up?"

"I'm not getting worked up. I was wondering how long it would take for you to start looking down on me. Now I know!"

"Looking down on you? Don't even go there. I'm saying all of this because I really care about you. If I didn't care I wouldn't even be telling you any of this."

"Man, whatever. You're just like them people at my mom's church."

"What do you mean by that?"

"They always act like their shit don't stink, like they ain't never made no mistakes in their life. I remember I got locked up for selling weed when I was in twelfth grade and they started acting all shady towards me and my mom. It was crazy. They supposed to be all saved and sanctified and everything, and they was making me feel like a piece of shit."

"Now that wasn't right. I am sure those people had issues and they were wrong and everything, but guess what—they're human. None of us are perfect."

"That's not how they act. They talk all that shit about how they supposed to be down for their fellow man and compassionate and they all act just the opposite!"

"In some cases, I agree. . . ."

"You think if I rolled up in my mom's church on Sunday and told Rev and all the congregation that I was nailing women for money and that I rolled with a nigga that killed somebody that they would welcome me with open arms? Them cats would start to throw holy water on me or some shit!"

"I hear what you're saying, but you have to remember one thing. None of the congregation at your mother's church, or the pastor, or me, have a heaven or hell to put you in. All that matters is your relationship with the Lord."

"That sounds good and all, but people still be trippin'."

"Look, people are going to trip until the end of time. You can't get caught up in that. All you need to know is that if you go to God and ask to be forgiven then it will be done."

"So if Dex goes to God and asks to be forgiven for being a lying-ass snake and for skinning Tony with a potato peeler and pouring acid on him, then God is just going to say, aight then, you straight! You think that's gon' be the case?"

Onyx closed her eyes real tight and dropped her head when I said that. She looked grossed out for a minute. It looked like she was going to have to get up and lose her turkey sausage over the railing.

"In the scheme of things it don't matter what I think."

"But it do matter what you think. I'm digging you like that. I'm feeling you enough to make you my main jawn. I need to know that you forgive me for all of the shit I been into before I can start getting religious and stuff."

"Trust me, if you can't learn to lean on God and go to him no matter what the problem, you're not going to be able to lean on me. My shoulders ain't that strong."

Onyx stopped talking and started staring across the river toward the Camden aquarium. Her voice was getting all choked up like she was about to cry. I kissed her on the back of her neck and started to rub her back. She was making me feel bad. I felt kind of embarrassed too, because this chick was making me soft. I looked around to make sure ain't nobody saw me being all sentimental.

It was crowded that day for a Friday morning. There was mostly white people down there walking their dogs and playing with their kids. I didn't give a fuck if they thought I was soft. But just when I was about to turn back around I saw his face.

That motherfucker was standing right behind a pack of people who were in line at the hot dog stand just staring at me and Onyx. She didn't notice, but I did.

Even though he was rocking a pair of black sunglasses, I could see clear as day that it was Dex.

31. I stood up from the bench and looked in his direction. When he saw that I noticed him he ducked his head and turned around. That nigga started speed walking down Penn's Landing in the opposite direction.

Onyx turned around and started tugging on my arm.

"What's wrong?"

"Nothing. I think I just saw Dex. Wait right here."

"Be careful. . . ."

I ran toward where I saw him standing. By the time I passed the hot dog stand he was out. I stopped and looked around but I couldn't see his ass anywhere. Just when I was about to turn around and head back to where Onyx was sitting, I saw him jet from behind a statue.

Dex was running toward the stadium steps that led up to the street. I'm thinking, what the fuck is going on with this nigga? I started running up the steps, skipping them jawns two at a time trying to catch him. That track shit was starting to kick back in, because I was flying. When I got to the top of the steps he was just running across the street. I screamed out the boaw's name, but he just kept on hustling like I wasn't behind him.

The light had just changed when I ran into the street on

Delaware Avenue, so I was dipping and dodging in between cars trying not to get my ass run over.

Once I got on the sidewalk I picked up the pace and started closing in on that nigga. I could tell he was getting tired and that he couldn't run much longer. By the time we got to Second Street he was done. He just stopped running right in front of the water plug on the corner and turned around. He was winded. I ran right up on his ass.

"What the fuck is wrong with you, Dex?"

"What . . . what you talking about?"

"What am I talking about? Nigga, I'm talking about you spying on me and then running when I saw your ass. And where the fuck you been hiding at? You know I got rolled on because of you and your nut-ass boaw?"

"Yeah . . . I heard about that."

"That's all you got to say about it, is that you heard?"

"What the fuck else you want me to say? I'm gon' see them niggas when it's time for them to be seen? Don't sweat that?"

"Don't sweat it. Pussy, I got my head kicked in over your bull-shit. What the fuck you talking about, don't sweat it?"

"Oh, now what . . . you ain't down for me no more?"

"I ain't that down for no motherfucking body enough to get dumped on and get dragged up the street. You acting like I was just arguing with them niggas. They was trying to put me the fuck under and you and your bitch-ass sidekick wasn't nowhere to be seen."

"Cuz, we had business to take care of, and plus I was down at the police station on Tuesday night when that shit happened."

"Police station?"

"Yeah nigga, don't play dumb. The police station. And them

pigs told me that you were down there too, running your mouth like a bitch!"

"What?"

"Yeah nigga, they told me you was down there trying to make it seem like me and Herb had something to with Tony getting killed."

When he mentioned Herb's name, that made me look around. He was nowhere to be seen and that made me feel real uneasy. They was always together, and now that Dex was spying on me, Herb wasn't around. That didn't seem right.

"I know the cops ain't tell you no shit like that."

"Why didn't they? They said you was ready to pin that shit all on us like we had something to do with it."

"Dex, can't you see that they're trying to turn us against each other? If they think that we had something to do with it then they gon' do that."

"Aight then. So how did they find out about Herb then? How the fuck do they know anything about him?! I'll tell you the fuck how. You went in there and told them that they should start looking at him, and since we roll together you basically told them to start looking at me!"

"Man, you losing your fucking mind. Tell me this, why are you even getting all hyped like this? If you and that nigga ain't have nothing to do it then you don't have shit to worry about, now do you?"

"What you trying to say?"

"You tell me, Dex."

"Man, everybody knows that the mob knocked that nigga off. I ain't trying to get all up in that though. . . ."

"Oh, now everybody knows that the mob knocked Tony off?"

"Yeah. Everybody knows."

"Whatever man, I'm still trying to figure out why the hell you following me."

"Why I'm following you? I'll tell you why. Because I always keep my enemies close, that's why."

"Enemy?"

"Yeah, you probably told that bitch everything like a dick-head. I know you did."

"Dex, what the fuck you talking about? Told her what?"

"You know you told her what we used to do for Tony and what we did with Archie's wife."

"I ain't tell her shit."

"Whatever man. Like I said, I'm keeping you close."

"Keeping me close! If that enemy shit you spitting is true then I should've put your ass in my back pocket, because you the fucking snake!"

Dex looked at me like I was crazy. He didn't expect me to come back at him like that. All that time he was walking around acting like he had everything under control, and now he was going to find out that that was not the case. I was sick of that nigga. I was sick of acting like everything was cool. Sick of trying to be loyal to that motherfucker. From that point on, it was on.

"Oh, so now I'm the snake?"

"Yeah pussy, you the snake. All bets are off, I don't give a fuck what happens to you and your slimy-ass friend. I don't want shit to do with y'all."

"You acting like you ain't have nothing to do with all of this. You was in there fucking them bitches just like I was. You was getting that cheese from Tony just like I was. You ain't no better than me. That bitch got you thinking you better than somebody, but you in this shit too."

"Yeah, I might've been in it. I can't deny that. But you can't even compare me to all the shit you done. You so damn shady that you don't even see it, but that shit gon' come back on you one day. I'm supposed to be your nigga . . . your cousin. If you'll stab me in the back you'll do it to anybody."

"When the fuck I stab you in the back?"

"Let's see, where the fuck do I begin? Let's start with when you stole my fucking money!"

"When I steal your money?"

"Don't play yourself, nigga. Your dumb ass stole my money when we was down in North Carolina and then you tried to act like we got robbed?"

"Who told you that dumb shit?"

"Ain't nobody have to tell me. Your stupid ass gave me the same hundred-dollar bill at Bluezette that night that was missing from my luggage."

"What the hell are you talking about?"

"I wrote a phone number on that same C note when we was in Durham, but I guess you ain't even bother to look at it. You acted all Big Willy like you was doing something by giving me some cheddar when it was mine in the first fucking place."

Where the fuck was the Kodak people that day? The look on that nigga's face had to break some kind of record for being the stupidest look ever. If I had a camera I would've just snapped the picture myself so I could keep it for the rest of my life. I knew I would never live to see another person look that damn stupid again.

I knew after I said that shit that we was going to be playing hardball, and I was right. Dex was salty and there was no telling at that time what he was capable of doing. I put that shit out there and just stood back to see what he was going to do next.

"Look, I don't know how I got that bill, but I ain't no thief.

Plus, I was with you when the money got stolen. So how I do that?"

"I don't know, but I know you did it."

"Aight then, but I ain't the only one on some ol' thief shit. Where my shit at, nigga?"

"What you talking about?"

"I'm talking about my tapes."

"Oh, so now they're your tapes."

"Yeah nigga, they my tapes. Where they at? I know you got the tapes because one of the hoes on my block said you had a plastic bag when you came out of my crib. And I know that you the only person who know about the hiding place."

"I lost them when I was getting rolled on."

"Then they should've been in the middle of the street when I got home, but they was gone."

"Maybe somebody on your block picked them up."

"Nigga, if you don't fucking come up with them tapes by the end of the day you gon' regret that shit the rest of your life!"

"You threatening me, Dex? I will knock your fucking head off, nigga. You don't want it with me!"

"What you wanna do, pussy!"

We was getting loud as shit at that point. The white folks who was walking by looked noid as shit. They were crossing the street to avoid us and staring. Me and Dex was about to lock that shit up right in the middle of high-saditty Society Hill. I knew that the cops would be there in five seconds flat if we started to rumble, so I backed off.

If I got locked up Onyx would've been stranded in Philly without me. I just backed off for the time being. I knew it was time for me to start turning them clowns against each other. I wanted to fuck up their whole program. I didn't want Dex or Herb to be able to trust each other.

"Look Dex, I don't know where the tapes are but it's better that they're gone anyway. Now you can't use them to blackmail me."

"I ain't thinking about blackmailing your bitch ass. You fucking with my money now, and I ain't having that shit."

"Oh, I know all about your fucking scheme."

"What?"

"Yeah . . . yeah. You think Herb is so damn loyal but he ran that shit down."

"What? You crazy. Herb ain't tell you shit."

"Then how I know about y'all scam to get them jokers who owed Tony to give y'all half? How I know about that?"

"Man, Herb wants to put a slug in your ass. He ain't tell you no wild shit like that."

"Then how do I know that y'all left Bluezette that night to go see a cat up in the Northeast who was acting like he ain't want to pay up on what he owed? It was the helicopter pilot dude, right? Herb know what the deal is."

Dex was steaming mad but he was trying to play it off. I don't know if he totally believed the bullshit I was spitting at him, but I knew I was making him have doubts about Herb. I would have no other way of even knowing that Dex knew somebody who flies a helicopter. I wanted them niggas to be at each other's throats.

"Look, I don't know how you found that out, but Herb ain't no snitch like you. I don't have to worry about him."

"Oh yeah, then where is he now? He probably has the tapes now and he's collecting your loot. Yeah. Where the hell is your boaw, Dex?"

"Oh, I know exactly where he's at and so does your bitch."

That's when it hit me. Onyx. I was so caught up in Dex that I totally forgot that I left her by herself on the water. Dex had this sneaky-ass look on his face like he knew something. I didn't say shit else. I just turned around and started running back toward Penn's Landing.

That fucking Dex lured me away from her on purpose. He wanted Onyx to be by herself.

32. I hauled ass back to Penn's Landing. I was in the zone, because I almost got hit by two cars and I didn't care. I just wanted to get back to Onyx.

When I got back close to the water I saw a crowd of people standing around in a circle near where we were sitting. There had to be at least twenty people. My heart almost stopped and my knees got weak, because I knew it was gon' be some shit. I almost didn't want to keep running.

When I got up to the people I pushed my way through the crowd until I could see her face. Onyx was sitting on the bench next to this wrinkled-ass white lady who looked like Barbara Bush and had her arm wrapped around her. I ran up to her and dropped to my knees in front of them. The first thing I noticed was that her clothes was dripping wet.

"Onyx, what happened? What happened?"

She put her arms around me and started to hug me real tight. The white lady just kept rubbing her back and shaking her head like she had seen some crazy shit. Onyx just kept hugging me and didn't say nothing. The lady started doing all the talking.

"When I looked up from changing my granddaughter's diaper I saw this fella push her over the railing."

"What?"

"They were tussling, and I'll tell ya, she was giving him a way to go at first. Then he just shoved her over the railing. He took off running that way. My son and his friend chased him but he got away."

"Which way did he run?"

"He ran that way after my son John approached him. John said, 'C'mahn fucker, won't you pick on somebody your own size.' He took off that way. These nice young men stepped over the railing and helped to pull her up."

She was pointing to two scraggly-looking white dudes with skateboards in their hands. I shook both of their hands and thanked them.

Onyx pushed herself real close to me and whispered in my ear.

"It was Herb. . . . We were fighting and he pushed me into the water."

"What? That pussy pushed you in the water?"

"Yes."

I pushed her back from off me so that I could look at her face. There weren't any bruises and she wasn't bleeding. I still was mad as hell though. I stood up and told the crowd that she was cool. I grabbed Onyx's hand and told her that we were out.

The old white lady grabbed my arm.

"Don't you want to wait for the police? You have to report this so that that monster can be found and arrested."

"Naw, that's cool. I just want to get her home. Thank you."

I put my arm around her and started walking fast as shit back to the street. I didn't want the police to track Herb down before I got to his ass. That would've been too easy.

Even though it was hot outside, Onyx was shaking because she was soaking wet. I know that she was mad shook up too. I flagged down a cab as soon we got back to Delaware Avenue and we hopped in that jawn fast as hell. Just like that we was out.

When we got back to the Marriott the first thing she did was jump in the shower. The water in the Delaware River looked and smelled disgusting, so I know she wanted to get that shit off her skin.

When she got out of the shower we started packing our shit up fast as hell. We weren't even talking, because she knew like I knew that there was nothing to say. We were on a mission.

It was a like three o'clock and we needed to be out. I knew that if Herb and Dex was able to find us at Penn's Landing, then them niggas probably had been following us all day.

When we had everything together we checked out of the hotel and got Onyx's car from the valet. I got behind the wheel, since I knew Philly better than her.

"Are you OK?"

"I've been better. I was more embarrassed than anything else. I can't believe he threw me in the water."

"So tell me what happened again."

Onyx told me how Herb popped up out of nowhere right after I left to chase Dex. He came and sat down next to her on the bench and just started talking shit to her. When she tried to get up and walk away he gripped her up and started getting hyped.

He accused her of stealing the money out of the hotel in Durham. Then he kept asking her where the sex tapes were. He told her that he knew she was in on it and that he was going to fuck her up if she didn't start talking. That's when Onyx said she slapped him in the face and then tried to run.

He caught up to her and grabbed her by the neck. She turned around and just started wailing on him. She said he was just slinging her around and trying to push her to the ground. Herb never hit her in the face but that pussy punched her in the back at least twice.

She hit him in the nuts and then he got real pissed and started to drag her back toward the railing. They tussled like the white lady said and then he pushed her over the railing into the dirty-ass water. Just picturing that shit in my head made me want to snap Herb's fucking neck.

"I'm just glad that you know how to swim, because I would've probably drowned."

"You can't swim? I been swimming since I was knee-high to a bedbug."

"So what do you think I should do first?"

"Well since you don't want to go to the police, I think you should go to the newspaper and talk to whoever has been covering Tony Salvatore's murder."

"I don't trust no damn newspaper reporters. One of them white folks might turn my ass in before I get out of the building. I think they be real tight with the police."

"But you're innocent. You didn't kill anyone."

"I know that and you know that, but it don't matter. Everybody knows that I roll with Dex. If I go in there and tell that lady what I know, she'll start snooping around and find out that I be with him, and she'll tell her little cop friends that I'm in on it so they can come lock me up and she'll have a big story. I can't trust them."

It was quiet in the car except for the radio. Colby Colb was on Power 99 giving away a trip to Jamaica. I wanted to call in and try to win that vacation so I could just be out and get away from all that bullshit. Onyx just kept coming at me.

"Come on, there has to be somebody there you can talk to."

When she said that, I got to thinking about who I could call. I don't know no motherfucking body at the news stations or papers in Philly. I was driving down Broad Street wracking my brain when it hit me. I knew it was a long shot, but I had to try.

I banged a left off Broad Street onto Callowhill Street even though there was a NO LEFT TURN sign there. Onyx grabbed my leg because I almost got us hit by a SEPTA bus.

"Sorry about that. I just got an idea. This is the newspaper right here. I have to find a parking space though."

"What are you going to do?"

"I don't know what the hell I'm doing. We'll see."

I had remembered a while ago seeing this reporter dude from the *Daily News* on *Philly After Midnight* talking about some hip-hop shit. He looked real familiar and it seemed like he was about my age but he might have been younger. I remember thinking he was a fucking noodle because he was up there saying that Jadakiss and Beanie Siegel spit a lot of violent shit and that their lyrics was ignorant.

That nigga didn't know what the fuck he was talking about. Me and Chen was talking on the phone watching it together, and Chen was like, the boaw probably listens to Salt-N-Pepa and Will Smith. I couldn't remember his name at first, but then it came to me. It was so damn off-the-wall I don't know how I could forget it. It was Mister.

Even though that nigga didn't know shit about the rap game, it looked like he had his shit together. Chen had said he heard that boaw was from South Philly, so I figured I would try to talk to him about that.

I parked and me and Onyx walked back around to the front entrance of the building. I was hoping that dude wasn't a snake. We walked in the lobby and went up to the guard's desk. It was an older white guy.

"Hello, I'm here to see Mister."

"Mister Mann Frisby?"

"Yeah, him."

"Hold up one second. Let me see if he's still here."

Me and Onyx were on edge. The guard's old hands were moving so slowly through the directory. It was like torture. He would look up the page and then back down and then back up and then back down. I wanted to do that shit for him. Finally pop-pop picked up the damn phone and dialed.

"Hey Yvonne, this is Harry out at the front desk. Is Mister Mann Frisby still here at the paper. . . . Uh huh . . . Oh I see . . . I see . . . thank you. Well sonny, he doesn't work here anymore."

"Are you serious? Damn!"

"Yeah, Mister Frisby left back in December or January I believe."

"Ok, thank you."

Me and Onyx turned to walk out of the lobby. I was irked and didn't know what my next step was going to be.

"Hey, are you friends of Mister?"

I turned around and looked up and there was this woman cheesing and walking toward us. I say looked up because she was some ol' WNBA-type. She had to be at least six-two, and was dark brown–skinned with sexy-ass legs for days. Honey was walking toward us like she was on the runway or something. I lied real quick.

"Yeah, we're his friends. You know there he is?"

"Hello, I'm Jenice. He left the paper some time ago."

I was like, fuck! I ain't know that nigga from Adam but I felt like I needed to talk to somebody young and black if I was going to talk to anybody at a newspaper at all. I tried to play it real cool like I went way back with that boaw.

"Aw man, I didn't know he left."

"Where do you know him from, high school?"

"Yeah."

"Were you on the track team at Overbrook too?"

"Yup."

That's where I remembered that nigga from. He ran for Brook. He was all right but I always blasted his ass in the 800. And the more I thought about it I think he might've been on the Oak Lane Wildcats track team that I ran for when I was a young boaw. She asked me my name and I told her and introduced her to Onyx.

"You know, I'm not surprised at all. All of Mister's friends who used to come visit him at the paper had very unusual names. Only Mister could have friends named Oshunbumi and Tanqueray."

"Yup . . . that's Mister for ya. So is he still a reporter?"

"Sure. I believe he freelances for magazines now and he's working on a book."

"What's the book about?"

"I've been sworn to secrecy, but it's really good. It's something I think you'll enjoy reading."

"Do you have his number? I need to get in touch with him."

I was like, damn, what the fuck is he writing books for? I needed his ass right then and there. She looked back and forth at me and Onyx like she was trying to see if she could trust us. I knew by the way she paused that her ass wasn't about to give up them digits.

"How about this. I'll call his house from the lobby phone and you can talk to him, but I don't want to just give his number out. You understand, don't you?"

"Of course."

She walked over to a phone that was hanging on the wall and dialed the number. I tried to see what she dialed, but she did it too fast.

"Here you go, it's ringing."

She walked across the lobby I guess to give me privacy, but I could still tell that she was trying to listen. His answering machine picked up. I could hardly hear his voice because it was this loud old Negro spiritual music on there. I just hung up thinking that dude was a fucking spaz.

"He wasn't there but thank you anyway."

"Do you want to leave your number? I'll make sure he gets it."

"No that's fine. I want to surprise him."

"OK, nice meeting the both of you."

She turned around and walked away. I felt like a dickhead. I was in there trying to track down somebody I ain't even know. Me and Onyx rolled out of there kind of heated. She scooped up a complimentary newspaper when we were leaving.

I looked over at the cover of the paper and I almost swallowed my fucking tongue. Dex had struck again.

33. I didn't say shit until we got in the car and I pulled away from the curb. I was looking in the rearview mirror like crazy. Onyx was looking at me like I was a dope fiend or something. I must've looked like I was losing it.

"What is wrong with you?"

"Nothing, I'm cool. I'm just trying to make sure we're not being followed that's all."

I lied of course. I was shook like a motherfucker.

The face on the cover of the *Daily News* was one that I'd never seen before, but the name jumped out at me like a damn Mack truck. The headline said that New Jersey executive Larry DiFillipo was tortured and murdered at his crib in Cherry Hill. I knew right away when I saw it that it couldn't have been anybody else but Tammy's husband.

The Larry boaw was smiling real hard with a cigar in his mouth on the cover of the newspaper. With everything else going on I had totally forgotten that Tammy said she wanted her husband killed.

I drove over to the Ben Franklin Parkway and parked behind the art museum. I needed to get my head straight and get a plan going. Me and Onyx got out of the Neon and spread the newspaper across the hood of the car.

That's when I started to give her the rundown. I told her that the man on the cover of the newspaper was the husband of one of the jobs that me and Dex boned. I told her that Tammy tracked me down and asked me to kill her husband but I told her I wasn't with that shit. I didn't tell her that I nailed her in a king-size bed at the Bellevue.

"So you think she asked Dex to kill her husband?"

"I know she got him to do it, because she said she was going to if I didn't."

"Are you for real?"

"Yes. That chick is playing hardball because she found out that he cheated on her."

"That's all? I mean, why didn't she just leave him?"

"Well you know, it's money involved too. Whenever shit gets crazy like this, you know it's loot involved. I think the boaw had a crazy life insurance policy or something. I'm sure she promised Dex a piece of the pie and his greedy ass took the bait."

They had a picture of Tammy on page two crying outside of the house. The reporter wrote in the story that she was too traumatized to talk to the press. If they only knew that she was the one who had his ass killed.

I got sick to my stomach the more I read the story. Larry DiFillipo was killed the same way Tony was. The acid, the potato peeler, the toes missing. Dex was going all out to make that shit seem like it was Mafia related. When I found out that Dex killed Tony I knew that nigga was off the hook, but now he was on some ol' other shit.

I was waiting for Onyx to bounce on me at any minute. I was taking that jawn through a whole lot of shit. At that point, I was scared I was going to lose her, but she was right there with me the whole way.

We hopped back in the whip and drove back to my house. I

knew it was risky going back around that way, but I had to do it. My mom wasn't home from work yet, so the house was totally quiet. I threw my bag on the living room floor and ran up the steps to go to my room. Onyx sat downstairs on the couch.

I should've expected it. Shit was everywhere when I walked in my room. All my clothes were all over the floor. The drawers of my desk and dresser were pulled out and my mattress was flipped over.

Dex must've come in my room looking for the tapes. He turned that shit out. It looked like he looked everywhere.

I didn't panic at first because I knew that the tapes were right underneath his nose. That nigga came and wrecked my shit and what he was looking for was closer to him than he thought.

I started to panic though after I realized that the tape with Herb and Dex was in the bottom drawer of my desk. I got down on my hands and knees and started tossing all the clothes and papers to the side trying to find that tape.

The drawer was pulled out and flipped over and the tape recorder or the tape was nowhere to be found. I was throwing shit all around that room like crazy. I looked under the bed, in folders, in my closet, everywhere.

I guess I was in denial. I didn't want to think about it, but I knew what the deal was. Dex had the tape. That nigga probably was somewhere listening to it again and again trying to figure out how I got that conversation on tape. I was on my knees in the middle of the floor, steaming fucking mad. I got him and he got me back. That shit was on.

I went to the top of the steps and told Onyx to come upstairs. When she came into my room I told her what the deal was. I told her that Dex had the tape and she knew right away how serious that was.

That was the only real proof that I didn't have shit to do with killing Tony. Herb and Dex said it out their own crooked mouths that they left me out of it. I needed that tape back so that I could prove that I was innocent if I needed to.

Right while I was explaining all of this to Onyx I looked up and noticed that the red light on my answering machine was blinking. I stepped over all the junk on the floor and walked across the room to my dresser. I had four messages.

> *What the deal, homey. This is Chen. Are you still rolling with me to First Friday tonight? I hope you ain't forget. Holla at your nigga and let me know what's crackin'. Aight, peace.*

> *Hey, this is Dynisha. Call me when you get this message.*

> *Yo cuz, unless you checking your messages from a phone booth or some shit, you can see that I wiped you the fuck out. Now if you want your shit back then you better remember real quick where them tapes is at. Don't think I'm playing with you either, pussy. You don't want it with me if I don't get them tapes back! You and that bitch gon' be toast if I don't get my shit. You heard me? The next fucking time we gon' tie her ass up and tie bricks to her shit so she go straight to the bottom of the river. Play with me if the fuck you want. . . .*

> *Yo, what the deal? This is Quan. I heard you got rolled on by the faggot boaw Yanni and his peoples. You aight? Hit me on my cell, 267-555-5411.*

I know Onyx was dying to ask me who the hell Dynisha was but she didn't say nothing. She just played it real cool like everything was sweet.

"I have a question. Why didn't he say anything about your tape on the message?"

"I don't know. Why you say that?"

"I don't know. I just think if he heard a recorded conversation between him and Herb that he would've said something about it and been a little bit more upset."

"I don't know."

"Think about it. He would've flipped."

"You're right."

"This may seem crazy, but I don't think he has the tape."

At first when Onyx said that I wasn't really trying to hear it, because I knew that he was the only person who could have possibly had the tape recorder. Then I just took a closer look around my room and I saw that more shit was gone than I noticed at first. My VCR, PlayStation, Game Boy, and Movado watch were gone. I was so fucking mad.

"You know what Onyx? You're almost right."

"What are you thinking?"

"He does have the tape with him and Herb on there, and the tape recorder, but you know what?"

"What?"

"He don't know he have it."

"What do you mean?"

"He came in here and took all my shit so that I would tell him where the tapes are. He probably just took the tape recorder and tossed it with the rest of the stuff, not knowing what was on it. It's brand-new and it looks like it costs a couple of dollars, so that's why he took it. Damn!"

"You may be right."

"I know that I'm right. That dickhead don't even know what he has, but I know one thing though. I have to get it back."

"How are you going to do that?"

"I don't know, but I have an idea."

Dex was trying to play Big Willy and I was gon' go right along with the flow as long as I got that tape recorder back. There was only one problem at that point. I knew that it was about to be on and I didn't want Onyx getting caught up anymore than she was already. I shut the door to my room so my mom wouldn't see what happened and we went back downstairs.

I tried to tell Onyx that I wanted her to go back to North Carolina, but she wasn't having it. Said she didn't want to leave. She said some shit about wild horses couldn't drag her away from Philly at that point. I don't know what I said or did to have this jawn all up on me like that, but damn. I didn't even hit it and she was all worried about me.

She was acting like I was her nigga for years or something, and I couldn't figure that shit out. I was used to chickenhead bitches who rolled out at the first sign of trouble. This jawn got thrown in the damn river and was still down with my ass. I knew she wasn't going to leave, so I just said, fuck it, and gave up trying. Even though she was a church girl, she was a soldier. I'm glad that I didn't fight it no more because my pretty little choir girl wound up saving my life. Onyx came through on some ol' SCI FI Channel shit.

I used her cell phone to call Dex, because I didn't want him to know that we were in the house.

"Yo nigga, you took my shit."

"Yeah and I'm gon' take more than that if you don't tell me where my motherfucking tapes are. . . ."

"Look bitch, cut the bullshit. We gon' hook up tonight so that we can get an exchange going on."

"Where the fuck you trying to meet?"

"I want to meet somewhere where there's a lot of people. I want you to meet me at First Fridays tonight at midnight."

"Where's it at this month?"

"It's at Brave New World at Seventh and Arch."

"Yo, are you going to have the same cell phone that you just called me on?"

"Yeah, why?"

"I'll call you at this number and you can come and meet me outside."

"Fuck no! I want you to come into the party and leave that pussy out in the car. If I see him inside that building it's gon' be on. I'll take care of his ass later."

"Don't you have to get dressed up for them parties?"

"No jeans, no Tims."

"So how we gon' do this? You want me to roll up in the club with your VCR and PlayStation underneath my arm."

"Leave my shit in the car with Herb."

"And what about the tapes. You gon' bring them into the party?"

"Don't worry about what I'm gon' do. You'll get the tapes. Just be there at midnight."

I hung up the phone and looked at Onyx. She looked nervous as shit.

"Is he going to come?"

"He'll be there. I just have to make a couple calls so that shit will go down the way it's supposed to."

I called up Chen and told him what the deal was. I knew I could count on the South Philly soldier who ate more greens and cornbread than me. He was hyped when I told him the plan. I needed somebody who was on point and who wasn't scared to go to war, and the boaw Chen was perfect.

And then I called Archie.

34. We had a smooth start to a rocky night. After I got off the phone with Archie I grabbed the keys to the car and we were out.

Me and Onyx checked into the Radisson out by the airport. After we put our bags in the room we talked for about fifteen minutes, and then we both went back to the lobby so she could use the ATM machine.

Onyx checked her balance, and it was a thousand more than when she last checked it. Archie came through. That bigheaded freak went to the bank like I told him and put the money in Onyx's account. They used the same bank so that shit went down pretty easy.

After that we took the hotel shuttle over to one of the rent-a-car places and rented a tight-ass Expedition with tinted windows. I didn't want Dex and Herb to see us coming. It was time to get down.

We were both dressed and ready to roll by eleven. Just looking at that girl made me want to drop to my knees and eat that coochie for like three days straight. It didn't make sense, she looked so damn good. She had on a pair of black capri pants that fit just right around all that thickness. I could sit a can of Pepsi on that donkey and it wouldn't fall off, that ass was so proper. Her shirt was one of them jawns where one arm was out and the other was covered right under her shoulder. She wore sandals that made her seem three inches taller. Her legs was bangin'.

Before we rolled out I started to push up on her and try to spark something, but I knew it wasn't worth it. I knew that if I started fucking that girl I was going to be in that ass all night, and we had business to take care of. Plus, she wasn't having it anyway.

It was bad enough that I was taking her ass to a party. Onyx ain't really into hip-hop and parties. The crowd is always real professional and tight at the First Friday jawns but sometimes it can get a little freaky. Especially when the reggae music gets cranking. She told me when we went to the mall that day that she hadn't been to a party since she was a sophomore.

I didn't know what that had to do with being a Christian. I liked to go out and get my jig on every now and then. I don't be getting high and pissy drunk when I go out. I just liked to be where the jawns were at, and nine times out of ten that's the hot spot.

We hopped in the Expedition and headed to North Philly to meet Chen. He was parked in his Lexus right in the parking lot of the McDonald's at Broad and Girard like we planned.

He got out of his car and hopped in the backseat of the truck. I showed him a picture of Dex and told him what kind of car they would be coming in. I didn't have one of Herb, but I described what he looked like and told him about the birthmark.

I was going over the plan and Chen was listening and all but he couldn't keep his eyes off Onyx. It was so obvious that he was feeling her. He didn't even try to hide it. That was a funny cat.

After we got squared away on everything, Chen hopped back in his Lex and sped off toward Brave New World. Me and Onyx drove around for another fifteen minutes or so before we went to Dex's block. His car wasn't there, but the upstairs light was on in Aunt Verdele's room. I could see her moving back and forth through the curtains, so I knew she was in there.

I was stuck. I didn't expect her to be in the house, because she was always at the bar on Friday night. That night was different though, because she was right up in the crib chilling.

"Damn!"

"Do you think she'll leave anytime soon?"

"I have no idea, Onyx. She could be in there all night."

"I have an idea, but it may be kind of insensitive."

"What?"

"You can call her from the cell phone and tell her you need her to pick you up."

"Huh?"

"Tell her that you are somewhere close by and that you're in trouble and that you need her to come and get you. That way she'll be out the house for at least ten minutes or so and you can go in there and get the tapes. We'll be gone by the time she gets back."

"That's a bangin'-ass idea to me."

I got on her cellie and called Aunt Verdele. I had no idea what I was going to say until I heard her voice. I just went with the flow.

"Hello."

"Hey Aunt Verdele, listen, I need your help."

"Baby, what's wrong?"

"I'm down near Richard Allen and I need you to come get me."

"What happened?"

"I got into it with these boaws down here and now I think they're going to come roll on me."

"Where you at?"

"I'm at a phone booth near Tenth and Brown, but by the time you get here I'll probably be waiting in the Chinese store."

"All right baby, I'll be there in like ten minutes."

"Yo listen, Aunt Verdele. If I'm not down here when you get here, don't panic. I called this girl I know and told her to come and get me too, but I don't know if she is really going to come or not."

"Oh OK. I'll be there."

She hung up the phone and started getting ready fast as hell. I could see her ripping and running back and forth across her bedroom while she was getting dressed. I felt bad for making her panic but I had to get her out of that house for at least a few minutes. I didn't want her to know anything about the tapes.

She was downstairs and out the door in like three minutes. She jumped in her whip and sped off. Her son might've been a shady bastard, but Aunt Verdele was a trooper. I laughed to myself because I knew she probably had a can of mace and a stun gun sitting right next to her in the passenger seat.

As soon as she turned the corner on her block, I jumped out of the truck and ran across the street to her house. I pulled out my key and opened the door. The living room was dark but the light in her bedroom and the television was still on. I didn't bother to turn the light on either, because the nosy-ass neighbors on the block might be watching. I went right to work.

I got up on the couch and leaned over the back until my hands could touch the floor. I started feeling around underneath the couch until I could feel the top of the bag. I was getting noid as hell because I couldn't feel the bag.

When I finally got a good grip on it I yanked it from underneath the couch and pulled it up close to my face. Everything seemed to be cool, but the bag seemed lighter than I remembered.

I put the bag down and got on my knees and lifted up the couch a little bit. As soon as I peeked under there I could see three tapes on the floor. I gripped the couch with one hand and reached over to grab the tapes with the other. I slid all three of them across the floor toward me until they were out from underneath the couch.

And then I made the big mistake. I started to stand up and just let the couch go, and it slammed to the floor and made a loud noise. I didn't even think about it at first until I heard the footsteps thumping over my head. It sounded like King Kong was moving down the hall toward the top of the steps.

"Verdele . . . Verdele . . . is that you? I thought you left out of here."

I froze for a split second and then I snatched the three tapes up off the floor and stuffed them in the Gap bag. The string was all popped and jacked up, so I just grabbed the bag from the bottom and jetted toward the door. By the time I started running across the living room I could hear the footsteps coming down the stairs.

"Verdele . . . who the hell is that?"

Once I got to the door I looked back over my shoulder real quick and saw the dude flying down the steps. It was dark but I could tell he was ass-naked. Dude was like six-five and looked like a bodyguard. He looked me dead in the face.

I pulled the door open, ran outside, and slammed the door behind me. I ran up the block to the truck and hopped in. I tossed the tapes in the backseat, started that jawn up, and pulled away from the curb like a madman.

When I drove by the house her friend flung open the door and ran out onto the step. He still didn't have one lick of fucking clothes on, but I don't think he even cared. He was straining so hard to see who was in the truck, but he couldn't see shit through the tinted windows.

I banged a turn at the corner without even stopping and sped off down Twenty-sixth Street. The next stop was Brave New World.

35. The parking lot across from the club was jam-packed when we got down to Seventh and Arch. The line for the party was all the way up the block. I drove by real slow and looked, but I didn't see Dex. It was about fifteen minutes past midnight, so I figured he was already inside waiting for me.

While I was cruising the block Onyx tapped me and pointed out the window to the other side of the street. Herb was sitting in the driver's seat of the Honda and another boaw who I'd never seen was in the passenger seat.

"Lord be with me! I can't believe that brute threw me in the river."

"Don't worry about that, Onyx. I'm gon' handle that nigga when the time is right."

"Don't you go doing nothing crazy. I just want him behind bars."

I ignored her comment. I knew that no matter what happened, I was going to get a piece of Herb before any goons in jail got their hands on him. I kept on cruising down Arch Street past Eighth, looking for somewhere to park. I called Chen on his cellie.

"Yo Chen, what's the deal?"

"Ai yo, your man Dex got here about ten minutes to twelve and he went straight into the club."

"Was he with anybody?"

"Naw, but he came with two boaws and they're sitting in the car outside of the club."

"I know, I saw them. Listen, as soon as I get a parking space I'm going to head for the club. Where are you parked?"

"I'm right in the parking lot across from the club. From where I'm parked I can see right inside dude's Accord."

"Aight bet. I'll see you in a few. . . . Wait Chen, you know what? I'm going to have Onyx drop me in front of the club and just circle the block so I can run in there and handle my business."

"Aight then."

I drove around the block and pulled back up in front of the club. I hopped out of the Expedition and Onyx slid over to the driver's side.

"Yo, just double-park as long as you can until the cops come and tell you to move. Then just circle the block until you see me come out. Pay attention, because I'm probably gon' be moving fast as hell when I bounce up out of there."

"OK, please be careful."

I shut the door and got in line. I looked over, and Herb and the dude in the car was gritting on me real hard like they wanted it with me right then and there. It took a lot of control for me not to step out into the middle of the street and call his ass out.

If my life was a book or movie, I know that would be the part where the cats reading or watching it would be mad as hell. They would probably expect me to pull that dickhead out of the car and take the guns to his nut ass.

I just chilled though, because I knew a rumble wasn't going to be enough. I wanted to do his ass dirty. I wanted to do some shit that would fuck up his whole program.

It took me a good ten minutes to get up in the club. It was wall-to-wall bitches. I almost forgot what I was in there for. Summertime in Philly was off the hook. They came in all shapes and colors. Chocolate honeys, red bones, and cinnamon hotties everywhere.

Biz Markie was the DJ that night, so the dance floor was packed. The bar close to the door was so crowded that I couldn't even see the bartender. Every other nigga looked like Dex—tall and dark-skinned with muscles.

I thought I saw him everywhere I turned. I walked around for about fifteen minutes, but he was nowhere to be seen. I felt like a fucking jerk walking around in circles looking for that nigga, so I just leaned against one of the bars that was off in the cut and flirted with a couple of honeys.

I had on a pair of dark gray khakis and a lighter-colored fitted shirt that made my chest and abs look tight. I was getting mad attention just standing there chilling. Them chickens had me feeling like I was "that boaw."

I was standing there rapping to this chick named Ginger when the snake finally showed his face. I happened to look up and he was standing on the balcony looking down at me. He waved his hand for me to come up. I told the honey that I'd be back and started walked toward the stairs to get to the other landing.

When I got to the top of the steps Dex was standing there with his arms folded, looking mad. Like I gave a fuck. There were tables and little couches all the way across the upper landing of the club. People were up there eating hot wings or just getting their drink on. Two jawns sitting at a table close to us got up and started walking down the steps. He was yelling damn there at the top of his lungs because the music was so loud. Biz Markie was mixing back and forth between Busta Rhymes and an old Michael Jackson jawn.

"What's the deal, nigga. Where them tapes at?"

"Slow your fucking roll, Dex. Have a seat."

I sat down in the chair and pushed the other one out with my foot. I didn't give a fuck that he was in a rush. I was in control. Dex thought that I was pressed to get back my VCR and Movado watch and all that other shit, but I couldn't care less about that. The watch was fake and I got the VCR from Wal-Mart for ninety-nine dollars any damn way. He had something way more valuable and he didn't even know it.

"Come on now, I ain't got time for all that shit. Where are the tapes?"

"The tapes is outside. You'll get them as soon as I get my shit back."

Dex jumped up from the chair.

"Herb got your stuff out in the car. Let's go get it."

"Naw nigga, sit your ass down. I got somebody out there who's gon' handle all that.

"Call Herb on your cellie and tell him that a Chinese boaw is about to come and get my stuff right now. If everything is there then he'll give him the tapes. Everything better be there."

"Aight bet."

Dex whipped out his phone and called Herb in the car. He was screaming into the phone with one hand over his ear. The music was cranking.

When he hung up he just looked down at he floor and nodded his head to the music. That motherfucker couldn't even look me in the eyes. He was trying to act so damn hard like he was running shit, but he knew deep down he was a fucking snake. He was dead wrong and he knew it. I never did anything to that boaw, and out of nowhere he just started trippin'. That money had him doing some crazy shit. I guess he thought getting paid was more important than being down for his cousin. That had me fucked-up in the head for a minute, but I didn't let it get to me. I tried not to think about it. I was on a mission. I knew what I had to do, and if it meant that Dex was going down then so be it.

He didn't have no love for me, so fuck it. That shit was on.

"What did Herb say?"

"He said 'cool.' He's waiting for the dude now. Who the hell is the Chinese boaw?"

"Don't worry about all that."

While we were in there gritting on each other, Chen was outside handling his business. That nigga needs to go put in an application for the CIA or something, because he was smooth.

He pulled my plan off big-time. Herb and that other cat probably saw him walk up to the car and thought everything was sweet since it was this short little Chinese boy. He caught their asses way off guard, because he wasn't the typical Chinese store boaw that they was used to dealing with. Chen was down for whatever.

From what he told me later that night, he walked up to the car and tapped on the window. He told them that he was there to get my shit and they looked him up and down before Herb reached into the backseat and handed him a loaded pillowcase with all my stuff.

Chen said he looked down into the pillowcase right in front of them to act like he was inspecting the bag. What he was doing was trying to see if the tape recorder was there. Once he spotted the recorder he turned his back and started to walk back to his car. He told me that he reached into the bag and popped open the recorder and scooped the tape. He stuffed it in the pocket to his sweatjacket real quick and turned around and walked back to the car.

He said that's when he started tripping on Herb and the other boaw.

"Yo, everything ain't in here!"

"What the fuck is you talking about? That's everything."

"Naw dude. There was a Kenneth Cole watch and a gold ring missing from his room too."

"There was only one watch and there wasn't no fucking rings."

"Naw dude, we can't accept this. This ain't cool. The deal is off."

That's when Chen shoved the pillowcase back through the window and turned around to walk away. He hit the cell phone on his speed dial and told me that he had the tape and to come outside.

I looked at Dex and told him that the deal was off because all of my shit wasn't in there, and I got up to walk away. He grabbed my arm and started getting all hyped and shit.

"What the fuck is you talking about motherfucker? Everything is in that pillowcase!"

"Naw, my boaw said that my Kenneth Cole watch and my gold ring wasn't in there."

"What nigga? You don't even wear no damn rings. I ain't never known you to wear a gold ring."

"Yeah Dex, well just like there's a whole lot of shit I don't know about you, there's a whole lot you don't know about me."

I pulled away from him and started to walk down the steps. He jetted down the steps right behind me. He was on my fucking heels so close that he almost knocked me down. When I got to the bottom of the steps I started to rush toward the door. Niggas was gritting on both of us because we was just pushing through the crowd, elbowing motherfuckers out of the way.

Once I got right up to the front door I had to stop because the crowd of people coming in the jawn was so thick that nobody could get out. Dex was right behind me. I could feel that nigga breathing on my neck.

"I know one thing. When we get outside my tapes better be out there."

"Man, you can talk all that shit you want, but you ain't getting shit. Matter fact, I ain't bring the tapes to the club, because I knew you would try to get over . . ."

"What! Pussy, why the fuck you playing with me? You gon' make me fuck you up—"

I didn't even let him get the rest of the sentence out. I turned around, caught that nigga with a two-piece. That was the first time me and Dex fought since I was twelve and he was thirteen. He whipped my ass back then, but that wasn't the deal that night.

He staggered back after I hit him and lost his balance. When I hit him he fell back into this pack of jawns trying to squeeze their way into the club. I took advantage of him being off balance and just started to hammer that nigga. He was falling to the ground and the jawns was hollering and screaming.

Dex bounced back up kind of quick and started swinging. He caught me right in the mouth the first time and swung real wide the next and missed. I hit that pussy with a uppercut and just started swinging haymakers at his ass. We were locking it up and I was definitely getting over.

Everybody was screaming and most of the niggas at the door was coming toward us so they could see the fight. A minute after we started rumbling we fell to the floor. That nigga Dex turned real bitch when we hit the floor, because he kept trying to bite me. I could feel that nigga's breath on the side of my face. He was on some ol' Hannibal Lecter shit. I was lighting up his head, just hammering him with short fast punches, since we were so balled up on the floor.

Just when I was able to push myself up a little bit and get my balance these two bouncer dudes grabbed me by my arms and dragged me from off top of Dex. While they were pulling me he kicked the shit out of me right in the nuts. That shit hurt like a motherfucker and went straight to my stomach. It felt like somebody reached inside of me and just started to twist my shit with their hands. It was killing me and it took me a minute to get myself back together.

When I look back on it I'm so glad these bouncers were dragging me, because if they didn't hold me up I would've fallen. Before I knew it they had dragged me out of Brave New World onto the sidewalk. Everybody in line started running toward me and crowding around. They had me hemmed up real tight against the big glass window in front of the club. I was tussling and trying to get away, but the cats had me gripped up crazy.

"Aight, aight. I'm outside now, y'all can let me go!"

"You need to just calm down buddy . . . calm the fuck down."

"I'm cool, I'm cool. Just let me go! I ain't trying to fight no more."

They held me there for about half a minute before they let me go and told me that I had to leave the club. At that point I still didn't see Dex. I guess the other security guards still had him up in the club.

When they let go of me I straightened out my shirt and walked right out into the street. I looked across the street in the parking lot, and Chen's Lexus was gone. The Honda was still sitting there, but Herb and the other dude were nowhere to be seen. I started to walk toward the corner of Seventh Street, and less than a minute later Onyx came flying around the corner in the truck.

She opened the door and slid back over to the passenger seat, and I hopped in. When I pulled off I saw Dex getting dragged out of the club by three bouncers. He was struggling with them, and Herb and the other boaw came over and started to pull him away. It was a big mess. All of the people who had been in line before the fight were in the street at that point, blocking traffic, since so much was going on in front of the door.

I was trying to squeeze by and speed away, but there wasn't enough room in the street to get by. I leaned on the horn but them niggas would not get out of the street. I looked in the rearview mirror and saw two cop cars trying to come through. Their lights and sirens was on. It was bananas out there that night.

I crept up more on the crowd like I was going to tap one of them with the bumper of the Expedition if they didn't move, and that's when they started to get their asses back on the sidewalk.

The window was rolled down, so when I drove by through that mess Herb and Dex looked up and saw my face. They looked mad as hell that I was rolling off and they were still caught up in all that shit.

I flashed them this cocky-ass grin like "yeah nigga, what" and they all looked like they wanted to smoke me. At that time I thought it would be a while before I saw them again, but I was wrong.

It wasn't even a whole hour before I saw them cats at the emergency room.

36. Chen met me and Onyx down in South Philly like we planned so I could get the tape and we could work out what to do next. He hopped out of his Lexus at the corner of Thirteenth and Fitzwater.

I could tell that Chen lives for that type of shit, because he was hyped as hell. That boaw was wired when he hopped in the backseat of the truck.

"What took you so long to get out of there, nigga?"

"Man, me and Dex started rumbling when I was trying to leave the club."

"What!?"

"Yeah, I beat that boaw down in there. Then the bouncers gripped me up and dragged me outside. They got his ass too, but they made him stay in the club."

"For real? I know that boaw's mad as shit. Especially since he didn't get what he came for."

"Did you get the tape?"

"What's my name, boaw? They don't call me Big Daddy Chen for nothin'. I get the job done."

Chen pulled the small tape out of his pocket and handed it to me. The first thing I did was put it in a little case and tuck it down into my sock. Onyx was just sitting there taking in all that shit. The whole time we were driving to meet Chen she was all nervous. She was breathing all fast and she kept looking out the back window. I knew that was the most action that country girl ever had. My little Holy Roller was getting a whole ghetto fabulous tour of Philly.

She looked at me from the passenger side of the truck like something was bugging her. I overlooked some major shit and she caught it.

"Now what are we going to do?"

"Now we kick into the second part of our plan."

"But wait. What about your mother? Dex has the key to your house and he can just let himself into your house. He may go there looking for you."

"Fuck yeah! I need to call my mom!"

I whipped out Onyx's cellie and called my mom's line. The phone just rang and rang. I was getting noid as hell because I didn't even think Dex would go back to my crib after he didn't get the sex tapes. Onyx was on point with that one. My mom didn't pick up until after the third time I called. She sounded like she was half asleep.

"Mom! Mom!"

"Who's there? Who's this?"

"Mom, it's me. What do you mean, who's this? You only got one son."

"Oh, I'm sorry baby, I was asleep. What time is it?"

"Listen Mom, you need to get up and lock the door."

"I locked the door before I came upstairs."

"Did you lock the top lock though?"

"I don't think so. Why?"

"Look Mom, get up and go downstairs and lock the door right now."

"What boy? What are you talking about?"

"Trust me Mom, you have to do it now. Go lock the top lock. I have my key if I need to get in."

"What's going on?"

"Just do it! Are you on your cordless?"

"Yeah, why?"

"I want you to stay on the phone while you go downstairs and lock the door. Stay on the phone so that I can hear what's going on."

"Jesus! Boy, what is going on?"

"Please just do it!"

I heard her get up and walk down the steps to go lock the door. She had an attitude with me, but I didn't care. I just didn't want Dex to stroll up in there again. After she locked the top lock she sucked her teeth and started talking to me again. She was wide awake now.

"OK, I locked the door. Now are you going to explain to me what's going on?"

"Now go and make sure the backyard door is locked too."

"You are really working my nerves. What is the problem? Are you OK?"

"Yeah, I'm straight. Just do it Mom."

"OK, I locked the back door too. Baby, you making me scared. What's going on?"

"Don't be scared, Mom. Look, I'll give you the scoop later. Just don't open the door for nobody tonight, even if it's Dex. Especially if it's Dex."

"Is that what this is about? Did y'all fall out again? I swear child, you and your cousin act like two women sometimes. What was it this time, one of them nappy-headed girls?"

"Mom, it's serious. It ain't a game. Don't let him in no matter what."

"I'm going back to sleep because y'all are tripping . . . Wait a minute, hold up. That's the other line."

She clicked over before I could tell her not to answer the phone. I knew that Dex figured she was in the crib but I ain't want her to be all obvious about it. Chen and Onyx were just staring at me while I sat there waiting for her to come back on the other line. I wish she didn't click over, because then I wouldn't have had to hear the bad news. The bad news that made me feel even worse. I wasn't ready.

When my mom clicked back over she was breathing real hard and yelling into the phone. She was losing it.

"Jesus! Oh Lord, please help me . . ."

"Mom! Mom! Calm down and tell me what happened!"

"Baby, that was Judy on the other line . . ."

"What happened?"

"She said that Verdele was in a car accident."

"What!"

"She crashed into a utility pole near Tenth and Girard. Judy said she might've been drinking and driving. They took her down Temple."

"Oh my God . . ."

"I'm going to throw something on and go down there to the hospital. Where are you?"

"I'm in South Philly. I'll meet you down there. Be careful, Mom."

I hung up the phone and just started to pound on the dashboard. I was mad as hell because that was my fault. I should've just snuck in the house and stole the tapes. I was thinking, why the hell did I make her leave that house? I knew that she drinks like a fish, especially on Fridays and Saturdays. I knew that I had fucked up big time.

When I told Chen and Onyx what happened they was in

shock too. Onyx felt real bad because it was her idea. She was damn there in tears.

Chen hopped out of the truck and got back in his Lex. I peeled off and started speeding straight down Thirteenth Street toward North Philly with him following me. Even though I knew it was mad risky to go down there, I knew I had to do it. I had to go and see Aunt Verdele. I didn't even know what I was going to say to her when I got there, but I knew I had to go.

My heart was beating fast as hell. I was whipping that truck in and out of traffic and running red lights like crazy. Onyx had her eyes closed most of the ride back to North Philly. I think she was praying. No, forget that. I *know* she was praying. She was rocking back and forth in the seat with her head down and her lips moving. She was talking so low she wasn't even whispering. I don't even know if words were coming out at all. She was in the zone.

I wasn't mad at her though, because I knew it would take some kind of God to make that situation OK. I sent my play aunt on a phony mission and now she was laid up in a hospital. Damn!

I think that was the fastest I ever got to North Philly from down Thirteenth and Fitzwater. The crazy thing is that I almost caused three accidents on the way to the hospital.

When we got there I just parked on the street right next to the hospital. Chen parked across the street from me. We all hustled to the emergency room not knowing what the hell was going to happen.

Like the white folks say, it was so intense.

I went up to the counter and asked if Aunt Verdele was in there. They told me that she had just been admitted not long before we got there and that we had to take a seat and wait. The last thing I wanted to be doing was sitting down.

I felt like I could hop on the track and run a mile, I was so amped. Chen and Onyx must've felt the same way, because they didn't sit down either. The emergency room was packed but it wasn't anybody for Aunt Verdele that I knew.

We waited for about ten minutes before we walked back outside and stood in front of the hospital. It was too crowded and crazy in that jawn for me to stay in there. I couldn't even hear myself think.

After we got there this one dude came in all shot up. His boaws carried him right by us. He was jacked up. Onyx grabbed me real tight and buried her face in my chest. That was too much Philly for her.

"I can't take all this. I'm going to go and sit in the truck, OK?"

"Aight cool. Here are the keys. I just want to make sure that Aunt Verdele is cool, and then we can roll."

"That's fine. I'll be in the car."

I handed her the cell phone and she walked away. Chen was smoking on a Newport and I was on edge like a motherfucker. Like five minutes later my mom came running up looking all crazy. She still had rollers in her hair and a bright orange scarf on. She was so caught up in trying to find out what happened to Aunt Verdele that she almost ran by without seeing me.

We all ran back to the counter and this time the chick told us that she could have one visitor. My mom didn't say nothing else. She just followed the lady back there.

That's when I started to think about what lie I was going to tell. I knew she was going to tell my mom that she crashed on her way to scoop me and keep me from getting rolled on. I didn't know how I was going to explain that. It turned out not to even be an issue. I didn't see my mom for the rest of that night, which I know for a fact was the craziest night of my fucking life.

Me and Chen were on our way back out the door when all hell broke loose. The dude who chased me out of Aunt Verdele's house was coming in while we were walking out. As soon as he saw my face he started trippin'.

"You . . . motherfucker . . . You was the one who broke in Verdele's house."

I just stopped and looked at him, because he caught me off guard. Everybody in the waiting room was staring at us like we were crazy. I didn't know what to do, so I just tried to play it off and kept moving toward the door.

"Man, I don't know what you talking about."

"Oh you know what the fuck I'm talking about! You ain't get to take nothing because I caught your ass, nigga! I checked everything in the living room and the basement and you ain't get a damn thing."

"Man, like I said, you got the wrong one."

He stepped to the side and blocked me from leaving. He didn't say nothing to Chen. He just looked at him and gave him this crazy mean look.

"You ain't gon' nowhere! Somebody call the cops."

Everybody was just looking at us like we were on stage acting out a play. Nobody said shit at first until this fat Puerto Rican lady got all in it. She looked like she was a little off, and I guess that's because she was.

"Ain't no need to call the cops, man. They parked right outside the hospital. You can just go to the door and yell and they'll come."

"Ai yo, mind your business, lady!"

"Who the hell you talking to, Jackie Chan? I chop your ass up and put you in some egg foo yung. Ha-chee-cha! Ha-chee-cha!"

"I got your Jackie Chan bitch. Don't make me karate chop your ass."

"Screw you, Bruce Lee! You ain't gon' do shit to me!"

This shit got real crazy. The chick jumped up and pulled out a

Rambo-looking knife on Chen and starts walking toward him. The nurses started screaming and everybody sitting near the psycho chick got up and started moving away from her.

There was so much going on that I forgot about dude blocking the door. I think he forgot he was blocking the door too. She lunged toward Chen, and he moved out of her way and reached down into his jeans pocket. Before I even knew what was going on he whipped out a can of mace and started spraying that shit right in her grill.

She started hollering and screaming, but she still was coming at him swinging that knife like a madwoman. That shit was off the hook. Everybody was screaming and trying to get out of the way.

The next thing I knew the doors to the emergency room came sliding open and two cops came running in. They flew right by me and Aunt Verdele's friend and headed for the loony bitch. They knocked the knife out of her hand and slammed her down on the floor. She was screaming and cursing and trying to rub her eyes.

The nurse ran from behind the counter and told the cop that the chick had been in there for two hours harassing every damn body. They were so focused on her that me and Chen just walked real fast out the door. We made it a good five steps before dude grabbed me by the arm.

"I ain't forget about you. Why was you in Verdele's house?"

"Look man, that's my aunt. I'm here to see about her because I heard she was in an accident. I have to go, so let go of my arm."

It smelled like he had been French-kissing Jack Daniels before he got to the hospital. That nigga was definitely a little nice.

"Tell me why you were in her house."

"Look dude, you obviously been drinking and maybe you think who you saw was me, but you're wrong."

"I ain't had that much to drink, nigga."

"Look, I'm going to give you five seconds to let go of my arm, or it's gon' be on."

"Oh yeah? You think I'm scared of your punk ass? Y'all young boaws think y'all can't get a good ol'-fashioned ass-whippin', but I'm ready like Freddy."

I just ignored him and looked down at his hand gripped around my arm. I was about to give Chen a signal so he could spray dude, but I noticed something even better. A shiny gold wedding ring was on his finger.

"Dude, tell me this. What the fuck you doing with my aunt Verdele when you're married?"

"What . . . what? Man, me and Verdele are just friends. That's my drinking buddy. What you need to do is stay out of grown folks' business and tell me why you was robbing her!"

"Nigga, that's my aunt. I ain't thinking about robbing her."

He loosened up his grip on my arm and I pulled away from him. That nigga was big, and I knew he probably would've smashed me, but I played it real gangsta. I got up real close to him and gritted on him hard as shit.

"Now tell me this, partner. What's your name?"

"Harry."

"Harry what?"

"That's all you need to know."

"That's cool, Harry. That's all I need to know. Let's make a deal. You need to stop saying that I was up in her house tonight, OK? Because if you don't I'll make sure I track down your wife and tell her that you been getting your old-ass freak on with my aunt."

"There's nothing between us. Like I said we drink together and that's all."

"Oh yeah? Do you get butt-naked with all your drinking

buddies? Huh nigga? I ain't think so. You was up in there nailing tonight, because just like you saw me, I saw you."

"OK, OK listen. Shut all that shit up about telling my wife. I won't say shit if you won't."

Just when we had squared all that away one of the cops came out and asked Harry if he was looking for a cop earlier. The cop said that one of the hospital workers told him that. Harry played it off and said he was cool. He didn't want no part of me. He didn't want the missus, whoever the hell she was, to find out that he sticks his stubby little dick in his drinking partner.

A few seconds later the other cop, who was black, came out of the emergency room with the crazy Puerto Rican lady in hand-cuffs. She was still spazzing out and screaming. So much was going on. The one cop, the white one, was still trying to talk to her, and the lady was trying to spit on all of us. Chen's cell phone started ringing while he was backing up into the driveway in front of the hospital, trying to get away from her.

His eyes got big after he was on the phone for a minute.

"Yo, it's Onyx. She said that Dex and them are here. They just parked and she said that them cats is . . ."

He didn't even get that shit out of his mouth before I looked up and saw all three of them coming toward us. Dex, Herb, and the boaw they was with in front of the club were walking fast as shit.

I don' think they even noticed us at first, because there was so much commotion in front of the emergency room door. They all looked like they were on a mission.

Herb noticed Chen first. I guess a Chinese boaw with a Sean John jean set on would stand out big-time. All of them niggas slowed down and looked around. Dex and his crew panicked big-time. They saw me and Chen standing there talking to two cops and Chen pointing at them, and they must've thought that we were snitching. They all turned around and jetted back to where they came from.

Both cops saw them run, but they didn't blink. They weren't thinking about them niggas. They disappeared around the corner. It was like they were the Three Stooges. The crazy thing though is that the joke was on me.

Like two minutes after they ran around the building and out of our sight I heard Onyx scream. By the time me and Chen ran around the building I saw the Honda Accord peel away from the curb. The passenger side to the truck was wide open and Onyx's gold bracelet was on the ground. Dex and his monkey crew took that shit to another level.

Them pussies kidnapped my girl.

37. Me and Chen jumped in the truck first. When I remembered that Onyx had the keys I grabbed the bag of tapes off the floor in the backseat and we switched to his Lex. We wasted a lot of time fucking around in the Expedition, so by the time we got in Chen's car and pulled off, the Accord was nowhere to be seen.

We were driving the wrong way down one-way streets trying to see if we could spot the car but we didn't see it anywhere. We were all up and down Broad Street, up and down the side streets.

I was going fucking crazy in Chen's car. He was driving fast as hell but it still seemed like he was going too slow. I felt like I needed to be in an airplane or some shit looking for her.

The shit that was running through my mind wasn't making it any better. I knew that those clowns hated me and were pissed because of what I did earlier that night. I kept thinking that they was going to do some ol' crazy shit to her.

I was so mad I was about to cry in that car. I had that girl all mixed up in that, and it wasn't pretty. Dex was all about getting that money, and I knew that anything that got between him and that cash would cause major problems. I was ready to have beef with him and Herb because I didn't give a fuck. I wasn't ready for them to get their hands on her though. I wasn't ready for that.

Calling the cops crossed my mind once or twice, but I knew I wouldn't rest until I got them niggas myself. I made up my mind that it all was going to be over that night no matter what. That shit was coming to an end.

It was like two thirty in the morning and we were still ripping and running all over North Philly trying to find them. What made it so bad was that every other nigga got a black Honda Accord, so we kept thinking that we saw the car but it was other people. By quarter of three I told Chen to go to my house. I wanted to get my burner and check my messages to see if Dex had called. It wasn't like he could call me, because Onyx had the cellie.

I ran up to my room and checked the messages but there was nothing on there. I got my burner and ran back out to the car. I was ready to drive around all damn night if I had to. I was ready to shoot all the niggas in the head as soon as I saw them.

I remember that Chen was driving down Ridge Avenue and he was talking nonstop about everything and I just tuned his ass out. I wasn't trying to hear anything. I kept thinking about Onyx and everything she was probably going through, and that just made me want to pray.

I knew that wherever she was she was praying too, and I figured the more prayer the better. My eyes were open, but I was definitely praying. I was talking to God like he was sitting right in the car with me.

I kept asking him to help me find her. I kept asking God to keep them niggas from killing her over what I did. I knew they were acting crazy and I didn't want her to get it. I kept asking God to help me over and over again.

It was kind of ghetto when I look back. I was asking God to help me find them, but I planned on busting a cap in all their asses when I did. It was crazy, but I just wanted to make everything right.

The sex tapes that Dex was losing it over were in the backseat of the Lex. I was so ready to give them jawns up that I didn't know what to do.

The next time I looked up at the clock it was four in the morning.

A few minutes later Chen's phone rang. Onyx's number came up on his caller ID. I was so damn happy I wanted to scream.

"Yo Onyx, wassup? Where you at? Where you at?"

I couldn't hear her voice at first, it just sounded real loud and muddled. After a few seconds I could hear Dex's voice, and then Herb's. They were having a conversation but I couldn't really make out what they were saying. I was so frustrated because I knew that Onyx had dialed Chen's number for a reason. I was so damn irked that nobody was on the phone though.

At first I thought they made her call so she could tell us to come and get her. I was hoping that's why, anyway. A few seconds later I knew that wasn't the case. Onyx started flipping out on them, and when she did that I knew exactly why she dialed Chen's phone.

She was talking nonsense at first, and Herb started screaming at her. He must've walked up on her, because I could hear him loud and clear after a while. I figured she must've hit the talk button on the phone, and it was hidden under her shirt or in her pants. Wherever it was them niggas couldn't see it.

Herb was getting real frustrated because she was babbling and crying and shit. To tell the truth I was getting irked too that I didn't know what the fuck she was talking about. And then it hit me. It hit me so hard I almost jumped out of the car. She was trying to tell me where they was at. I had the call on Chen's speaker phone in the car.

"Please let me go, I don't have anything to do with this. . . ."

"*Shut up bitch, I know that nut-ass nigga told you what the deal was. . . .*"

"*Look, if you guys do anything to me you're going to make me tell my friends Terry and Andre to come and see you. . . .*"

"*Do I look like I give a fuck?*"

"*You can say that now, but when Andre and Terry get together it's going to be ugly. Everybody knows what happened when they got together . . .*"

"*What the fuck are you talking about?*"

"*I may not be making any sense because I'm not from Philadelphia and I don't know where I am but I know I'm on Andre and Terry . . .*"

"*No bitch, you're on crack. Shut the fuck up . . .*"

"*I'm not crazy, I just know that when Jaime went to Vegas she had to escape . . . she had to escape. . . . The fake Callahan and her crew were coming to get her and Steve wasn't there.*"

"*Yo Dex, this bitch is a loony tune. I don't even know how your wack-ass cousin can put up with this trick. . . . She over here talking about your aunt going to Vegas and shit. . . . She's a fucking noodle.*"

She was quiet after that, but I was still hyped as hell because I had a good idea where she was. Me and Chen were flying down Broad Street at that point and I told him to bang a left on Pine and get down to Third Street as fast as he could. I knew where they took Onyx. She told me as clear as day, even though I knew it sounded crazy to everybody else. Chen was just as confused as Herb.

"Yo, what the hell is your girl talking about? She wasn't making no damn sense."

"Yes she was, Chen! She's on the roof of a hotel on Third Street! I think it's the one that they're still building."

"How the hell do you know that?"

"Man, she just told me. She just fucking said it on the phone."

That's when I started to run it down to Chen while he was running through red lights all the way down Pine Street. When Onyx was talking about Terry and Andre I knew right away that she was talking about wrestling. She knew just like I did that Hulk Hogan's real name was Terry. And when she said Andre the first thing that came to mind was Andre the Giant. Any real wrestling fan from back in the day knew that both of them cats fought at the third WrestleMania. That's how I figured out what street she was on.

When she started talking about Jaime being in Vegas I knew she wasn't talking about my mom Jaime. My mom ain't go nowhere near a casino. She was talking about Jaime Sommers, the Bionic Woman. There was an episode where she went to Las Vegas and had to fight these things called Fembots that looked just like humans.

When they started chasing her in that episode she ran up to the roof of the hotel and escaped by jumping up on a helicopter. The reason she said Steve wasn't there was because the boaw who played the Bionic Man wasn't on that episode. It all made sense. It my have sounded like bullshit to everybody else but I knew what she was trying to say, and she knew I would know.

Chen's phone dropped the signal. I started to call back but then I figured they would hear the phone ring and they would take it from her. He called up some of his partners in South Philly and told them to meet us down there, and we kept on speeding toward the hotel. I was praying again that I got her clues right and that she was really there. It was freaking me out that they had her on the roof of a building.

When me and Chen got down to where the building was it was dark as shit. The sign hanging on the gate said that they were building the La Fleur Suites. I knew right away that it was the right place because Dex's Honda Accord was parked half a block from the building. It looked like the hotel was almost finished but there weren't any windows in yet. That jawn was about as tall as it was going to get.

The first thing me and Chen did was go to Dex's car to see if he had left my shit in there. The pillowcase was on the floor in the back. Luckily they left the doors open, so I just went in and got out my tape recorder. I knew I would need that more than anything else.

We couldn't see what was on the roof from the street, so I grabbed the plastic bag with the tapes from the Lex and we rolled out. Chen grabbed a flashlight out of his trunk. The gate was open, so we just walked right in past the cranes and all that other shit they used to put up buildings.

Once we got in there it was totally dark. I lost count of how many flights we went up, but it was a lot. It was crazy because we were trying to get up there quick without making any noise. I wanted to get up on the roof so bad it was killing me.

Chen turned off the flashlight and we stood still in the dark whenever we thought we heard somebody walking down the steps. That's what took us so long.

We was almost to the roof when Chen's cell phone bit us in the ass. That jawn started ringing, and his phone rings to the beat of one of Jay-Z's songs. He cut it off kind of quick, but it was loud. He looked down at his caller ID and saw that it was one of his niggas from in South Philly. He wanted to go back downstairs and meet them, but I couldn't wait that long. I told him to call the dude back and tell him that we were going to the roof. I didn't want Onyx to be with them zero-ass niggas for another minute. Chen called them back and whispered the information, and then we kept on going.

We didn't think that nobody would've heard that phone, but we were wrong. Me and Chen was creeping real smooth up the steps when we both heard something click. I looked up and Herb was standing at the top of the landing with his heat aimed right at me. The other cat they were with was looking over his shoulder. I started to reach for my gun to just blast his ass, but I knew he would get me before I got him, so I just chilled.

The other dude patted us down and took my gun and Chen's flashlight. He was taller than Dex and was real husky and light-skinned like he was almost white. He had red hair that was nappy and in a little blowout. I never saw him around the way. I didn't know who that nigga was. Dude must've been a mute or something, because I don't remember him talking at all that night. I just remember his scream. That loud, crazy scream.

When we got to the roof Dex was standing near the ledge of the roof talking on his cell phone with Onyx gripped up by the arm. Both of their backs were turned to us until Herb turned on the flashlight. He had a flashlight too, and he aimed it right in me and Chen's face.

He was looking at us with this crazy look of shock.

"What the fuck? How did y'all find us here?"

"We followed you, that's how, nigga."

"Nobody is talking to you, pussy! I was talking to my cousin."

Dex put his cell phone in his pocket and started walking across the roof toward us. I just ignored him because I was too busy trying to see if Onyx was OK. It was so dark that I couldn't really see her face until they really got up on us. The first thing I noticed was that she was crying. She wasn't bleeding or anything the way I pictured in my head all the way up to the roof. She was just scared and upset.

"How the hell did y'all get here, I said!"

"Look Dex, I ain't come here for all this talking. Let her go so that we can roll. I brought your tapes, so now we're even."

Herb handed him the bag of tapes and Dex looked through it real quick, and then handed the bag back and took the gun out of Herb's hand. Dex still had Onyx's arm all gripped up, and he walked up close to where we were standing. He looked like he was about to explode he was so damn mad.

"How the fuck did you find us up here, and don't tell me no bullshit or else I'm gon' have Herb bust a cap in your ass."

I was happy as hell that he took the gun from Herb. He probably wasn't going to shoot us anyway. He seemed like the kind of cat that talked a lot of big gun talk but probably didn't ever squeeze a trigger in his life. I was more worried about Dex having Onyx all hemmed up. I knew Dex was about to do something off the wall, so I just started talking. I knew by the look on his face that it was on. I knew it was time to divide and conquer.

"Damn Herb, you're going all out to play this shit off. . . ."

"What the hell are you talking about?"

"Oh come on, you need to stop frontin', because the game is over. You know me and you planned to get Dex for the loot after y'all collected it all. . . . But you know what? The more I think about it, I can't let you do that to my cousin."

"Nigga, is you crazy? I don't fuck with you like that!"

"Come on, Herb. You trying to tell me that you ain't tell me about how Dex killed Tony? You ain't tell me that?"

"I ain't tell you shit like that, pussy! You need to stop lying and . . ."

"OK Herb, then how did I know that Dex skinned Tony and

poured the acid on him to make it look like the mob did it. How did I know that?"

Herb had this crazy look on his face. I had him fucked-up in the head. Dex was looking back and forth between us like he didn't know who to believe. I know that he trusted Herb and that was his nigga, so I didn't expect him to just jump on my side and believe me. I just wanted to put some doubt in his head, and that shit worked. It worked because that little bit of doubt turned into a whole lot of doubt.

"Hold up cousin, what is you saying? You saying you knew that shit all this time and you ain't say nothing?"

"Yeah, because me and Herb was waiting for y'all to collect all the money so that he could steal it from you and we could split it."

"You're talking shit. . . ."

"How you think I knew where y'all were at. He called me up and left a message saying that y'all were up here on the roof. And the reason I found out all the other stuff is because he taped y'all conversations."

"What!"

"Yeah, I have one of the tapes right here . . ."

I bent over real slow and pulled up my pant leg. I reached into my sock and pulled out the small minicassette. I motioned to Chen to hand me the tape recorder out of his inside jacket pocket.

"Wait a fucking minute! I don't know what the fuck he talking about Dex. I ain't never tell him none of that shit and I ain't never taped a motherfucking thing."

"OK, well let's listen to this shit to see what cuz is talking about."

I put the tape in the recorder and rewinded it to the beginning. I hit the play button and pushed the volume up all the way. Dex snatched it out of my hand and put it close to his ear.

Everyone was quiet, even Herb, while the tape played. Both of them clowns had stupid-ass surprised looks on their faces. Herb really looked dumb because he couldn't figure out why the hell I had a tape of their conversation.

Dex clicked it off before it got to the end.

"When did you tape this fucking conversation, Herb?"

"What nigga, you believe this lame? You gotta be kidding me!"

"Why wouldn't I? That sounds like you on there and I know it's me so . . ."

"I don't know how the fuck he got that tape."

I was loving it. I was waiting for that moment damn near all summer.

"Listen Herb, stop denying it and come clean."

"Pussy, you know you're lying! You fucking liar! Yo Dex, don't believe him."

Dex just held up his hand to his lips and closed his eyes. His jaw was tight as hell and it looked like he had a instant migraine headache.

"I'm about to smoke both of y'all, because I don't know who is telling the truth."

He pushed Onyx away from him and started aiming the gun back and forth between me and Herb. She ran over to me and hugged me but I didn't hug her back. I leaned real close to her though and whispered in her ear.

"Onyx, go the way Jaime went and stay there as soon as I say run."

She nodded and I pulled her off of me and made her stand behind me next to Chen.

"OK cuz. You're going to believe him over me, as far as we go back?"

"Why shouldn't I?"

"Because he's going to get you for all your cash, that's why."

Before Dex could react, everything just started to get buck wild. We all looked up at the same time because of the noise. And then we could see the bright light from the helicopter. I thought it was the cops at first but Dex didn't seem paranoid enough for it to be the pigs. The dust and shit on the roof from the construction was flying everywhere. We all started choking and coughing and trying to cover our eyes.

I told Onyx to run, and she took off like a damn cheetah. She never looked back. She just ran to the door that we all came through and disappeared.

That's when Dex jumped into action. I looked up in time to see him aiming his gun at Herb. He let off two shots and both of them hit him in the legs. He dropped to the ground and started screaming. I knew he was screaming because his mouth was wide open. I couldn't hear shit through all the noise.

Dex turned around to me next and aimed the burner right at my chest. I just knew that was it. I didn't think he would hesitate for one minute to blow a hole in my chest, and I was right. As soon as he was about to do it, the high yellow boaw pulled out the gun that he took from me and let two shots off at Dex. He missed both times.

Me and Chen dropped to the ground.

Dex fired back twice and hit him in the arm. Then he turned around and started running toward the helicopter. The boaw fired two more wild shots that didn't hit nothing, and then started to chase Dex.

As soon as Dex got to the helicopter he turned around and fired a few more back at dude and just tore his whole shit up. Dude, who I found out later from all the newspapers was named Kashif Taylor, started stumbling backward. He had his back to us, but I could still tell he was fucked-up.

He tried to turn and run but all the wind from the helicopter was whipping his ass around. Dex shot him one more time in the back and that's when he started tumbling toward the edge of the roof, and just fell off. I'll never forget that as long as I live. Even with the helicopter going, I could hear him scream.

There was so much commotion going on that I never even heard or saw Chen's boaws come running up on the roof. They grabbed us up off the ground and started pulling us to the exit. Herb was crawling across the roof on his stomach trying to get out.

I turned around just in time to see Dex open the door to the helicopter. Right when he was getting up in there I saw something fall to the ground. As soon as he shut the door, that helicopter lifted off right away. I never saw the pilot's face, but I found out exactly who he was later on.

While Chen and his boaws was running toward the door and Herb was crawling on his stomach, I was running in the opposite direction. I wanted to see what fell from the helicopter.

There was no light up there at all, but I was still able to find the bag. It was a trash bag that was knotted up and tied real tight.

I ripped it open and put my hand inside and felt what I thought I would. It was cold hard cash. When I counted it later on I saw that it was $7,020. Dex probably didn't miss that shit.

When I was on my way off the roof Herb was still crawling his way to the exit door. He was moaning and screaming about his leg, and to tell the truth I felt a little sorry for him. But not sorry enough to help him. I left his ass up there. I stepped right over him like he was trash in the street and never looked back. Some people might think that was ignorant but if I would've done what I wanted to, he would've been laying right up on that roof with a snapped neck. From what they said on the news a couple of days later, Herb made it all the way down to the eleventh floor by the time the cops got to him.

He's sitting in jail now. Broke and with two bullets in his legs.

I ran down the steps to what was going to be the lobby of that hotel and went to get Onyx. She was right where I thought she would be, hanging on the built-in ladder inside the elevator shaft.

When she jumped down into my arms she squeezed me real tight. She was crying and hysterical, but she was happy to see me alive. I was happy to be living too.

I was happy that I was going to be around after the credits rolled for the summer of 2001.

38. The whole month of August was crazy. My whole life got turned upside down in one summer and it was hard trying to get it back together.

The newspaper and television people were on my block almost night and day. The lady who lives four doors down from us told the *Tribune* that she always knew that I was into something bad. Ms. Josephine told the newspaper that I was always causing trouble. I guess she still didn't get over my beating up her grandson when we were in seventh grade. I never said anything to that lady, and they were using her and a lot of other people to make me look bad.

The old me would've walked down the street and cursed her out. I was pissed off. Even people who hardly knew me was all up on the news talking like they knew everything about me. All of a sudden they were experts on me.

The craziest thing that happened is that I actually started going to church again with my mother. I went twice in August and the day before Labor Day. It was tight. Of course everybody was looking at me and whispering all three times, but I didn't care.

Onyx told me it was going to be like that, and I knew myself that certain people would be trippin'. Some of those same people who sat up in there trying to act like they were better than me were turning more tricks than a little bit.

I just wanted something different. I was burned out dealing with the streets. I hustled weed, sold illegal cable boxes, and had sex for money. It got to the point where I felt like I had been there and done that with everything.

The only thing I didn't go all out for was God. At least that's what Onyx said. She said I needed to start reading the Bible more often and going to church. I listened to her and started reading the Bible every day but everything seemed the same. First of all, I didn't even understand everything that I was reading. Some of it was so confusing. I was ready to give up, but I didn't. I was in the house all the time anyway, so it was something to do.

Me and Onyx talked every day for at least two hours on the phone. I knew that our bills for August was going to be mad high. I didn't care though, because I had to talk to her. Her and my mom were the only people I felt like I could trust after everything that went down. They were the only people who I knew wouldn't turn into snakes on me.

Me and Onyx would pray on the phone together. She was the first person I ever did that with. I guess after all I put her through, she felt like she had to pray for me all the time.

Our conversations got real deep. She told me that I should write a book about all that happened to me. I told her that I would think about it, but I knew I wasn't going to. She said that my story may inspire people who been through something, but I didn't agree.

I told her that most Christian people who cracked open the book would just put it down as soon as they read that me and Dex were nailing chicks for loot. I knew that the real Holy Rollers wouldn't even read far enough into the book to see how

I'm trying to change my life. They would see the beginning and judge me from jump street.

I was really down on myself. I felt like a bad person because of all that went down. I heard Onyx when she was telling me that God forgives, but I couldn't wrap my brain around that. It's not that I didn't care, but on the real I just knew I had already made a place for myself in Hell. I just couldn't see God letting me up in Heaven like everything was cool.

Onyx just kept telling me that as long as I went to God and asked for forgiveness and accepted Jesus that I would be straight. I thought that was so cheesy at first. That's the way they make it seem on TV movies and all, but life is harder than that. It's hard to go from being bad to good and holy, like I'd never done no dirt.

I thought if I told the preacher at my mom's church what I did with those women, that he would probably ban me from every church in Philly. I was wrong though, because my mom asked him to talk to me and I found out that he used to gang war back in the day. He told me right to my face that he jacked up a lot of dudes real bad back in the '60's.

He told me that a few of them were so beat down when he left the scene of a big street fight that he don't know if they lived or died. That's what made him go to God. I was like, damn, if he can preach then I can at least try to get it together.

I couldn't believe that the preacher at my church used to be a thug boaw. That blew my mind, but it made me feel what Onyx was saying even more. It's like, if God wants to turn you around he can do it. I figured out after living through the summer of 2001 that I could do anything.

All my dawgs were acting funny around me since word on the street was that I snitched, but I didn't care. They didn't know the real story. I didn't care what they thought. I knew that I wasn't perfect, but I wasn't no snake like Dex. He was the one.

Life was crazy in August. Herb caught all the heat because the neighbors all identified him as the one who they saw coming and going out of Tony's house. His face was on the front of every newspaper in the city.

Dex got off scot-free. The last time anybody saw him was when he hopped in that helicopter on the roof of that hotel and disappeared. The cops found the helicopter in a field in the Northeast. The pilot was slumped over the controls with a bullet in his head.

They said on the news that there were tire tracks from an SUV on the grass, which went across the field and then disappeared. Dex was just like them tire tracks, because that boaw was ghost. Onyx kept telling me not to be bitter, but I couldn't help it. I wanted him to pay for all he did, and he was somewhere chilling with all that money.

I was broke. The little bit of money I did get from off the roof I wound up giving to Aunt Verdele to help her get a new car. Me and Onyx both agreed that I had to do it. I felt bad because she was on her way to help me out when she crashed and I wasn't even in danger.

A lot of people would call me stupid for giving up the loot like that, but I had to do it. And the crazy thing is that I started out broke when I first started working for Tony and I was right back at square one.

I came close to death just for some quick cash, and at the end of the summer I had nothing to show for it.

39. I was sitting up in my room yesterday thinking that my crazy summer wasn't as much like a book or movie as I thought. I mean, books and movies have crazy endings where there's a shoot-out or somebody gets locked up or something happens to shock the hell out of people.

I don't read all that much, but Onyx does, and she's always complaining about books with jacked-up endings. She says that a good book or a movie should blow your mind and make you think.

Like I said, I haven't read that many books so I can't speak on that. Now movies are a whole different story. I watch a lot of them jawns and I know which ones are off the hook because of their endings.

I mean, everybody loved flicks like *The Sixth Sense* and *The Silence of the Lambs* because of the way they ended. I hated *The Talented Mr. Ripley* though. That was beyond stupid. That jawn was the worst. When *Ripley* ended I threw my soda at the screen and just cursed. I wanted my coins back, for real.

But when I think of all the stuff I went through over the last few months, I think that maybe somebody would want to read about it or see it on the TV screen. It's just that the ending would suck.

Dex didn't get locked up. Herb did, but so what? He's a dick-head. It's not like he got killed in a hail of gunfire after trying to escape the police. That's what people want to read at the end of their books.

Meka hasn't been heard from either, but I don't know if she hooked up with Dex or if he did something to her before he rolled. I figured I would just keep watching the news to see if they found a black girl floating in the river.

Archie didn't betray me and send some of his fellow pigs to kill me. If that would've happened then maybe it would be good enough for the end of a book. Maybe, but it didn't.

Me and Onyx didn't run off to Vegas to get married and live happily ever after. I mean, she digs me and all, but she said I got a lot of issues and that I have a lot of work to do on myself be-fore I can really be a good man for her. I'm not trying to be a deadbeat and my woman is a lawyer. I'm not trying to look like lame.

With books and movies, people like to see the bad guys get it real bad. And I guess from my eyes, Dex and Herb were the bad guys. Like I said, the ending would probably suck since they both are still alive and Dex is out of the picture.

That pussy-ass cousin of mine called me like eight o' clock this morning when I was in the kitchen making my mom breakfast for her birthday. Even though she's not into zodiac signs, she's a Virgo and they need to be treated like queens. I was shocked as hell when I picked up my mom's phone and he was on the other end. He sounded dumb as shit.

I should've just banged on him since I had nothing to say. I went through so much over that clown and we were supposed to be family. He almost fucked up my life and now he was calling like nothing ever happened. That was the first time I heard his voice in more than a month, when we was on the roof of that hotel.

At first he tried to deny that he killed Tony, and then he said something about him using us to get rich. He said that he wasn't with nobody getting rich off his work, so he erased him so he could get some major cash. I just listened. I didn't say shit. There was nothing that he really could say. Just hearing his voice though was enough to make me want to snap his neck.

I'm happy that I wasn't killed or didn't have to go to jail, but part of me still wanted to get revenge on Dex. It wasn't right that he just skipped off like that without anything happening to him.

But the more I thought about it the more I kept hearing Onyx's voice telling me not to be filled with hate and rage. She kept telling me to let it go. I told her that I felt some kind of way that Dex just got off like that. Even though I was learning to talk to God every day and learning about what it means to be a Christian, I was still mad. Hearing him on the phone acting all blasé and cocky didn't make it better.

He was carrying on about how he was about to come up big-time and he wanted to hook me up too. I guess the boaw thought I was stupid. I didn't want no part of him. He said something about getting a call from a producer who saw one of his pictures on the Internet who wanted to put him in movies.

I couldn't believe my ears. After everything he had done I would think he was going to lay low for a minute. This nigga was sitting up there telling me that he was about to move out to L.A. to be a porno star.

I was thinking he has to be the stupidest person on the face of the earth. He killed at least three people and he thought he was going to just start making flicks like nobody was going to find out and dime on his ass.

Dex said that this rich big-time stock broker dude was putting his money behind a new line of movies with thug-type niggas. He said that he had a meeting with the man in an hour and that he was going to tell the dude about me too. I told him not to even bother. I didn't want no part of it. Onyx was the only woman I felt like dealing with, and I told him that. I told him that all of that madness was over.

"Cuz, you crazy if you miss out on going out Cali."

"I ain't missing out on nothing."

"What? They got the baddest jawns in the world out there. All of them bitches look like Trina or J Lo, for real."

"That's cool, but like I said I don't want no part of that. I don't get down like that no more."

"That jawn got you acting all holy and shit. Her pussy must be tight. Tell her big Dex said hi."

"Man, I ain't telling her nothing. . . . Look, I gotta go. It's my mom's birthday and I'm making her breakfast."

"OK, tell Aunt Jaime I said happy birthday. I gotta get ready to run anyway. I got a meeting with the big dogs at nine o'clock on the 105th floor and I'm trying to get there early. I'm trying to get his paper."

"Aight then, Dex, whatever . . ."

I hung up the phone and finished making my mom's food. When I was walking through the living room the blinking red light on the caller ID caught my eye. Before I walked up the steps I put down her glass of orange juice and pushed the button to see where Dex was calling from. It was a 212 area code and it said phone booth, so he had to be in New York somewhere. I knew it couldn't have been Philly because we don't have buildings that tall.

I took my mom her grub and gave her a kiss. She was cheesing from ear to ear. My cooking wasn't all that, but she loved when

I cooked for her. Before I walked out of her room she reminded me to call Onyx in Durham because it was her birthday too. I remembered though. The two ladies in my life had the same birthday, so it made September 11 hard to forget.

Coming in March 2005 from Riverhead Freestyle

WIFEBEATER

THE NEW NOVEL FROM MISTER MANN FRISBY!

Turn the page for your sneak preview
of the first chapter . . .

RIVERHEAD
FREESTYLE

MONDAY, NOVEMBER 10, 2003, 8 A.M.

I knew it was going to be a hell of a day when me and my daughter looked up to see a scandal so intense it almost burned our eyes out.

It would be a long time before anything on my nineteen-inch RCA would ever catch me off guard like that. At two years old, Brie had no idea what her eyes were focused on and would not remember any of it. I was grateful for that because I was two years away from turning thirty and I didn't know if I could handle it myself.

It was a dreary, nasty November day. The weather lady called it "brisk" but from my point of view it felt like Russia in the dead of winter. I remember the weather so well because I dressed Brie in five minutes flat and we went flying out the front door. People stared but I didn't care. It was rainy and windy and my little daughter was being hauled through South Philly in my arms without a hat on and only half her head braided. By the time I reached the corner of Twenty-third and Christian, at least four women rolled their eyes at me in disgust.

I hooked her up the best I could, considering my hands were shaking like crazy and I had to piss like a racehorse. Nothing that she was wearing matched. She had on a pair of peach tights, a dark green turtleneck with red polka dots, and a pair of hot pink rain shoes that my aunt had given her as a gift. Brie's hair was only half braided because I started taking it out the night before. My neighbor, Jar-u-queesha, had made my daughter look so pretty when she'd cornrowed her hair the week before, but at that point she looked like an extra from *The Color Purple*.

Brie's mother and her conniving lawyer would have loved to catch that Kodak moment. Minerva wanted to see me slip up so bad. My ex prayed for the day when I would crumble under the pressure of being a single dad. She wanted full custody, but Michael Jackson would have Wesley Snipes's complexion before I let that happen.

That crazy-ass morning changed everything though. As flaky and unreliable as Minerva could be, I started to think that her ghetto fabulous rat trap in North Philly would be the safest place for my little princess. Before I left the house I picked up my cordless and hung it up a hundred times because I was tempted to call somebody, anybody, and tell them what we had seen. But I kept stopping myself. It was hardly a conversation to have with anyone, let alone over the phone.

I was instantly paranoid. It wasn't so much the *what* as the *who* that made it so off the damn hook. And that's not saying that the *what* didn't take the cake too.

I have replayed that morning so many times in my head. Brie woke up at about seven that morning, fussing because she wanted to watch a particular Teletubbies tape for the umpteenth time. It was cool at first. I used to get a kick out of seeing my baby mesmerized by those four colorful creatures, but after about six months of playing that tape I wanted to go through the TV screen and give Dipsy, Laa-Laa, Po, and Tinky-Winky a straight-up rumble. I laughed sometimes picturing myself throwing them off a cliff one at a time.

I was real groggy when she woke me up, because I had been up until five in the morning trying to write a paper for an on-line course I was taking that cost like four hundred dollars. The paper was overdue, and it didn't look like I was going to be finished by the extended deadline either. Being a full-time solo dad with a two-year-old at home was way more time-consuming than I had ever thought it would be.

Brie woke me up the way she does every morning, with one of those wet, sloppy kisses. It did the trick every time. I jumped up right away before I could fall back asleep and before Brie could start bawling out of control. My eyes were barely open as I looked for the VHS case with her favorite characters. Before I could find the case, my eyes stopped on a tape that was sitting upright and not in a sleeve. The label had dingy, yellow tape on the side and it read: *Teletubbies (5-Hour Marathon)*.

I knew right away that I hadn't seen the tape before. It made me wake up real quick. I was just standing there digging between my cornrows when it hit me. My mother and her three coworkers had taken off work a few days before to go to a huge flea market in Norristown. She had definitely mentioned something to me about buying Brie some new tapes, but it went in one ear and out the other. I had been on the phone with the people from the electric company, pleading with them to keep my electricity on for at least another week when my mom and Ms. Judith dropped by. PECO was on my back tougher than Verizon and it had me vexed that day. I could hardly remember my mom's visit, let alone her leaving a bag of flea-market toys and three new tapes for Brie.

All of Brie's stuff blended together after a while anyway, so I could hardly tell a new tape, DVD, or toy from the old ones.

Half the time it was all one big pile of madness. Everything talked. The yellow school bus sang nursery rhymes when she pushed it, the ambiguously sexed doll baby recited the alphabet, and most annoyingly, my baby's new Elmo doll sang the *Sesame Street* theme song in Spanish. That damn thing could probably do the Harlem Shake if you squeezed it the right way.

So, when I saw that one of the tapes had five hours of Teletubbies on it, I grabbed it off the shelf with the swiftness of a Ninja on crack. Those overstuffed characters kept her glued to the screen and quiet and that's what I was looking for that morning. All I needed was maybe two more hours of sleep and I would have been straight. I wish.

Brie was already settled into her plush little yellow Teletubbies chair when I popped the tape into the VCR and went downstairs to the kitchen to get her something to eat. I was tired as hell so I kept it real simple. I poured her a bowl of Honey Combs. I was too tired to even put milk in the bowl. The kitchen was bordering on filthy and I wanted to get in and out. I made my way back into my bedroom, or our bedroom I should say because she never slept in her own room at night.

I handed Brie the bowl of cereal but she never took her eyes off the screen. The Teletubbies had Brie in the zone. I stretched back out across my king-size bed, *our* king-size bed, and dozed off. It was November 10, the day after my sister's birthday. The last thing I remember before our lives took a dramatic turn was Brie leaning back in her chair and watching those four colorful bastards dance around the grassy hills as if they were high on that shit.

I was sleeping hard at first. It was the kind of snooze that you fight somebody for interrupting. About twenty minutes or so into my semi-coma, Brie woke me up tugging on my arms and whining. I was more confused than annoyed because she always, without fail, watched the Teletubbies quietly until the credits rolled. Wild Rugrats couldn't drag her from in front of the screen. I was halfway in dreamland, halfway in reality when the sounds that filled my room jolted my brain.

It wasn't the normal PBS type of sounds. It was a far cry from Bert & Ernie kickin' it on *Sesame Street*. What I heard that morning was more like the sounds that fill my bedroom when Brie goes to visit her grandmother, and Nia from Thirty-third Street comes to visit me. Of course I thought I was still dreaming. I sat up and Brie was standing at the edge of the bed. At first she was blocking my view of the TV, but I could still hear the grunts, moans, and laughter as clear as day. I reached forward and picked my baby up so that I could get a clear look at the screen.

Like I said, it wasn't so much the *what* as the *who*.

I was stunned. There's not shit else I can say except that I was stuck on stupid. My first reaction was to cover my baby's eyes but it was already too late for that. I realized later that she had already seen about five minutes of the action on screen before I woke up and stopped the tape.

At that moment I vowed that I would never tell Brie about what her precious little eyes had witnessed. That all went out the window when my name, and hers, started to make newspaper headlines. When the smoke cleared, I knew I would have to break it all down for her one day. She was definitely going to have questions, and I knew that I would have to do my best to break her off with honest-to-God answers. But in the meantime, what a way to start our week.